AT
THE
TID...

A...

by

Thomas H. Raddall

Introduction : Allan Bevan

General Editor : Malcolm Ross

New Canadian Library No. 9

McClelland & Stewart Limited

The Canadian Publishers
McClelland and Stewart Limited
25 Hollinger Road. Toronto

0-7710-9109-5

THOMAS RADDALL, who tells us that he is a Bluenose who has lived and played and worked most of his life among the Bluenoses, is one of the relatively small group of Canadian authors who earn their living by the pen. Primarily a writer of fiction, he has also tried his hand successfully as a historian. In the stories included in this volume, Raddall appears in the role for which he seems to me to be best suited—as the writer of historical fiction.

The historical novel, and the same applies to a short story in the historical tradition, presents a broad picture of a society that actually existed some time in the past. The fiction writer is not as rigidly tied to facts as is the historian and may be forced by the demands of his creative muse to make some minor distortions of historical facts in order to achieve the artistic unity his form dictates. For this he should be forgiven. In historical fiction we seldom find an exact historical account of events, or even a completely objective portrayal of historical figures; we should, on the other hand, have a convincing re-creation of a world inhabited by people who think and feel and talk and act in a manner consistent with their own time in history.

The successful fiction writer who sprinkles historical figures among his fictitious characters tells us, not what has actually happened, but what might very well have happened if characters such as those he has created had called on Governor Wentworth of Halifax, or had talked with Sam Adams of Boston, or had ridden with bloody spurs behind the impetuous Duke of Kent. Raddall's readers probably know that the Duke of Kent did live for a time in Halifax, and they may also know that the energetic Duke believed in flogging defaulters and hanging deserters; but few readers are well-enough acquainted with Nova Scotia history to know whether the characters appearing with the Duke are historical or fictitious. In the true tradition of historical fiction the Duke, together with other historical figures, appears in these stories faced by situations that never existed; but as long as these situations could very well have existed, as long as the Duke acts and the fictitious characters with whom he appears act as they would have acted under the imaginary conditions described, then the story is true and the author is obeying the unwritten laws of the *genre*.

In his use of actual figures in imaginary crises, in both his historical novels and his historical short stories, Raddall creates true-to-life situations and treats his readers with respect. As a writer he lives up to the standards he has set for any artist: "His obligation is always to the truth." As we read his fiction, his people come to life for us, struggling or laughing, praying or fighting, as the early Nova Scotians must have done two centuries or so ago. The facts are less important than the atmosphere, and, although Raddall's facts, I have been assured by historians, are exceptionally accurate, it is through the conjuring up of real people living in a real world that his stories come to life.

As Raddall himself has said, the creative writer is driven by a personal demon to try "to capture with ink and paper the spirit, good or evil, of mankind"; he must write with "absolute honesty," and he must make his work readable. Judged by the matter, the admirable verbal resurrection of a dead society, Raddall's historical stories are eminently successful. But the writer of fiction, historical or otherwise, needs to be prepared to see his work tested by standards related to the methods he has used to communicate the particular truth that lies behind the material.

Raddall has little sympathy with "novels that begin and end nowhere, with strange perverted creatures in human form who speak a language never heard on land or sea." His own stories deal with a situation that forces his characters to make decisions and to act in such a way as to bring about the solution that ends the story. The stories usually begin at the beginning, which are as a rule very good indeed. For example, note how the attention is attracted at once by such opening sentences as these: "Justice Martin Bunt went down the harbour on a spring afternoon in 1778 with mingled curiosity and distaste—a trifle more distaste than curiosity" ("At the Tide's Turn"); "In the beginning the site of our town was a low wooded slope beside a tidal river in a most lonely stretch of the Nova Scotia coast" ("Pax Britannica").

Led on by the skill of the author, whose creative imagination seems to function most vigorously when he reconstructs the past, the reader soon finds himself carried away to Oldport in 1778, with the troubled townsmen distressed by the suspicions of both their New England cousins and the King's representatives in Halifax ("At the Tide's Turn"). Or he is introduced to

Colonel Sumter Larrabee of Tarleton's Legion as the "tall hawk-faced South Carolinian" brings his defeated Loyalist troops to Oldport for one cold and disastrous winter before most of them move on ("A Harp in the Willows"). After we are successfully oriented in time and place and rubbing shoulders with a character or group of characters, we are presented with the situation —some critical problem that faces the characters and demands a solution. As the story proceeds to its climactic ending, the characters passing through minor crises on the way, Raddall creates suspense and appeals to our sentiments of patriotism, our sense of the pathetic, and our sense of humour. One event leads on to the next, characters come into contact and conflict with each other, conversations take place (and Raddall handles the difficult task of creating individualized and realistic conversation very well indeed), and the story runs along easily and naturally until its conclusion.

Raddall is no stream-of-consciousness technician; actions and conversations reveal motives, and the characters take clear, easily defined shapes. There is no probing into the darker regions of the consciousness, no psychoanalytical exposure of character. The plot is more important than the characters, who are nearly always simple, "flat," uncomplicated beings driven by fairly obvious motives. Such characters, consistent and convincing in their broad, clear outlines, are not out of place in the historical short story. Colonel Sumter Larrabee, for example, who is the best of the Oldport characters, is always seen objectively and from the outside, even his famous diary being little more than an account of facts. His actions are always consistent with his Tory principles, his pride in his family background, in his possessions and his privileges, but rarely are we afforded a glimpse behind the objective façade. He has enough character for the type of story in which he appears, enough to serve as an actor in the story that is unfolded. Raddall, of course, is a realist, and perhaps we know the stiff-necked but delightful Colonel as well as we know most of our acquaintances.

A novelist has several hundred pages in which to develop characters, involve them in a major predicament and several lesser ones, and then resolve all problems. The world of the novel can expand in time and place to include a whole panorama of society or several generations of characters. In the short story such leisurely expansion is impossible. Instead of an extensive view of man, either in time or space, there has to be a much more restricted view, concentrating on only one aspect of life. For example, in Raddall's *His Majesty's Yankees* we are introduced to a great crowd and a great variety of characters—Micmacs, Yankees, Loyalists, historical and fictitious characters—all swarming across the pages of the novel. There is room for all, and all contribute to the vivid and comprehensive picture of life in Nova Scotia almost two centuries ago. In an Oldport short story, the author has to restrict himself severely, each story dealing with only one of the many themes that are interwoven in the novel. This need to condense and concentrate no doubt accounts in part for the sudden and dramatic climax that usually ends a Raddall short story.

It is not easy to decide which of Raddall's stories should be classified as historical; he has admitted that the richness of the Nova Scotia past has, for him, "an insistent way of intruding upon the story," and even his stories of contemporary life are coloured by his awareness of the past and its impact upon the present. In one of his stories ("A Muster of Arms") Raddall has the Reverend Mac explaining to the two policemen from the outside the reasons for the Nova Scotia-ness of Nova Scotia:

> The trouble with you and Quinn is that you're from the West where everything was born yesterday. The East has a settled history going back three centuries. You're up against the fact that these people have roots going down out of sight—out of your sight anyway—and they're proud of their roots because they've clung to their own soil all this time. They don't depend on books for their history. They've got it right in their own heads, family tales passed down carefully from generation to generation, and a family pride as fierce as anything in Norman England . . . Look here, did you ever stop to consider what kind of people settled this country? It took a bold man to venture here and a steadfast woman to follow him. No attraction for the rich, no field for the merely clever, no ease for the sluggish, no security for the craven or the weak. Nothing but hardships and danger and just a chance of wringing a living out of the woods and rivers and the sea. So they came, the bold and steadfast, and they cut the woods and ploughed the clearings and fished the rivers and the sea. They had to fight with savages for a foothold and with the climate for existence, and time and again they had to defend, with arms, the things they'd won from both. Struggle, struggle, that was the story, all down through the years.

In this volume, however strong the historical element is in tales of contemporary Nova Scotia, the stories selected are clearly set in what we now see as history. Most of the stories have been chosen from those with an Oldport setting. There is no organic unity in these assembled tales, but there is a line of development through the stories of Oldport's first settlement, the trials of the early settlers during the American Revolution, the arrival of the Loyalists, and the gradual coming of age of the society dominated by Sumter Larrabee. The Oldport stories seem to me to be Raddall's best; when he writes about the first inhabitants of his own town, he has an especially perceptive, penetrating, and compassionate eye. But there are other good stories, and two involving the Duke of Kent are here included, as is the warm and humorous story of Kezia Barnes, in "The Wedding Gift." The story of the singing match that takes place in a blacksmith shop some place in Nova Scotia in 1872 ("Blind MacNair"), gives us, as well as its wealth of ballad references, a brief glimpse of the American Civil War and its impact on Nova Scotians. The most recent historical event that serves as a backdrop for a story is the Halifax Explosion of 1917, described from the point of view of a young boy in "Winter's Tale." There are many others that could have been included, some of them probably as good as any of those selected.

The Reverend Mac's admiration for the early settlers shines through Raddall's stories. He writes about the past with knowledge, understanding, humour, and affection. The stirring account of a pioneer society struggling for existence against savage men defending their rights and against an untamed wilderness of unfriendly rivers and of dark and foreboding forests, with the life-and-death-giving sea as their only connection with the civilization left behind, always appeals to some instinct in man. When such a story is well planned and well written, as is the case with Raddall's historical stories, there is added to the interest in the material an aesthetic pleasure that turns each story into "a tale which holdeth children from play, and old men from the chimney corner."

ALLAN BEVAN

Dalhousie University
May, 1959

CONTENTS

At the Tides Turna

IN the beginning the site of our town was a low wooded slope beside a tidal river in a most lonely stretch of the Nova Scotia coast. Not exactly lonely, for the river ran fifty or sixty miles into the peninsula and made a very easy highway for the canoes of the Micmacs, a people hostile to intruders, especially those who spoke the English tongue. In the fighting for Acadie the Micmacs, blood allies of the French, had played a bloody part. But in the end they were out-matched by frontier fighters as ruthless and as cunning as themselves. One of these was Silas Bradford, the founder of our town.

Bradford is a fascinating figure even now. He must have fascinated his contemporaries. Who else could have led them away from the peace and security of Cape Cod, the home of their pilgrim fathers, to settle in this Indian-haunted wilderness which the English called Nova Scotia, the French called Acadie, and which the Micmacs were quite sure was Megumaage? He had come first to the peninsula in 1745 and joined that amazing army of raw New England militia which conquered Louisbourg. Afterwards he and his company of rangers remained in the peninsula to curb the raids of the Micmacs. The regiment of British regulars at Annapolis were helpless outside their palisades. When Halifax was founded in '49 its garrison was little better off. The white inhabitants of the province were almost entirely French in blood and hostile in sentiment—and closely allied to the Micmacs in all ways.

And so for years the ranger companies under men like Bradford carried on a single-handed war against the savages. Of that struggle perhaps the less said the better; a merciless business conducted by canoe and afoot in the wilderness, dependent always on surprise for success—a long and hungry journey in utter stealth, a sudden volley of shots and yells, a closing rush with the tomahawks rising and falling, and the little circular patches of skin and hair dripping red from the belts. Both sides had their victories.

Sometimes the scalps were traded for blankets and hatchets in the French posts toward Quebec, a currency as good as *louis d'or.* Sometimes they went to Halifax for the British governor's bounty—any price from £5 to £50, depending on the circumstances, and no questions asked. A patch of clotted hair might be a man's, a woman's or a child's—who could tell? A bloody chapter. . . .

When the British made the second and final conquest of Louisbourg in 1758, Silas Bradford was there with his armed sloop and his rangers, an amphibious company very useful in the coastal creeks and in the forest about the town. Young Wolfe, the brigadier with the red hair and the absurd chin, was even then fermenting plans for Quebec in the following year, and bespoke, amongst many things, Silas, his rangers, and his sloop. The rangers went to Quebec, and it was one of them who first pointed out to Wolfe that now famous path up the cliff before the Plains of Abraham. But Silas himself had other plans.

In the destruction of Louisbourg he foresaw the final overthrow of the French empire in America. The time was ripe for a matter he had cherished many years, a settlement of his own people in the promised land. He went back to Cape Cod, the place of his birth, and his old neighbours flocked to hear him. The itch for new settlement was strong in all New England. The vast lands to the west, so far from the sea, had no charm for these fishermen sons of the pilgrims. It was the peninsula of Nova Scotia they saw in all their dreams, a great wharf thrusting out toward the cod banks.

Pious men, these, singing psalms through their noses precisely as they talked, for they were Yankees of the Yankees, gaunt powerful men with nut-cracker faces and shrewd eyes, who drank much rum and feared nobody but a God who was always very near and talked through his nose to them.

"A fine place to dry fish and handy the Banks," Bradford told them. "We'd ha' moved our families there long since if 'tweren't for the French and Injuns."

"They say there's good farmland along Fundy Bay," said Increase Nickerson. "Cleared and diked by the 'Cajun people that was took off in '55. To be had now for the takin'."

"That's for farmers," Bradford snorted. "We're fishermen, us Cape-Codders. That Nova Scotia province must always depend in the main upon the fishery, and the south and east coast is the place for it—handy the Banks, an easy run to Halifax or Boston, and none o' that Fundy tide, where your harbour goes out to sea twice a day and leaves your vessel on her beam ends in the mud."

He spread a map before them and thrust a thick finger at the inlet where our town now stands. "There's Kebamkoogwek. Meanin', The-River-has-a-Bar-at-its-Mouth." .

"Humph!" they said.

"Ah, but the river scours a channel in the bar, with twenty feet good water on common tides and a goodish bit more on the springs. What d'ye want? It's schooners you've got, not seventy-fours. Within the bar the river takes a turn to the west and there's a tidal pool, sheltered from all winds. That's the place for us. A brook runs off the hillside big enough to turn a saw-mill, grist-mill, anything ye want. The whole land's a forest that's never heard the sound of an axe—shipbuildin' timber growin' by the waterside—and there's a salmon fishery in the river mouth good for a thousand barrels a season."

"Then why didn't the French settle the place?" demanded Micah Daggett.

Bradford grunted. "Farmers! They'd no real taste for the sea. The French must have their hands and feet in the dirt always. Well, there's more rock than dirt at Kebamkoogwek."

Then Judah Merricombe spoke the question in all their minds. "What about the Injuns?"

"Look'ee here," Silas Bradford said. "In my father's time they hanged women for witches at Salem. 'Cause why? 'Cause they were afeared o' what they didn't know. So 'tis with people don't know Injuns. Injuns ain't a danger but to men that's afraid o' the shadows in the forest. Tell you I've been in those parts nigh fifteen year, fightin' Injuns their own way, and beat 'em at it. D'ye know what they call me? Mel-ke-ga—Strong Fist, that is. Ay, and they've other names for me, come to that. Noo-je-na-ba-de-ga—The Slayer—and after we drove out the 'Cajun French and burnt their farms it was Pe-jis-to-wa-ya-luk—He-Smokes-Them-Out. D'ye think they'd provoke me lightly? I tell you I was trained in a rough school that held the only good Injuns were the dead 'uns. Strike, strike first, and strike hard—that's the secret, and waste no time on words. *They* know. I'm not saying this to boast."

"We must have room for the flakes to spread and dry our fish," Judah objected. "Means an almighty big stockade for a few men and boys to guard when we're off to the Banks."

"Are ye men or what?" Silas Bradford cried. "I'll have no stockade about me. We'll build our settlement as if 'twas on Cape Cod, for look'ee here, a stockade's a bad thing. People inside come to think upon it as the limit o' their world. The savages see it that way too. I'll have none of it."

"We've got wives and younkers to think of," Amos Harding said.

"Ease your minds, then. The Injuns have wives and younkers too. They've learned their lesson. Wrote in blood, it was. Besides, they're a scattered, wanderin', shiftless people. The mad priest Le Loutre managed to gather a few hundred *kenaps* now and again, wi' the promise o' blankets and arms and some trumpery for their women; but he never held 'em long, 'specially after they'd got mauled in a fight or two. Besides, Le Loutre is gone now. His bishop at Quebec disowned him and sent Father Maillard to preach peace amongst the tribes. Ye've nothing to fear but your own fancies. Words! Words! Great God, I am no talking man. D'ye want to go or not?"

"People's goin' to Nova Scotia from all New England," Increase Nickerson said.

"Us too, then," Amos Harding said, "afore someone gets to Kebamkoogwek ahead of us."

So they agreed and formed a Committee of Proprietors, in the New England fashion (in Old England they would have called themselves a Company of Adventurers), and came to Kebamkoogwek in the summer of 1759, when Wolfe was hammering at the gates of Quebec. Sixteen schooners lay in the tidal pool above the bar. Women stared over the low bulwarks at the forest where the axes rang; quiet, unsmiling Cape Cod women in heavy homespun gowns, relieved by a bright handkerchief about the shoulders; the hard-working, child-bearing pioneer women who married at sixteen, were middle-aged at twenty-eight, and very often dead at thirty-five.

Each settler had a measured strip of water-front with all the land that lay behind it, and so our town began as a procession of clearings along the shore, linked by a rough track where the yoked oxen struggled to haul sleds (they had no wagons) amongst the boulders and the stumps. The first homes were crude log huts with puncheon floors, stone-slab hearths and chimneys of clay moulded over sticks.

But Silas Bradford built himself a proper house at the very start. He was rich in the light of those times. The Nova Scotia governors had paid him well for his sloop and his services: and in the background, in the dark scalp-hunting years . . . well, the prices had been good and paid in gold. He brought his material ready-sawn from Boston, beams of red pine, oak posts and joists, white pine scantlings, planks and clapboards, spruce flooring, windows of real glass, doors—he forgot nothing, not even the bricks for the chimneys, nor the great slab of mahogany for the mantelpiece in the parlour, nor the delft tiles for the hearth. A provident man.

It was strange to him that the others clung so to the sea in their building, as if it were a refuge to be kept at hand. Silas chose his land deliberately at the north skirt of the settlement, at the edge of the forest where the river flowed down from the mysterious interior. As for the town street, he scorned the track that clung thus to the harbourside and cut out a road running straight up the slope into the forest, and built his house to face it, calling it Wolfe Street after his old commander, and so it is known to this day.

They wanted to call their settlement Newport, because it was just that; but someone pointed out that there was a Newport in Rhode Island, founded by Antinomians from Massachusetts Bay, and therefore not quite respectable, and Bradford said bluntly, "Call it Oldport and be done with it. It's old enough. The Injuns say their great god Glooskap camped here when the world was young."

And Oldport it was, and is.

They saw a few Indians in the Fall, canoes stealing up-river in the dusk, hugging the far side of the pool; but there was nothing to fear from these furtive wanderers. Oldport kept a musket over its mantelpiece, ready to hand, and let defence go at that. The first winter was hard. They still tell tales of it in our town. The river froze, and the tidal pool as well, and the great mass of ice in the pool rose and fell with the tide, breaking along the shores, swaying its tremendous weight against the banks with the winds, freezing again on the slack.

The makeshift wharves of that first summer were crushed to matchwood, and some of the vessels sank at their moorings. Food ran short. They had relied on the hunting, and the hunting that year was poor. For fresh meat they snared white hares in the frozen swamps. Flour was a luxury. Chiefly they lived on codfish caught and dried the previous year, and on smoked salmon and old ship-biscuit. They suffered a disease which may have been scurvy or a form of beri-beri, but which they considered a malady of the country. Yet they hung on. An enduring people.

As soon as the ice was out of the river they patched their vessels and set out for the fishery on which their lives and fortunes depended, leaving the boys and old men to get firewood for the women. They felt their town secure. Had not Silas Bradford said so, and wasn't he there, the grim strong man, to face whatever problems might arise?

A few days after they sailed for the Banks, Ichabod Limard came rattling at Bradford's door, the stout oak door fetched all the way from Boston. Ichabod was a tall pale youth from the Maine backwoods, where he had been scalped with a number of other unfortunates in one of the French-Indian raids. His coarse yellow hair stopped at a patch of pink skin on the top of his head, crudely circular like the tonsure of a monk, where the scalp had healed. The muscles of his face had gone slack, as the muscles of scalped heads do, so that his features dripped downward like soft wax, a mass of thick wrinkles and heavy jowls, with the eyes peering light blue through the slits. His mind had warped, too.

Silas opened the door and the poor half-wit stood gibbering in the warmth of the Bradford kitchen, in his torn and patched drab homespun breeches and grey woollen stockings, a coarse linsey shirt and ragged blue coat. There was still much snow in the shadow of the woods but where the sun fell the ground was bare, with greasy mud in the hollows. Ichabod's moose-hide moccasins soiled the hooked rug on the kitchen floor.

"Injuns?" Silas said. "Well, what of it?"

Mrs. Bradford turned an inquiring eye. She itched to order this filthy ragamuffin out of doors—messing her clean floor!—but she was vaguely alarmed.

"All the men away at the fishing," she murmured, as if Silas did not know. She was a little afraid of Silas, a grim man, and touchy on some subjects. She had asked him once, soon after they were married, if he had ever scalped a woman—a tactless question.

He answered abruptly, "Be still, woman." His grey eyes had gone hard and cold, like the ice in the edge of the woods. She folded her hands and said no more. He took a musket from the moose-horns over the mantel, poured a stiff charge from the powder-horn hanging on the wall, measured it with the ramrod, poured a little more, thrust home a wad, two balls, another wad. He examined the gun-flint, primed the gun, nodded, and leaned the musket against a chair.

He exchanged his shoes for a pair of moccasins and pulled on a shirt of caribou hide, his ranger shirt, the sleeves fringed from wrist to shoulder with dangling leather points. His old ranger cap of racoon fur hung on a nail, its glossy tail dangling. For some queer whim he rejected it and put on his thrice-cocked blue Boston hat, his ship hat, crisp and stained with salt, one peak torn by the flying grape at Louisbourg. It gave him a certain air of authority, perhaps, that the fur cap lacked.

He slipped a tomahawk in his belt, slung on powder horn and bullet pouch, caught up the musket and was gone, all in a potent silence. Mrs. Bradford saw him step across the stones and stumps of "Wolfe Street" and vanish amongst the pines, moving like a lean cat in his moccasins. Silas struck back upon the ridge and followed it for a mile in the bare hardwoods on the south side of the crest, where the spring sun had melted the snow and his moccasins left no tracks. Then he turned toward the river.

On the north slope, where the April sun never fell, the snow lay deep and crusted in the green gloom of tall pines and hemlocks. He wished he had brought his snowshoes but the crust bore him well enough. A fool's journey, he told himself. The poor half-wit had seen half a dozen peaceful hunters and multiplied them by four. He was always seeing Injuns.

Silas perceived the camp smoke now, and moved more cautiously. From the bare branch of a great oak on a spur of the ridge he looked straight down upon the camp, fifteen wigwams or more, some in the edge of the woods, the rest pitched on a flat of dead grass at the riverside. Children moved about the fires, a few curs slept in the sun. Beside one of the fires a group of young squaws were playing *al-tes-ta-kun*. They used a platter finely carved from knurl of maple, tossing the little bone discs and catching them expertly. At each throw they bent forward, heads together, watching the fall of the discs, counting those with the lucky mark uppermost, and the spillikins they used for forfeit passed from hand to hand.

Their caribou-hide smocks and leggings were soiled with the grease and soot of winter fires. They wore fillets of red cloth about their heads but the long black hair flittered about their shoulders with their rocking movements. The rattle of dice and the giggling laughter came up very clearly to the man in the oak. They were keeping no watch. Were these people peaceable or simply ignoring the presence of the white settlement just below, knowing its impotence? There was no sign of men or canoes. That was ominous.

Silas descended the tree carefully and walked down to the camp. The snow crust held firmly to the very edge of the trees but in the sunny wild meadow by the river the brown grass was bare. He stood there in plain sight with the musket in the crook of his arm. For a long time he remained thus, a statue in a shaft of sunlight through the trees. The young squaws were intent on their game. An older woman came from a wigwam, waddling toward the river with a brass pot in her hand. She saw Bradford and froze at once. They stared at each other.

One or two of the players looked up, regarding the woman curiously, and followed her stiff gaze to the man in the edge of the woods. Then the whole camp was watching him, even the children, all in utter silence. The curs, sensing trouble, roused from their slumbers and snarled, but like the women, they were awed by this still intruder.

"*Kway!*" said Bradford in his strong voice. "Greeting!"

They did not answer. All those black eyes were wide and frightened.

"Where are my Meeg-a-Mahg brothers?"

Again silence.

Bradford said softly, "I see that my daughters have no tongues and I am sad, for my warriors take the hair of silent women."

A young squaw spoke hurriedly. "*Wis-ko-ma-ya-sa*—they have gone to hunt moose."

"My daughter lies! I see the rock where my brothers have been grinding paint. They have taken the canoes. Do the Meeg-a-Magh paint for the hunt? Do they hunt moose in canoes? *Tal-sut-um-un*—how does it sound to thee?" He could see wrinkled female faces peering from the wigwam flaps. One spoke.

"There is one canoe, an old one. Behold, it is in the bushes by the river."

Silas gestured fiercely. "Take it then, and fetch my brothers. I would have talk with them."

"They would not come," the old woman said sullenly.

"Tell them Pe-jis-to-wa-ya-luk stands in their camp, my daughter. They will come." None moved. The old woman withdrew, frightened, into the wigwam. Silas turned his cold eyes to the hesitating young squaws.

"What pleasure shall the young men find in the arms of dead women? Who is to shelter the child when the wigwam burns? Go, while there is time!"

Two ran to a clump of alders on the bank and put off in a canoe, an old thing with gunwales chipped and splintered on hard portages, the sides a mass of bark patches and daubs of black gum. They paddled rapidly downstream and disappeared around the bend.

A long wait. Bradford said no more. The women watched him beadily. After a time they began to steal glances into the woods at his back. He had expected that. The warriors would land their canoes below the point and creep through the woods to see what was afoot before showing themselves. His position there was awkward, for he dared not take his eyes from the women. They were as quick with a tomahawk as any of their men.

He stepped over to the group of young women silent about the forgotten game, and squatted where he could watch them and the woods, with the musket across his knees. They shrank away from him, and he said quietly, "Won-to-ko-de—it is peace." In swift side-glances he kept an eye on the river but nothing came around the bend. From the woods came the cry of the loon; not the maniacal laughter but the long call, three minor notes, a mournful sound.

He murmured, "The loon has no feet for branches, my daughters. Call my brothers to the fire. I wish to make talk."

A young matron—he had noticed her anxious gaze toward the staring children—stood up quickly and flung back her head, pouring the loon's wild laughter from her throat. In a moment, magically, an Indian stood in the open at the edge of the meadow. There was no movement, no sound. He materialized. The *kenap* wore nothing but a leather breech-clout and moccasins. His round Micmac face was streaked with red and orange paint. His brown body shone with bear grease. The coarse black hair was gathered on the top of his head with a thong—the Micmacs did not shave the head leaving nothing but a scalp-lock like the continental tribes—and a single eagle feather was thrust through the knot. He carried an ancient French firelock and a glittering steel tomahawk. A stone tobacco pipe was slung about his neck by a thong.

"Won-to-ko-de," called Bradford, without rising. They could not shoot him where he sat without risking the squaws. The warrior advanced boldly and squatted facing the white man at a safe distance, just beyond the reach of a tomahawk. He stank of sweat and rancid bear grease. Evidently the return had been made in some haste. Bradford found some grim humour in the thought of the other *kenaps*, stripped and painted for war, cooling their sweat now in the icy gloom of the trees, with the snow crust under their feet—perhaps beneath their bellies. They could not stay there long. They were tough, but not as tough as that.

Silas called out in his ringing voice toward the trees, "Ho! Is thy sagamore afraid, my brothers, that he send a *kenap* to make his talk? What medicine is this?"

Instantly the bushes parted and a tall Indian stepped into the sunlight. Like the other he was stripped to breech-clout and moccasins; but the moccasins were gaudy with rows of coloured trade beads, a pewter crucifix hung from a thin brass chain about his neck, and he wore on his head a silver-laced cocked hat of the kind worn by French officers at Louisbourg and Quebec.

The sagamore was painted more elaborately than his *kenap*. A black stripe encircled mouth and nose, overlaid with stripes of red ochre, and his eye-sockets were flaring scarlet cups. He carried a fine fowling-piece with a chased silver lock-plate. Silas stood up as he approached. They dropped their guns carefully and held up their right hands.

"Kway!"

"Kway!"

"I am called Kwemoo, the Loon," said the sagamore calmly.

"I greet thee, O Loon. Men call me Strong Fist. I have other names."

The fierce black eyes gleamed in their scarlet sockets. "The trees of the forest know the fame of Strong Fist. Ayah! His medicine is all-powerful. Did I not fire a ball at him by the waters of Tawópskek ten summers gone? And did not the Strong Fist brush it aside? Ayah! This thing I saw!"

Silas remembered that, an ambush almost in the shadow of Fort Anne. He had been shifting his tomahawk from the right hand to the left, and the ball glanced from the moving blade.

"Behold, I come to make talk with my brother," he said smoothly, "and find none but squaws and children in his camp. Have my brothers made war medicine?" A rhetorical question. War medicine was plain on their faces.

"Behold," retorted the sagamore, "we have watched my white brother's village and saw none but squaws and children. Where are the white warriors?"

The inevitable question! They had seen the weakness of the town. Still, The Slayer's bold appearance in their camp puzzled them, as he intended it should. Silas hoped that his famous presence there amongst their women and children would poison their spirit with precisely the same fear he knew himself. A subtle notion. Yet he was not a subtle man, and felt a sickening doubt of his ability to accomplish what he wished.

There was no blinking the uncomfortable facts. The Loon was no petty patriarch. These painted *kenaps* were the advance patrol of a tribe moving down the river from the winter hunting grounds in the interior, a pack of human wolves, lean and famished after the hard months in the snow. Ordinarily they would scatter up and down the coast in little fishing camps for the summer; but Oldport, a shining new temptation, lay between them and the sea. The thought of the defenceless settlement weighed on Silas like a stone. He cursed his blind confidence. This was what came of trusting other things than guns! For the first time in his life he faced a situation in which words were the only possible weapons, and heard a mocking laughter ringing out of all the past. This was Silas Bradford, the fighting man who believed in nothing else, who left the talking to men with a taste for it and held them in contempt—even the founder of Halifax, the man Cornwallis, whom he had liked otherwise.

He seemed to see Cornwallis now, treating patiently with petty chiefs who stank the council room and shed lice on the carpet, nursing their self-respect, sending them away with gifts, seeing that the guard presented arms as they passed, striving for the goodwill of those savage ragamuffins—Cornwallis the aristocrat, with a fleet in the harbour and regiments at his beck! To Captain Silas Bradford of the rangers all that smacked of cowardice, a paltry compromise with evil. Words! Words! Words, when any sound man knew the only good Injuns were the dead ones!

Now, suddenly, he saw what lay behind that madness. The Englishman had looked forward to a time—to this time—when small settlements would spring up along the coast, impossible to garrison, dependent for their prosperity, indeed their existence, upon the goodwill of the savages. But all that was past and far away. What words could serve now, here in this wild meadow, in the presence of these staring squaws, the wooden-faced *kenap* and his chief, the menace lurking in the trees and moving down the river?

The Micmacs had a smattering of bastard French but no English at all. Silas spoke Micmac well, but he had no respect for it, a grunting tongue that crammed a sentence into a single word and again took half a minute's gutturals to express what an Englishman could say in a second. In Micmac oratory the circuitous approach was the only decent way to the subject, you talked in circles, in rhetorical questions, in queer flowery figures of speech. They had a weakness for eloquence and could be swayed, as Le Loutre had swayed them against the English. Could he, the man who did not believe in words, talk them out of their war paint when they knew their own strength and surmised his weakness?

But did they know his weakness? The sagamore kept darting a suspicious gaze across the river, and staring toward the high pines at the top of the ridge. It dawned upon Bradford suddenly that the Indians, noting the absence of white men in the town, suspected a trick, an ambush—more, a raid upon their camp. His presence there was proof of it. He had deceived the squaws with some such pretence but he was astonished that the warriors should believe it also. How long before they guessed the truth?

"Why have my white brothers made their village at Kebamkoogwek?" demanded the sagamore harshly. "The river is ours, O Strong Fist. These are our hunting-grounds."

"We do not want your hunting-grounds, O Kwemoo, for we are ship-men who must go upon the Big Water for fish. We want only peace in this place."

The sagamore grunted, "Behold, long ago when I was a young man we made a peace with the English. Was it not broken? Behold, ten summers gone I went to Chebuktook with other sagamores of the Meeg-a-Mahg and Maliseet peoples and made peace with the English again. Did we not make our totems upon the white bark? Did not the English sagamores make theirs in the name of their great sagamore Joj across the Big Water? Did we not bury the hatchet? Who dug it up again? Konwallich turned you and your leather-shirts upon us. He gave you gold for scalps of our people."

"Not before the Meeg-a-Mahg broke the peace," insisted Bradford vigorously. "Who took the hair of his red-coats outside the palisades of Chebuktook? At Tawopskek? Was not this in the Meeg-a-Mahg country? Men do not scalp themselves."

"It was done at the Otter's bidding," muttered the sagamore sullenly.

"Ayah! There is much blood upon the hands of Le Loutre. Now he is gone. So be it. The English now are at Quebec, O Kwemoo. Louisbourg is no more. There is no stone upon another."

"Onontio has strong medicine," said The Loon doubtfully.

By this name the Algonkin tribes knew the king of France.

"The medicine of the great sagamore Joj is stronger. Behold, the French have gone from all the Meeg-a-Mahg country. Did we not take them away in our ships? Did not we burn their villages?"

"The snow melts in the spring sun, O Strong Fist. But is there not another winter and another snow?"

Silas was getting nowhere, and meanwhile the rest of the war party had been slipping from the chill woods into the sunlight. Some stood tense in the edge of the meadow, watching the silent green mass of the hillside. The rest grouped themselves about the speakers. The rustle of moccasins behind him tried Bradford's nerves in a new and painful manner, his ears strained for the whistle of the descending tomahawk, all instinct crying out, urging him to leap aside and make a fight for it. But he stood motionless with thumbs hooked in his belt, steadying knee and hand and eye, serving a bitter apprenticeship in the strange art of diplomacy.

All the *kenaps* were stripped, greased and painted for war. He counted twenty-three. Their ribs and the powerful ropes of muscle stood forth in the brown hairless skin—it had been a hard and hungry winter but there was no weakness in them. All were armed with good steel tomahawks and guns of various worth. One young *kenap* had in his belt a matchlock pistol with a huge butt beautifully chased, a thing of unguessed age. At every waist dangled one or two crooked-knives, made from scraps of metal on the old savage pattern, with short blades and large curved hafts, and sheaths of leather ornamented with beads and dyed porcupine quills. Some wore necklaces of bear teeth which, like the grease on their bodies, were supposed to give them the strength of Moween. Others had tobacco pipes slung about their necks. All had powder horns and bullet pouches. Bradford wondered what they contained after a winter's hunting.

One of the *kenaps* spoke up boastfully. "The Meeg-a-Mahg will drive the English into the Big Water. Then Onontio will return to his brothers."

He had a villainous squint. Silas stabbed a finger at him.

"*Ankaptaan!* Behold! He looks two ways and sees only his nose, and that he calls Onontio!"

The shadow of a smile passed over the tall sagamore's face. Silas turned to him, but included them all in the wave of his big hand. Out of his aching fear for the women and children in the town below, his memories of Cornwallis, his own half-anger, half-remorse—out of these and yet from nowhere that he understood, the words he wanted rushed to his mouth at last.

"O my brothers, this is thy hunting-ground, and the river is thy path between winter and summer. So be it. My people have made their village where the river meets the tide, for though they must live upon the earth like other men their living lies in the Big Water. So be it. The land is wide, the Big Water is wide, and all we are very small. The great wigwam of the sky covers us alike, and the stars look down upon us, and all we are very small. When the young moon comes, a virgin upon her back, does she not shine upon us all? When she has met her lord the sun beneath the world and returned ripe to the sky again, does she not shine upon us all? Who does the sun warm in spring? Who does he burn in summer? Behold, when the wild goose flies southward in the fall of the year his wings fan up the cold wind from the north, and does not the north wind blow upon us all? The snow—is it deeper for my brothers than for me? Does the fire warm one man more than another? The hunting is poor, and behold, you hunger. The fishing is poor, and behold, we hunger. Is it not the same hunger?"

"*We-la-boog-wa*," grunted the sagamore. "These are good words."

"Behold, my brothers, He-who-looks-at-his-nose talked of war It is easy to talk of war. Squaws, children can talk of war. But when the blood flows, what talk can put it back? Behold, the Meeg-a-Mahg are mighty warriors. The French are mighty warriors. The English are mighty warriors. Have they not proved themselves, all through the time of our fathers and our own? And is the hunting better? Are there more fish in the Big Water? The smoke in the wigwam—does it smart the eye less because a new scalp dries upon the pole? There is a time for war and we have had much war. The death-cry of the warrior has silenced the birds in the forest. The wailing of the squaws is as the east wind in the reeds. Is there no time for peace?"

"These are the words of a coward," the squinting *kenap* said

"My brother cannot see beyond his nose. How brave is that?" The young squaws giggled. The *kenap* scowled.

"Behold, how handsome is this man, my daughters! What one among thee would not take him to her arms? That one is surely blind of an eye and cannot see from the other!"

The squaws laughed aloud now. The young braves stirred un easily. The white man was goading He-who-looks-at-his-nose deliberately. The young men were keen for war, yet they feared to speak, for they were proud and the white man had a barbed tongue, and the laughter of squaws was a clinging thing. All this the white man knew.

The squinting *kenap* sprang, swinging high the tomahawk, and Bradford stepped forward swiftly and struck him full in the face with that ham-like fist, a tremendous buffet. The *kenap* lay on his back with the blood spurting from mouth and nostrils

"Ayah!" murmured the squaws. "Truly this is Strong Fist."

"He wanted blood," Bradford said quietly. "He has it. Let him suck well on it. Behold, I have come amongst ye alone. Is there fear in my heart then? Yet I talk peace! And I speak for all the English here upon the river. Is there fear in these words?"

"There is no fear in the English," said the tall chief gravely "if they are all like thee and thy leather-shirts, O Strong Fist. I have known them many moons, and the blood of the Meeg-a

Mahg flowed wherever they went. They kept their faces high and had the heart of Moween the bear. The forest was their pathway, the river their drinking-pot, they took the war path in the summer heat and in the winter snow, and there was no staying them. These things we know. But how are we to know if Strong Fist means these words of peace?" And saying this the sagamore turned and cast a meaning glance toward the forest on the ridge.

Silas put forth a hand toward the ridge, as if a regiment of his leather-shirts were there concealed. "O Kwemoo, there is one way to know, the ancient way, the only way. Let us bury the hatchet together—here!—and may the curse of all the evil spirits in the sky, the forest, the rivers, and the sea fall upon him who breaks the peace!"

The *kenaps* drew back a little, uneasy at this invocation of evil. All the superstition in their bones had come awake. There was a silence. He-who-looks-at-his-nose lay like a dead man, eyes closed, blood oozing slowly from his nostrils and drying in thick dribbles over the paint upon his cheeks. The children stared at him, fascinated.

The Loon spoke suddenly. "O Strong Fist, these are good words. Let us bury the hatchet as you say." His intent black eyes regarding his own fine weapon reluctantly, then flicked to the shining steel in Bradford's belt. Silas considered swiftly.

"O Kwemoo, the burial of the hatchet is a custom of the ancient time. Let us then bury *koon-da-wa-se*, a stone hatchet, as the ancient people did."

The Micmacs had long since discarded stone weapons, but some of the finer specimens were preserved as keepsakes, he knew well. The sagamore made an imperious gesture to one of the squaws. She trotted away to a wigwam and brought out a tomahawk of the olden time. The head was of a dark stone like nothing Silas had seen in Nova Scotia, taken in some far war perhaps, or passed through the tribes in the way of trade. Its edge was much broken.

"Behold," The Loon said doubtfully, "our children have played with this thing upon the rocks. Is this good medicine?"

This or nothing, Silas thought. Aloud he cried, holding the thing high, "Behold, my brothers! Is not the edge broken? So does the hatchet grow dull with much war! Have we not taken it from the hands of children? So do the fathers bury the hatchet, that the children may live in peace!"

He flung the tomahawk out over the river, and it went looping end over end and disappeared in a small feather of spray.

"*Talaak*? Why?" asked the sagamore, astonished.

"That no man dig it up again! Let there be peace between our peoples till the rivers run dry and vanish from the earth. Is it well?"

"It is well," they chanted.

The Loon turned his bright black gaze to the still woods on the ridge.

"Let my white brother now call his *kenaps* to the stream, that we may wash our faces together in the custom."

"O Loon," Bradford said softly, "there are no warriors. They have gone in their great canoes to fish far out upon the Big Water. See!"

He poured forth the long yowling war-whoop of the Mohawks that his rangers had made their own. There was no answer from the hillside. Nothing moved. The woods lay breathless under the beat of the sunshine—breathless and empty.

Two or three warriors of the Meeg-a-Mahg came to their feet fingering hatchets, muttering that Strong Fist had tricked them into peace. The sagamore rebuked them sternly.

"O fools, the hatchet has been buried. So be it. Strong Fist has the heart of a bear. Behold, he came alone into our mist and with his naked hand smote down He-who-looks-at-his-nose. What one of you would go into the English village with naked hands? Let such a one say if there be shame in peace between brave men!"

With an immense dignity he strode to the river's edge and fell upon his knees, washing the war-paint from his face. The others followed, silently, and the unpainted Bradford knelt beside them and went through the ritual, drenching face and beard. The squaws withdrew in haste to the wigwams, for it was not good that women should look upon these things. Where the *al-tes-ta-kun* players had sat the fire was dying. A thin wisp rose blue from the embers straight into the April sky. The smitten *kenap* lay a little distance away, making snoring sounds. His nose was broken.

The dice lay in the maple-wood platter where the squaws had dropped them, in a litter of the forfeit-spillikins. A warrior returning from the stream scattered them contemptuously with a sweep of his moccasin. The men formed a wide circle, squatting about the thin smoulder of the fire, with Bradford at The Loon's right hand. A stone pipe was fitted with a reed and its bowl was filled with the harsh tobacco of the Meeg-a-Mahg—leaves of the wild *ta-ma-wa* mixed with shreds of willow bark. The sagamore lit it with a coal and sucked in a great whiff, closing his eyes and letting the smoke curl slowly from his nostrils. He passed the pipe to Bradford.

The pipe went round the circle, was filled, was passed again. Thus they sat for hours, in a profound silence, while the sun dropped down the sky and the squaws whispered together in the wigwams. And so it was that with the coming of the dusk there came upon our river and our town a peace—a peace that never was broken.

JUSTICE MARTIN BUNT went down the harbour on a spring afternoon in 1778 with mingled curiosity and distaste—a trifle more distaste than curiosity. He was curious to know the meaning of the smoke and thunder which had filled the harbour mouth since mid-morning, setting all Oldport agog. And he was going to present his compliments to His Majesty's Navy, which he had no reason to love; going in fact at a peremptory command from Captain Milligan of H.M.S. *Blonde*, and in one of the frigate's boats, rowed by eight powder-stained tars and steered by a jaunty young midshipman.

There were several reasons for Mr. Bunt's discomfort. One was that he was suffering from scabies—"that lothsome Distemper call'd the Itch," as he wrote himself—a common ailment of the times, when people spent long winters muffled against the cold, and bathing was considered dangerous. On the previous night he and his wife had anointed themselves with the usual remedy, a mixture of brimstone, tar and tallow, to be kept on for two days and nights. The midshipman in charge of the boat had given Bunt no time to wash, change his linen or even to tell his wife where he was going.

"You smell like hell," said the midshipman wittily.

"That," answered Mr. Bunt astonishingly, for he was a pious man, "is just the way I feel."

Mr. Bunt was in his forties then, and chief magistrate of our town, a burly red-faced merchant with a smattering of New England law, a supreme honesty, a touching faith in the future of Nova Scotia, and a wistful longing to be somewhere or something else. Greatness had been thrust upon him when Silas Bradford, the founder of our town, went off to the siege of Havana and died of fever there in '62. The people of Oldport, in the New England fashion, looked to the justices for leadership, and they elected Mr. Bunt to fill Silas's big shoes—a rôle for which Martin felt inadequate.

Not that Martin Bunt lacked courage—he had fought bravely enough in the colonial militia at Louisbourg in '58. But now that he was twenty years older and a deacon of the church, and possessed a struggling trader's business and a shrewish wife, with two daughters at school in Boston, he had learned to put discretion and valour in their proper places.

The other justices we need not consider much. Justice Daggett was very old and feeble, and he left the town in the midst of its greatest troubles and went to a Heaven where presumably there was no taxation, with or without representation. As for Justice Benajah Thripps, he is a story in himself; a cold, shrewd, tireless man without fear or conscience, who played both ends against the middle throughout the American Revolution, invested in privateers on both sides, never hesitated to betray the ships and possessions of his friends, and after the war removed with his family and fortune to the neighbourhood of Salem, Massachusetts. There he lived the rest of his days like a prince, with a great house, a staff of negro servants and the finest carriage and horses in that city of wealthy freebooters. It is related that after his death his body lay in state for a week in the great hall of his house, "embalmed" in cayenne pepper, an object of devout curiosity to the folks of Danvers and Salem. If there is any justice beyond the grave the material of his embalmment was a portent.

Two men in the Oldport of those times might be considered well educated: the Reverend Peleg Potter, a graduate of Harvard College, a godly but tipsy soul who repeatedly was asked to leave but stayed to the end of his days; and Mr. Amasa Barriman, of Yale, the schoolmaster who played the violin so charmingly, and gave singing lessons and lectures on "musick" in the Meeting House on week-day evenings. In the midst of the Revolution Mr. Barriman left without any asking, indeed without warning, leaving an unfinished sum in the shape of debts, and a mournful male chorus of creditors.

For the rest, our townsmen were very ignorant of the great world and the machinery that was to grind them slowly in blood and tears. Their news came by letter and pamphlet and word of mouth from their friends and relatives in New England. They had the right of sending a representative to the Nova Scotia legislature—a right which they exercised indifferently because no man could spare the time or indeed the cost of his tavern bill at Halifax.

Once or twice Mr. Bunt went down, a shabby and awkward stranger amongst the legislative swells. The rest of the time our town was "represented" by one of the Halifax merchants and lawyers who then, with the governor's favour, directed the colony's affairs, and Oldport considered itself favoured indeed if this representative addressed a note of thanks to the constituents he had never seen.

The town itself was run simply, on the New England model, a little democracy in which the justices and militia officers were selected by vote, and paid by fee or subscription—when they were paid at all. Like their pilgrim fathers (most of them came from Cape Cod) they appointed a day of prayer and fasting each spring and a day of feast and thanksgiving every fall, and observed them religiously. Christmas and Easter passed almost unnoticed, except in the way of prayer—it would have been unthrifty as well as "Popish" to have too many holidays. But on the King's birthday the militia company straggled to Battery Point (without uniforms and with no weapons but their hunting-guns, a queer collection) and fired a salute from the two 12-pounders, relics of the French wars, which then constituted the sole defence of the harbour.

For years they had watched with a shadowy disquiet the growing hostility of the older colonies toward the mother country, but they had no suspicion of the tragedy in store for themselves. Their sympathies lay where one might expect, though there was a wide and deep difference between sympathy for the cause of rebellion and agreement with what came out of it—the utter separation of the colonies in America from the rest of the British world.

It was no small part of their trial that when the Revolution began, the governor's seat at Halifax held the violent and stupid Legge, astonished to find himself head of the lone Atlantic colony not under the rebel flag. He bombarded the home authorities with petitions for troops, seeing sedition where there was only doubt, and rebellion wherever a few young hot-heads erected a "liberty pole" or refused to take the militia oath without a reservation against fighting their New England kin. The suspect Yankee settlements, of which Oldport was the biggest, he visited with a heavy hand.

He seized the honest if poorly spelled letters of our merchants and searched them avidly for treason, took away the two sorry cannon which were Oldport's only defence against rebel privateers, forbade all intercourse with New England (where of necessity our fishermen had to buy the farm produce they could not raise themselves), and harried the inhabitants with oaths of allegiance, abjuration, and supremacy.

As if this were not enough he sent a frigate to keep watch on Oldport loyalty—and Captain Dudington of *Senegal* was the contemptuous high-handed sort best fitted to arouse rebellion where there had been none. Dudington lay in our small harbour from Christmas '75 to April '76, stopping and searching every petty coaster, seizing whatever seemed contraband to his jaundiced eye, pressing the youngest and ablest men into the King's service as he pleased—(Justice Bunt protested as chief magistrate and was called a "bloody rebel" for his pains)—and sailed away just at a time when privateers were swarming out of Salem and other rebel ports to harry the Nova Scotia coast.

Our town was unarmed and helpless. Rebel privateers boldly made a rendezvous of an uninhabited harbour six miles to the west. His Majesty's fleet made no effort to drive them off. But the drunken crew of a Halifax privateer, licensed by Governor Legge, made free with our town for several days, insulting the people and threatening to "burn the rebel nest over their heads"; and a self-important lieutenant visited a sessions of the peace at Justice Bunt's house, posted sailors armed with pistols at the door, and stood over Bunt himself with a drawn cutlass "to see that the King's justice was done, by God!"

Upon a Sunday the Reverend Peleg Potter preached a memorable sermon from Isaiah 9—*The Syrians before, and the Philistines behind; and they shall devour Israel with open mouth. For all this his anger is not turned away, but his hand is stretched out still.* He was slightly drunk, but when the Reverend Peleg was only slightly drunk he was very eloquent indeed. Oldport came to see its tribulation as the wrath of God, a thing to be endured and not questioned. But even pious Martin Bunt wondered sometimes *whose* hand was stretched out still, and where his groping people might find it. All this and much more was in his mind as the frigate's boat carried him over the river bar and down the narrow bay on that April afternoon of 1778.

The *Duc de Choiseul* lay against the wooded east shore, on the reefs which have been known ever since as Frenchman's Ledges. Her three masts stood but she was badly holed and half full of water, careened at a sharp angle, yards acockbill, gear hanging all anyhow and a shot-riddled canvas flapping in great dismal rags. The paint of her visible port side was scarred with shot-marks. Three of the lower deck ports had been blown into one, a yawning hole that made Bunt's eyes bulge, seeing the thickness of timber and plank..

"A stern chase an' then hammer-an'-tongs for two hours," the middy said. "Then Monsoor ran her on the reefs. His flag was fouled aloft, I think. He didn't get it down quick enough to suit

Old Milly, at any rate. She heeled to port first, after she struck aground, an' we fired into her again, just as a lot o' the poor devils were pourin' up from the lower deck. Barrin' that it was a jolly fine fight."

He was a pert pale youngster of fifteen or so, the pimples of adolescence enlarged and blotched by the diet of the midshipmen's berth, and he was pleased with the fight and himself and the prospect of prize money.

"Didn't know we was at war with the French," murmured Mr. Bunt.

"Pshaw! We're always at war with France."

Bunt could see the French crew, a vague human mass in the edge of the fir woods, and a number of men roosting like gulls on the rocks by the shore, watching *Blonde*'s sailors swarming over the wreck, and the frigate's boats plying back and forth. The midshipman steered under *Blonde*'s stern. Her ports were all open, some of the guns protruding, others run in for loading, just as they had stood when the fight finished, and her deck was a litter of ramrods, sponges, match-tubs, long wooden cartridge-boxes with their rope beckets, and linstocks stuck in the planking by their pointed iron butts. In the waist was an ever-growing mass of stuff salvaged from the Frenchman. A few splatters of blood, rope-ends, ragged holes in the bulwark, and one or two splintered grooves in the deck witnessed that *Blonde* had suffered, but it was evident that "Monsoor's" shooting had been poor.

The midshipman led the way down a dark companionway and Bunt found himself in the captain's quarters, stooping to avoid the deck beams. The bulkhead between the main cabin and the sleeping compartment had been torn out, probably at the outbreak of war, and replaced with a canvas screen. Captain Milligan arose from a small desk in the inner compartment and greeted his visitor civilly—something new in Bunt's experience.

Besides the desk there was a cot and a twelve-pounder in that confined space. The gun had been cast loose from its frappings and run up to the open port with the train-tackles; and it had been in action, for a handspike, ramrod, and sponge stood beside it and despite the breeze through the port there was a sharp smell of burnt powder. The captain was a dry alert man in white cotton stockings, a pair of stout grogram breeches and an old blue coat with tarnished buttons—evidently his battle rig. There was a black smudge on his right cheek.

"Please sit on the cot," he said, and Mr. Bunt sat down, hat in hand.

"You're the chief magistrate of the town yonder?"

"Yes," Mr. Bunt said heavily. He had been through all this before, aboard the *Senegal* and others, though with much less civility. In a moment the purser would appear and there would be a demand for fresh beef, and the town would have to provide it—at the purser's price.

"Will you drink with me? We've had a busy day, sir, and speaking for myself I can do with a stiff 'un."

"Thank ye kindly," murmured Mr. Bunt. Captain Milligan roared for his steward, a sudden clap of vocal thunder that sounded like a report of the gun at Bunt's knees. Over a pair of stiff 'uns they regarded each other.

"Shall we drink to His Majesty?" asked Captain Milligan, watching Bunt with one eye.

"Why not?" said Bunt. They stood to drink, and Mr. Bunt, unaccustomed to the low deck beams, struck his head with a violence that filled it full of sparks. Captain Milligan appeared not to notice.

"I've sent for you," he said briskly, "because we've a full two hundred prisoners on the shore yonder, some of 'em wounded. I want you to accommodate 'em in the town for a day or two, till I've stripped the wreck. Then I'll take 'em off to the hulks at Halifax."

Mr. Bunt shifted uneasily. "We've got no buildin' big enough to hold 'em, sir, barrin' the Meetin' House, which belongs to the Lord's sarvice. Add to that, sir, the town's very poor and food scarce at this time o' year. We couldn't feed twenty, let alone two hundred."

"Ah! Well, billet 'em, man, billet 'em. Two or three to a house if you like. As for food, I'll have beef and biscuit delivered from the wreck to you. Have 'em come to you each morning, say, for the day's allowance. Messes of ten, say, and ten pounds of beef and ten of biscuit to a mess. I'll make it better if we can salvage enough. They'll miss their wine most, I fancy. Tell 'em it's the fortune of war and hard lines all round." A competent man, Milligan plainly expected competence in Mr. Bunt. "You understand," he added, "you'll be responsible for 'em."

There was a disconsolate lift and droop of Bunt's thick shoulders.

"We've no means of stoppin' 'em if they choose to run off. Cap'n, if that's what ye mean."

"Nonsense! Got a militia company, haven't you?"

"Yes, but no arms, no powder, no shot, nothing."

The captain regarded his visitor curiously. The stiff 'un was working within Martin Bunt. There was an odd note in his voice and a gleam in his eye.

"What's the matter?" demanded Milligan.

Mr. Bunt regarded his shabby hat and his large red hands. He wanted to talk—to talk a lot. He wanted to tell somebody the troubles of his town and people. Instinct and sour experience warned him to hold his tongue before this captain of the Royal Navy, but suddenly his tongue was past holding.

"Well," he burst out, "ye've treated me like a man, the first o' His Majesty's officers to give me a civil word in three—yes, in five years, goin' back afore the Rebellion. S'like this. We come here in '59 to make a settlement, from Cape Cod, nearly all of us. Bin a few come from Conne'ticut since, an' one or two from Boston. Every grown soul in the place today's a native o' Noo England, the heart, d'ye see, o' the—ahum!—Rebellion. All our relations live there. All our friends, barrin' a gen'leman or two in Halifax."

"I see."

"Not yet ye don't, sir. That ain't the half of it! We're mostly a fishin' people that has to git a livin' out o' the sea. The land's poor. We can't raise half, no, nor a quarter o' the grain an' roots we need. The rest we must buy in Noo England. There's no ch'ice about it. Yet the Halifax gov'nor forbids it! Ag'in, to buy we must sell—an' with us it's fish or nawthin'. Dried cod, salt alewives, smoked salmon—that's our livin', an' we have to take our pay in trade, an' trade where we can. That means a trade three-cornered like, 'tween Nova Scotia, the West Indies, an' Noo England. The West Indies take our fish and give us what they've got—rum, sugar, and molasses for the most part. Noo England gives us provisions an' mannafactered goods for the rum and the rest."

"Humph," Milligan said. "But taxation's at the bottom of this American trouble. What's your opinion on that?"

"I told ye we have to take our pay in trade. Cash is scarcer than ...."

"Than loyal men in Oldport?"

"Ah, don't joke, sir," Mr. Bunt implored. He was sweating a little with emotion, or perhaps it was only the drink. "Don't ye joke about loyalty, sir. That's a serious word. S'like this. We seldom see more'n a few pounds cash in the run of a year. Consequent, we don't take taxation very kind, bein' a self-supportin' people that asks nawthin' o' gov'ment but to be let alone. When the troubles begun acrost the Bay o' Fundy we knowed Sam

Adams an' John Hancock was at the bottom of it, and knew 'em for what they were. Jest the same, we didn't like the princ'ple o' the Stamp Act any more'n Boston folk. When 'twas repealed in '66 there was a celebration here in Oldport that lasted two days. We got the news June the third, an' the nex' day—'twas the King's birthday but no harm meant—we burnt an old house for a bonfire."

"The house of a loyalist, I wager!"

"Loyalist?" Bunt turned the strange word on his tongue.

"The rebels call 'em Tories."

"Ah! No, sir. 'Twas a li'l old empty hut that was built when we come to this place in '59 along o' Silas Bradford—Bradford o' the Rangers, that died o' yeller-jack at the seige o' Havana. A mortal pity Silas ain't alive today. Silas always knowed what to do. Silas 'ud know what to do now about the way we're bein' squeezed atween the King and the rebels."

"What do you mean?" demanded Milligan.

Justice Bunt opened his big hands expressively. "The rebel privateers is ravagin' our coast, takin' up our vessels—I've lost two myself. The King's gov'nor at Halifax took away our arms an' left us helpless to defend our property. We've asked ag'in an' ag'in for protection, an' all we've got so far is accusations o' treason."

"You've the protection of His Majesty's Navy, Mr. Bunt," Milligan said stiffly.

"All we've seen o' His Majesty's ships so far," Bunt said grimly, "has been press-gangs and searchin'-parties."

There was a long silence after that.

"D'ye know any reason why the Frenchman yonder"—Captain Milligan jerked his head toward the open port—"should run in here when we overhauled him?"

"None, sir."

"Suppose, Mr. Bunt, I told you she was laden with arms and ammunition for the rebel army, and had rebel colours in her flag locker, and a letter addressed to one Morris, a member of the Congress, from Silas Read, who's Benjamin Franklin's right-hand man in Paris?"

"I know nothing of it, sir."

Their eyes met and stared hard. Captain Milligan stepped to the port with his hands beneath his coat-tails. The bowsprit and the riddled spritsail of the French ship were just visible as *Blonde* swung at anchor.

"Well, we nabbed her at any rate," he said with satisfaction. "The Chevalier de Sucay on board too, and that other mysterious fellow who calls himself Jet D'Eau, hiding in the cable tier. I believe you, Bunt. The rebel army needs this stuff too badly to risk it on a chance revolt in Nova Scotia."

He said this very innocently and shot a quick hard look at Bunt's face. It was an honest face, full of genuine perplexity. Captain Milligan prided himself on his judgement of men.

"Mr. Bunt, a man in my position's got to do his duty and ask no questions."

"Yes,sir."

"At the same time, Bunt, I'm a man and I've got my opinions. It's my opinion you've been damned poorly handled."

"Yes, sir."

"There's been nothing but stupidity in this American affair. There was no need of trouble to begin with—a group of money-grubbing merchants on both sides—and the war's only making a bad matter worse." He added gloomily, "That's not for me to say, of course."

Another silence. Martin Bunt stared at the lees in his glass.

"You understand, Mr. Bunt, I can do nothing for you—nothing absolutely."

"I understand that, Cap'n."

"I can't go shoving my oar into provincial affairs."

"No, sir."

"I am a man without influence, absolutely without influence, Bunt." Captain kept throwing these remarks over his shoulder as he stood at the port, as if to stand off a Bunt in close pursuit. "One unfortunate move and I'd find myself on the beach at half-pay."

"I understand, sir."

Captain Milligan turned and faced Bunt abruptly. "I'm going to salvage all the Frenchman's cargo that I can, and take it to Halifax with the prisoners." A pause. Then, indifferently, "After that the wreck—it'll go to pieces in the first southeast blow, mind—is anybody's as far as I'm concerned."

Mr. Bunt came to his feet. "Thank'ee! Thank'ee, Cap'n! We...."

"Don't thank me, man!" barked the captain of the *Blonde*. He jerked his head once more toward the wreck of the *Duc de Choiseul*, swarming with his men and boats. "You can thank," he said with a grim smile, "Mr. Silas Read, of Paris."

Three days later Martin Bunt heard that name again, but in a very different setting and in quite another voice. A small boy had brought him a mysterious message in the dusk, and he had gone to Mrs. Hewler's tavern near the fish-lots, and found in

her small sanded taproom his younger brother Caleb, Justice
Benajah Thripps, and a long lean man with heavy-lidded eyes
and a Salem drawl.

"This," young Caleb said eagerly, "is Cap'n Jonathan Cogsley,
an' wants a word wi' ye. Marty."

"Cap'n o' what?" said Justice Bunt suspiciously. They had
the air of conspirators, sitting about a single candle with the
curtains drawn, elbows together on a small table, with mugs of
untasted beer before them.

"O' the privateer *Lizard*, in Congress service," drawled the
stranger. He recited particulars in an amused voice, as if he
were reading off a bill of lading. "Now lyin' an' bein' in the
haven known as Port Gambier, two leagues to the west, an'
ready to receive cargo duly consigned—the restraints o' princes
an' rulers an' all other dangers o' the seas notwithstandin'.
Cal'lated to pay ye an official visit yes'day, Marty, but we seen
that English frigate's upper yards jest in time, an' sheered off.
Come overland s'afternoon, I did, shanks mare, a-purpose fer
to see ye."

Mr. Bunt turned a pair of enquiring blue eyes on his fellow-
justice, Benajah Thripps, but the light of the coarse tallow dip
came between; over the flame he could see nothing but a
blurred sly smile.

"What d'ye want o' me?" he said to Cogsley.

"All the goods ye took out o' the Duck de Shozzu 'smornin',
arter the frigate sailed fer Hal'fax. There was—lemme see—"
Cogsley flicked his hard grey eyes toward Benajah Thripps for
an instant, but Justice Thripps was staring at the ceiling—"several chists of arms, a keg or two o' powder, a keg or two o'
balls, an' a box or two o' flints. Funny how that Englishman
come to overlook 'em, warn't it Marty—all tucked up nice an'
dry in the half-deck as they was? Yes, sirree!—an' ye salvaged
'em fer the rightful owners like the Patriot ye was—eh?"

"I salvaged 'em for our militia company," Bunt said stoutly.

"Bah!" snapped Justice Thripps.

"An' ain't givin' 'em up without doo authority," added Martin
Bunt defiantly. "What are ye doin' here wi' this man, Caleb?"

"Caleb's j'ined my crew at Port Gambier along o' half a
dozen other smart lads from your taown," Jonathan Cogsley
said.

"Ye lie!" snapped Bunt, and looked at young Caleb.

"It's the truth," said Caleb Bunt. "Marty, we've been drove
an' cussed an' abused, an' it's come to the point where we've

got to fight one way or t'other. Might's well be this way, as I see it."

"Them guns," put in Captain Cogsley, "was consigned to us at Port Gambier by Mister Read, the Congress agent in France. 'Twas reckoned safe, up here on the coast o' Nova Scotia where nobody'd suspect, an' we could run the guns an' stuff safe into Boston where that blunderin' Frenchman was sure to git caught. How'd that noisy frigate captain git on to the game? If there's been blabbin'—well, no matter, that's all spilled milk. Marty—I'll call ye that, for we're all good friends here, ain't we?—I call upon ye to deliver up them guns or suffer the consequences."

"What consequences?" Mr. Bunt demanded bitterly. "Ye've stole half our vessels now—you an' the other privateers."

"We could take the rest."

"They could take an' burn the town, come to that," added Justice Thripps glibly. "Ye've got to think o' the town, Marty. There's twenty sail of American privateers cruisin' 'tween here an' the Cape."

"No doubt," answered Bunt. It was strange to hear that word "American" on Benajah's lips. It seemed to set apart the people of Nova Scotia, as if the Bay of Fundy had achieved the width of the Atlantic. "On t'other hand we've now got sixty muskets, with flints, powder, and ball. We'd make it a right lively burnin', we would, Benajah. Besides, Cap'n Cogsley, this ain't Port Gambier, where the men-o'-war daresn't go for fear o' the shoals, amongst the islands. Bring your privateers into this narrow bay of ours, where the first passin' frigate 'ud catch 'em like flies in a bottle? You ain't so fond o' fightin' as all that."

"There's always night," drawled the Salem man.

"Look'ee here, Marty," urged Benajah Thripps. "Ye've got to figger this out like a sensible man. D'ye realize what it means—this French ship? I bin talkin' to one or two of her officers that spoke English. It means France has reckernized the independence o' the American colonies. Means France'll j'in the war herself in a matter o' months. Means England'll be fightin' fer her life afore the summer's out. She'll have to call the fleet home. Take away the fleet an' what's left? A few reg'ments o' redcoats firin' muskets into a continent! Tell ye, Marty, it means the end o' the King's rule in America. Nova Scotia—yes, an' all Canady—has got to go the way o' the rest. Don't ye see that?"

"All I see," Martin Bunt said stolidly, "is you're askin' me to give up goods that belong to us by right o' salvage, under threat o' vi'lence."

"Make your ch'ice," Captain Cogsley said, sprawling in his chair.

"An' remember," Benajah warned, "this is final, Marty. It's King or Congress—no three ways about it."

"Them that ain't fer us is ag'in us," affirmed Cogsley.

"It goes deeper'n King or Congress," Bunt said slowly. "What I see is lor on the one side—hard lor in lots o' ways; lor that's poor-conceived, lor that's administered wrong—but lor for all that, somethin' ye can depend on, put your faith in, somethin' ye can build a business on. And on t'other hand nawthin' but a lot o' Committees o' Safety, an' Sons o' Liberty, an' Patriots an' what not, all makin' lors unto theirselves an' not one knowin' or carin' what t'other's doin'.

"Some day, mebbe, the Congress'll git the upper hand o' the King's troops. Afore that, though, they'll have to git the upper hand o' the Committees o' Safety an' the rest, an' then ye'll be payin' taxes an' duties an' tidewaiters' fees an' t'other things ye think ye've scuttled fer ever, an' buyin' tea from John Hancock, say, at John Hancock's price. Then, mebbe, there'll be lor an' order south o' Fundy Bay, an' mebbe the left hand'll know what the right's doin'—but I ain't chuckin' my hat over the moon on the chance o' 'mebbe.'

"Today ye call yourself a privateer in Congress service. Where's your commission? Eh? Where's your letter-o'-marque? Ye've got none! No more has fifty other sea-thieves out o' rebel ports that's ravagin' our coast. Salem's fattenin' on stolen goods; so's Machias, Gloucester, Boston, all of 'em. D'ye tell me the Congress knows a whisper o' the thieves swarmin' acrost Fundy Bay in whaleboats, shallops, anythin' that'll float, an' lyin' in our lonely bays an' cricks for the first unsuspectin' fisherman or trader? In a week they've got a ship; an' a gun there an' a swivel there, and a bar'l o' powder somewhere else, an' away they go in the name o' Congress, robbin' and burnin' as it suits 'em, sendin' a boat to every defenceless settlement an' demandin' money an' supplies. Ye can't tell *me!* I've had to deal with your kind, talk polite to 'em, give 'em what they wanted these past three years—men that I'd ha' kicked off my wharf in or'nary times. I knew more'n one of 'em for what they were in my old days in Noo England—a lot o' gaol-birds an' wharf-rats turned pirate in the name o' Liberty! If that's liberty ye can have it an' be damned!"

"Then ye won't give up the guns?" drawled Captain Jonathan.

"Not while I can hold a gun myself," said Justice Bunt. He

arose from the table, jarring the beer mugs and the candle, and slammed the tavern door behind him.

Outside, in the cool spring night, where the first frogs were piping cheerfully, a hand and a whisper caught him. Bridget Hewler, mysterious in the shawl drawn about her head, plucked him toward the stable shadow saying in her rapid Irish voice, "Wisht, Misther Bunt, sir. This way a bit if ye please!"

"Woman," Justice Bunt said sternly, "ye've harboured all kinds o' rascals in this den o' yours, but this . . . ."

"Whisht!" cautioned Mrs. Hewler again. "Now don't ye come the pious deacon over me, Misther Bunt, sir, when there's matters more important. That Salem spalpeen's afther more than guns, I'll have ye know. His privateers ain't at Port Gambier by a matter o' leagues. They're layin' off Batthery P'int this minute . . . ."

"What!"

"Not so loud. Wisht, for the love of God—would ye be havin' 'em burn the house over me head? There's two av 'em, the *Lizard* an' the *Civil Usage*—an' what kind av name is that for a boat?—an' anchored jist ayont the bar, they are. They've got two boat-crews lyin' at Misther Thripps' wharf, an' come moonrise an' the tide they're takin' out the Bermudy schooner that anchored in the sthream yistiddy."

"Ah!"

"An' the Bermudy captain such a gintleman, too! Gave me two shillin', he did. 'Wan for the dhrink, an' wan for the sound av a Kerry voice ag'in, says he. Now don't ye go jawin' me about harbourin' rogues an' desarters an' 'scaped rebel prisoners, Misther Bunt, when there's captains stay at me house. Besides," she chuckled, "where's the harm givin' a sup and a bite to some poor divil on the run from Halifax?"

"Hush, woman," Bunt growled. "You're one o' the kind that's made things hard for all of us. Is this a change o' heart?"

She laughed in the darkness.

"If ye must know, me poor husband was from Cape Cod, himself, an' 'Bridie', says he, 'niver thrust a Salem man.' There y'are. So help me God!"

It would be magnificent to record that Justice Bunt, mounted on his old brown horse, galloped up and down the town street on that April night in '78 crying "To arms!" or "The rebels are coming!" or some other shibboleth fervent and ringing that would look well in the history books. He did nothing of the sort. On foot, in his big muddy shoes, his wrinkled grey stockings, his rusty black breeches, his shabby blue coat, his old-fashioned round hat, Martin Bunt went quietly from door to door, knocking gently but insistently.

Most of the militiamen were abed, for in those simple days Oldport folk retired soon after candle-lighting. Each came blinking to the door, holding high the home-made dip of yellow tallow, showing a good deal of hairy leg below the flannel shirt, and heard a voice whispering hoarsely out of the darkness.

"It's me, Bunt. Put on your clo'es an' join me up the street. Mum's the word!"

Bunt avoided the lanes running down to the waterfront, thinking of the privateersmen lurking at Justice Thripps' wharf. He kept east along the main street, tacking from side to side as the militiamen's doors occurred, working toward the fish-lots and Battery Point. In five minutes the first aroused caught up with him and shared his labours. They assailed him with eager whispers but he told them nothing. In twenty minutes the street was full of flitting shadows and gentle knockings and the dry rustle of men's voices hushed and tense.

From the harbour not a sound. A faint mist hung over the water. In that haze lay the Bermuda schooner, further hidden by the jumbled sheds and stores and lofts of the waterfront. The moon was just rising.

Battery Point was covered in scrub spruce and fir, all gnarled and twisted by the sea winds. Great whinstone boulders stood amongst the trees. At the tip of the point was a small patch of greensward where the old cannon had stood before suspicious Governor Legge took them off to Halifax. This was where the river finally melted into the tide, and the harbour bar ran across like a threshold a few feet submerged. The ship channel lay close in with the point, a good stone's throw, an easy musket shot.

Bunt's ox-cart was waiting in the clearing with the black man, Caesar, and Bunt's store clerk, Ogden. Caesar had taken off the ox-bells, wisely, for the big brutes stood swaying their heads in the great wooden yoke, uneasy at the presence of all these whispering men. Bunt threw off the old topsail which covered the wagon, and musket barrels gleamed in the moonlight. He and Ogden served them out. Caesar passed out flints, powder, and shot.

Mr. Bunt paused with a musket in his hands, seeing an unexpected face in the queer light. "That you, Joel Thripps?"

"Yes," Joel said.

Bunt hesitated. "I might's well tell ye, Joel, we're goin' to stop some Salem picaroons from cuttin' out the Bermudy schooner. They've had two boats at your father's wharf all evenin', waitin' for the tide. They've slipped her cables by now."

"Well?" Joel said.

"Ye know your father's mind, Joel?"

"What's that to do with mine? Give me a gun!"

Bunt passed him the French musket without a further word.

"And one for my brother Zoeth."

Bunt passed down another.

"Where's your brother Reuben?" He made his voice casual. He knew all about young Reuben Thripps.

"Gone in the Salem privateer along o' your own brother Caleb."

"Um!"

The clearing was full of men in hastily donned homespuns, loading and priming the French muskets in the first flush of the moonrise. From the west, where the roofs of the wharf sheds were beginning to shine, came a distinct creak of thole-pins and the cautious dip and swirl of oars. It was not long before they saw the dim bulk of the Bermuda schooner swimming ghostlike out of the haze, with two boats ahead, towing laboriously. The Salem men had awaited full tide to get the deep-laden Bermudian over the bar, and so lost the benefit of the river current.

As the moon drank up the haze Bunt's militia could make out the privateers, a pair of schooners at anchor close in with the point, on the seaward side of the bar. There was a glimmer or two about the decks, and suddenly there came a rattle of hand-spikes and the rumble and shrilling of ungreased gun-trucks—the privateers casting loose their cannon for action. The militia-men grouped themselves about Bunt with expectant faces.

"Looks like our trouble's come to a head," he told them hoarsely. "But it may be we can work 'em out without bloodshed yet. Take post amongst the trees and rocks, lads, an' let me do the talkin'. My own brother's in one o' them boats. God knows I don't want his blood on my hands."

"Phoo! You reckon they'll give up the schooner without a fight?" Roger Hartley snorted.

"What's your mind on that, lads?" Bunt said quietly.

"Have it out with 'em—tonight!" demanded Bushnell, sergeant-major of the town company.

"Ay!" snapped Joel Thripps. "An end to this pull-devil pull-baker, Martin, and if hell's our portion—take it!"

"Easy to say, that," Bunt murmured. A savage note in all these voices distressed him. They had been tried too long, that was the trouble. The fanatic spirit of their Pilgrim forefathers had welled up in them, but the Pilgrim patience was gone. Their mood was for fighting, and it mattered little whom they fought. It seemed to Martin Bunt that if the approaching boats had been a press-gang from one of His Majesty's ships they would have said the same things in the same way, with the same hard grip on the musket stocks. Upon such chances . . . but the voice of the Reverend Peleg Potter broke the silence and the trend of Bunt's thought in a stroke.

"The Philistines be upon thee!" cried the parson through his nose. He was cold sober now, and pointing a musket toward the water.

The privateers' boats were close and clearly visible in the moonlight. With their jerky efforts the tow-line rose to a taut bar, flinging a shower of glittering drops, and then drooped and dipped a long bight into the harbour again. Martin Bunt, unarmed, mounted a boulder at the waterside and hailed them.

"Ahoy!" answered a voice from the foremost boat. It was young Caleb Bunt. There was no mistaking that voice or that figure—for he stood up as he spoke. Bunt knew, with a chill at his heart, that this must have been arranged by the shrewd Cogsley in case of challenge. The boats ceased all movement and the pale faces of the oarsmen glimmered, facing all toward the dark hump of the point and the lone figure of Martin Bunt, clear against the moon.

"Caleb, tell your thievin' friends to give over towin' that vessel!"

"She's only a Bermudian," Caleb answered. "No skin off any back in Oldport."

The voice of Jonathan Cogsley spoke. "Give way ag'in, boys hearty now!"

"I warn ye, Cap'n Cogsley, if ye don't give over we mean to stop ye!"

"You an' who else, Marty?" There was mockery in the Salem voice. The oars were dipping again.

"The town militia! Stop, I say!"

"Keep a-rowin', boys." Cogsley's voice, assured and amused. Toward the point he called, "Wouldn't fire on your own countrymen, Marty, would ye? Not you! Why, there's young Caleb in the boat astern. Fire on your own brother? Not you, Marty! You go on home an' take the militia with ye, afore they git hurt." And he turned and hailed, "*Lizard*, ahoy!"

The nearer of the anchored schooners answered with a cheer ("a great amount of huzzaring & Strong Languige," Justice Bunt wrote afterwards) and lanterns appeared boldly on her deck, and men were plain, crouching about the cannon with glowing red dots of slow-match ready in the linstocks. She lay little more than a cable's length from the tip of the Point, with her guns trained on it and upon the looming wooden target of the lower town beyond.

"Fire a shot," Jonathan Cogsley declared, "an we'll blast ye off o' that p'int like hens off a roost, an' give your town a dose o' hot iron fer good measure. Go home, ye herrin'-chokers! Home, ye Blue Noses! Home to bed an' prayers else ye suffer fer it, or my name ain't Jonathan!"

The oars were not missing a stroke. Martin turned his voice to the second boat.

"Caleb! Caleb, boy! Out o' that boat with ye, an' swim for it! On'y a few strokes to the rocks here, Caleb!"

"Not me!" Caleb cried, rowing hard with the rest.

"Caleb!" screamed the man on the rock, like a woman.

"Give way, boys, an' let the fool holler!" shouted Cogsley's voice. "Backs into it, now! Pull! Pull, my bully boys! Another cable's length an' she's over the bar an' ours. *Lizard*, there! *Lizard*, ahoy! Give us a toon!"

From the *Lizard*'s deck came the rattle of a drum and the thin tweet of a fife playing *Yankee Doodle*, the old jingle of the French war that the New England rebels had made their own. It roused some thoughtful echoes in Martin Bunt. To that same tune, twenty years ago, he and his company of New England rangers had marched toward the walls of Louisbourg, fighting for King George. A jaunty song, born nobody knew where, it had a knack of picking up the feet when they were weary with the day's march and the musket heavy on the shoulder.

The words were silly, he thought. "Yengees"—that was the way the Mohawks pronounced "English" in the early days. Now, Yankee betokened a separate race. All the story of the Revolution was summed up in the changed meaning of a word. And there was blood in that change, and sweat and tears, and all the pully-haul of ideals and greeds and passions that now convulsed the seaboard of a continent and no man yet understood.

What the outcome would be he could not guess, though he knew the deep sources of the rebel strength and saw the weakness of the King's in the very presence of these privateers, unmolested on the Nova Scotia coast. The permanent separation of the colonies and the mother country seemed no more possible than the separation of Nova Scotia and New England, or the fact that young Caleb sat yonder in the Salem boat under the menace of sixty Oldport muskets.

He had no notion that tonight's events in Oldport would prove a sign and portent for the hitherto neutral Yankees of Nova Scotia. Nor could he see the five years of fratricide to come, with a host of rebel craft raiding and pillaging the Nova Scotia coast, and a swarm of Nova-Scotiamen, keen of aim and bitter of heart, taking a savage price upon the coast of Massachusetts. Nor could he foresee the post-war hegira of loyalists from the States and their influence upon the affairs and destiny of his town and province, nor for that matter the swelling flood of Highland immigrants who would make the province truly a New Scotland in the half-century ahead.

All that was hidden in a future too uncertain and remote for a sane man's pondering. The present was problem enough, and for the present Martin Bunt could see nothing but the Bermuda schooner, her spars agleam in the moonlight, the phosphorescent swirl of busy oars, the Salem privateers beyond the bar, and somewhere above all these like a physical presence the shadow of his twin gods, Lor and Order, accusing and demanding.

"For the last time," he called resolutely, "will ye give over?"

There was no answer. The oars rose and fell. The Bermudian swam along the moon path toward the Point slowly and surely, like fate itself, and the drum and fife and the voices from the *Lizard* and *Civil Usage* began to chant again—

> Yankee Doodle went to town,
> A-ridin' on a pony,
> He stuck a feather in his hat
> An' called it macaroni.

"Fire!" said Justice Bunt, fetching the word deep from his boots. The French muskets shattered the night, and like an echo came the clash of tangled oars and a horrid chorus of screams, oaths, gasps, and gurglings all mingled with a frantic splashing in the harbour water. Dimly, Bunt saw the Bermuda schooner lose way and then drift slowly into the tidal eddy within the Point, like a horse coming home instinctively to stable. The militia reloaded and fired now at random, Bushnell cursing to no purpose.

And now a ragged thunder from the anchored privateers, and a whirr and tearing in the scrub trees and bushes of the Point like a flight of woodcock driven up from cover, a voice crying out in pain amongst the rocks, a cut twig falling lightly upon Bunt's old round hat, a sound of hail on the roofs of fish-sheds and houses beyond, and torn shingles flying and falling in the silence afterwards like brittle autumn leaves. The two boats settled and vanished, oarsmen and all. Sixty well-aimed muskets at close range. . . . Ah, Caleb, Caleb!

The privateers slipped their cables, well knowing the sound of their gunfire was a dangerous advertisement to seaward, where the king's ships prowled.

"We'll be back!" cried a defiant voice from the *Civil Usage*— a promise kept.

"We'll be waitin'!" answered Joel Thripps; and that promise was kept also.

Mr. Bunt had a notion to reprove Joel for this bravado, unseemly to his sober mind. But he kept silent. His cheeks were wet. The powder smoke had stung his eyes—or so he said.

OBIE CALLATT belongs to the Oldport branch of the Canadian Legion. He never pays his dues—usually the Colonel pays them for him—and when in the course of our ritual the Colonel asks "Is any comrade in need of aid?" Obie never fails to rise and state his need. We have secured jobs of various kinds for Obie, at least half a dozen a year for all the years since 1918, but they seldom last longer than from one Legion meeting to the next, and when the question is put, Obie rises in the silence and looks sad.

"The trouble with me," he says ingenuously, "is I'm too light fer heavy work and a bit too heavy for light work, so I'm out o' luck all round."

Obie served in a Canadian forestry unit somewhere in the interior of France during the 1914-18 war, and somehow managed to cut his foot with an axe. The foot healed nicely. Today, at forty-five, he can show a surprising turn of speed when there is a fire or a dog-fight or some other free entertainment at the next street corner. But at other times he develops a terrific limp and may be seen hobbling from door to door along the back streets, weeping over a starving wife and children, holding impressionable housewives breathless with tales of shot and shell, waving his army discharge paper in his right hand and holding his left palm at the ready.

At first we were disturbed at this and felt that he should have a pension, and sent him off to a Medical Board at Halifax. Obie came back after a week and a letter followed, saying in part, "This man appears to be suffering from an ailment sometimes known as "Injun fever," the chief symptom of which is a chronic disinclination to work. It may manifest itself in a limp, a hobble or even a crawl, and usually is accompanied by a persistent thirst. We regret to say, however, that the malady, in the present state of medico-military knowledge, is neither curable nor pensionable."

We let the matter drop at that. A legion branch must draw the line somewhere if it is to preserve its self-respect. We came to look upon Obie as an Act of God. Still, I was very angry when one day I walked up the path to Larrabee House and saw Obie pocketing a quarter-dollar—his usual levy upon the housewives of the town. Miss Letty could not afford to support Obie's curious disability, even for half an hour. I was about to speak my mind, but Miss Letty, who could always read my mind with embarrassing ease, turned from the verandah table where the afternoon tea was spread, put a cup in my hand and told me to sit down.

"This poor man," she said, black eyes snapping, "has been telling me things. The country's ungrateful, the government's incompetent, the Legion's indifferent, and what's a poor wounded hero to do?"

"Work!" said I rudely.

"I must be goin'," announced Obie hurriedly.

"You'll stay right where you are!" Miss Letty said, and when the last of the Larrabees used that voice and look, with her fine white hair, her large and brilliant black eyes and that long strong mouth, it was the command of an empress.

"You're going to finish your tea and eat at least half a dozen muffins before you go. You said you were hungry, remember!"

And to me she said casually, "Promised to tell you how my great-great-grandfather Sumter Larrabee came to Oldport, didn't I? Well, sit back and try to look as if you enjoyed balancing a tea-cup. It's not a bad story, and this poor neglected saviour of his country may even find a moral in it somewhere. Let me see. Sumter Larrabee first came to Oldport . . . ."

Sumter Larrabee first came to Oldport on a day of early winter —1st November 1783, to be precise. A memorable date for him and for Oldport, though neither knew it at the time. A boat from the transport *La Sophie* landed him and Major Blount at the shipyard, in what was then the centre of the town, and they came striding over the litter of chips and shavings and past the rough parade ground of the town's militia and hailed a townsman to point out the place of business of Mr. Justice Bunt.

Bunt was chief magistrate in Oldport then, and owner of a West India trading-business, and he was watching from his counting-house window as they approached, a pair of strangers in an unfamiliar green uniform, one tall and dark, the other thick-set and blonde, and the tall one limping a little in his riding boots. The sight of those uniforms probably reminded Bunt that eight years of war had passed over Oldport like a summer tempest, black while it lasted, and shot with lightnings and much sound and fury, but already fading fast.

To the southward the independent states of America were an accomplished and triumphant fact. Nova Scotia alone of the seaboard colonies was British still. In the latter part of the war the seamen and ship-owners of Oldport had busied themselves in privateering against the Americans, taking a sharp revenge for their losses at rebel hands but somehow regarding it as a business like any other. But now the fishery and the West India voyages and most of the old life had been resumed.

Oldport had not even waited for the official word of peace— a forgone conclusion since '82. As early as April 1783 the American prisoners were released from Oldport gaol, and on May 5th a Yankee schooner came in boldly and warped up the river to The Falls, where her crew set about catching alewives for bait as they had done before the war. In August, H.M. brigantine *Brandywine* came in and removed to Halifax the detachment of the King's Orange Rangers who had garrisoned the little fort on Battery Point since '79, and now the blockhouse and the earth-and-log ramparts and the shabby wooden barracks stood empty and deserted.

And probably Mr. Bunt sighed a little at the sight of the strangers' uniforms. The pre-war life of Oldport had been extremely dull. The war's alarms and excursions, the speculation in privateers, the presence of a rollicking hard-drinking company of rangers in the town—all these had made sparkling times. The townsfolk had learned to dance, an astounding innovation in a settlement of Pilgrim blood straight from Cape Cod, and Mr. Amasa Barriman, that accomplished scapegrace, had taught them how to sing.

It must have seemed to Martin Bunt, under those first grey skies of winter, that his town was dropping with a sort of chill resignation into the poverty and monotony of the olden time. He was given to morbid spells Ten years before in a spasm of depression he had written in his journal, "I think Oldport is in a Decay and may be Manny Yeers befoar tis more than a Fishing Vilage."

What his town needed badly, though he did not say and probably did not know, was an infusion of new blood; and here and now, walking up the rutty street, was the very stuff.

"Mr. Bunt?" said the tall officer—that was Sumter—stooping to clear the lintel of the counting-house door.

"At your sarvice," answered Bunt, a term he had learned during the war.

"My name's Larrabee, sir, late of the British Legion, commonly known as Tarleton's Legion, and this is Major Blount of the same corps."

"Honoured," murmured Bunt politely. Their accent was strange to him. He could not place that slurring of the r's— "suh, La'abee, Tahlton, majuh, coah"—which gave such a queer music to their speech.

The officers warmed their hands at his fire. They were shivering, although the day was not cold as Oldport measured cold.

"You're about to have neighbours, Bunt," said Colonel Larrabee.

"Neighbours?"

"Two leagues off—but what's two leagues between loyal subjects of His Majesty? Our corps, or what's left of it, is now in transports off Port Gambier, with their wives and families— nigh on three thousand people, sir—intending a settlement there."

Mr. Bunt gaped. "Eh?" he uttered stupidly.

"Any objection?" snapped Sumter, and his black eyes and the hard blue eyes of Major Blount examined Bunt suspiciously. They had expected a welcome in this last loyal province, and this man obviously disapproved their coming, and through his nose—like a Yankee!

"Why—uh—none, sir, none. In a way, that's to say."

"Way?" they said together.

Martin Bunt shifted his thick black-stockinged legs and squared his shoulders, as if pronouncing sentence at a sessions of the peace.

"Look'ee here, gen'lemen, Port Gambier ain't a fit place to settle twenty people, let alone three thousand. 'Tain't even a good harbour, jest a bay all open to the east'ard, which is where the weather comes from in these parts. Good anchorage inside Spectacle Island an' that's all ye can say for it."

(I have mentioned Miss Letty's gift of mimicry, I think. When she quoted Bunt thus, with the nasal drawl, the monotone, the drooping eyelids, the head cocked to the right, it was Cape Cod to the life.)

"Then why," demanded Blount in a voice like the edge of a sabre, "did the rebel privateers make a rendezvous of that place, all through the war? That's our information, sir. And I reckon that's why the Governor at Halifax granted Port Gambier to our corps—to plant a loyalist population in that rebel nest. The place must have advantages."

"Ah," said Bunt, serious as death, "but the rebels wasn't settled there, sir. It's different when ye can slip cable for the open sea, the first sign o' weather. Listen, sir; the land at Port Gambier is just a mess o' rocks and wire-birch and scrub pine, the shore's a sand beach for the most part, runnin' off shoal a great way. The stream that flows into the head o' the bay—the on'y likely place for a settlement—ain't navigable on account o' the bar.

"Why, gen'lemen, we looked that place over very careful when we come this way in '59—an' give it the go-by, thankin' the good Lord for the harbour two leagues further on, what we call Oldport now. If there was room at Oldport I'd make bold to say ye should do the same; but there just ain't room here in Oldport for a whole corps and their families. Why don't ye go to Hal'fax or Shelburne?"

Colonel Larrabee gave a great snort at that. "Shelburne! There's ten thousand loyalists at Shelburne now, tumbling over each other for want o' room, and the place not fit to support a thousand. Halifax? Halifax is no better—thousands more loyalists there, and the Governor setting up tents and the deckhouses of ships along Granville Street to shelter 'em over the winter. Nunno! We've been granted lands at Port Gambier and to Port Gambier we go. We're Tarleton's Legion, sir—a corps that fears no venture, asks no quarter, and takes no nonsense!"

"On the aidge o' winter?" There was a queer crack in Mr. Bunt's voice, and no wonder. He considered them, or the Commissary-General, or the Crown Land agent, or all of them together, entirely mad. These men were from the deep South, he knew now; for Tarleton's corps was famous, of all the loyalist troops the most dashing, the best led, the most relentless, and, therefore, the most hated by the rebels. Men from Carolina plantations, most of them, with their women and children, planning to settle in a sandy Nova Scotia bay where none but seasoned fishermen could hope to make a living, and in November—when there was no fishing, nothing, and the first snow flying!

"I well know winter's hard in these parts," Sumter said, "and that's why I'm here to see you. The ships can't wait long in that open bay. Our men are putting up tents along the shore but we must have timber and boards at once. We must have huts and barracks to house three thousand people, sir, before the weather turns severe. That comes about Christmas time, we're told."

"Never can tell about cold weather," replied the uneasy Bunt. "Sometimes it snaps down awful quick. Timber? We've got a couple o' sormills on the river, at The Falls, two mile above Oldport; but all the stuff we've sored since the fall rains has been shipped to the West Indies. There's no logs cut, an' no snow for haulin'."

"Then," declared Colonel Larrabee, "you must get your people to work at once. You must get logs out to the river somehow. Damme, sir, we never had snow for logging in the South. I tell you we must have half a million board feet at the very least—before Christmas!"

"Impossible!" gasped Bunt.

"Nothing's impossible to determined men, sir! Is it the pay you're concerned about? We've authority to draw on the Governor for the expense of getting settled in Port Gambier for the winter. Is that good enough? Eh? You'll be paid the current price for your timber and nails and what not. For God's sake, sir, don't quibble over money at a time like this!"

Sumter Larrabee nourished a fine Southern notion that a Yankee would sell his own mother for sixpence, provided nobody offered seven; and what were these people of Oldport but Yankees living on the wrong side of Fundy Bay?

"Ain't worryin' about pay," said Justice Bunt with dignity, a rather crushing dignity. "It's your people I'm afeared for. I tell ye, sir, I've bin in this country thirteen year summer an' winter—sogered at Louisbourg with Wolfe afore that—an' I know what I'm talkin' about. 'Tain't a fit time nor place to set down people that ain't used to cold weather."

But Martin Bunt was wasting his breath, of course. Behind those grim visitors who walked like cavalrymen and talked like negroes was all the bitterness of a civil war in which they had risked everything on the losing side. For two years since the surrender at Yorktown they had eaten out their hearts in captivity or as refugees in New York, watching from that distance the confiscation of their estates and properties by "patriot" committees eager for plunder, knowing that any man who had fought for the king could look for no hope or mercy within the confines of the victorious states. And now that New York itself had been evacuated, now that there was no refuge but the coasts of Nova Scotia or the bleak forests of Canada, the men of Tarleton's Legion could not look a gift horse in the mouth.

And so, with Bunt's honest promise to do his best, Blount and Larrabee returned to the transport and sailed around the cape to Port Gambier where the others were waiting. A narrow strip had been cleared in the woods above the beach, and there in long precise rows were the pitiful shelters, some army tents secured for them by Colonel Mollison in his last days as Wagonmaster-General at New York, and the rest mere scraps of old sail canvas donated by the transports in the bay. There huddled the women and children from Carolina, Georgia, Florida, holding forth their hands to the blaze of fires. A few dozen slaves had deserted the old plantations to follow their masters into exile, and white and black men worked together for the benefit of all.

After three days the ships weighed and sailed; and those three thousand exiles, men, women and children, gathered on the windy shore and waved them out of sight. With those fading sails went their last link with the old homes and a way of life they would never know again, and the women wept; but the men stood silent with hard raised faces, as if the eyes of their enemies were upon them still. Now and throughout their misfortunes they maintained their old discipline, the spirit of the corps they had made famous. Tarleton would have liked that.

A pity Tarleton wasn't there. Then if ever they needed his infectious young laugh, his large daring eyes, his witty rosebud mouth, his headlong courage. But Tarleton had gone to England to write his story of the Southern campaign with a pen as reckless, as unsparing as his sword; and there he stayed, the finest British leader of light troops in his day, wasted in sour memories, and women and wine and Parliament.

For their last and most terrible campaign, the battle for existence in a northern winter, Tarleton's Legion was commanded by the able Scot, Colonel Mollison—and Mollison in turn leaned heavily on the tall hawk-faced South Carolinian, Sumter Larrabee. Mollison soon ordered Larrabee to take up his station in Oldport, saying, "Those people doubtless will do their best, Sumter, but ye must be there with 'em, drive 'em, harry 'em at the logging and the sawmills. We must have wooden huts and barracks in two months or perish—the tents'll be no shelter after Christmas."

And so, temporarily as he thought, Colonel Larrabee came to Oldport with his wife and five small children—Allan a babe in arms—and seven negroes from the old plantation by the Wateree. With him also went two dozen of his Carolinians to lend a hand at the logging. For his family and servants Sumter purchased two decrepit huts in the pine-woods at the western skirt of the town; and on the first evening he slipped an arm about Kitty's waist, watching Black Hagar rocking Allan in the cradle before the fire.

"I little thought I'd bring you to this, my dear, when I went courting the belle of Savannah."

And Kitty, slim and lovely for all her child-bearing and the troubles of war and persecution, flung back that dark head of hers.

"Sumter!" In that one cry was all the burning courage of the lost cause.

The cold set in early that year, one of the longest and hardest winters in Oldport history. Snow whitened the ground soon after the Legion landed at Port Gambier but it was not deep enough for sledding until January. At The Falls, under the worst possible conditions, Sumter and his mixed company of loggers worked all through November and December. The Oldport folk long since had cut all the timber handy to the little sawmills. Sumter had to go back on the ridges, and every log had to be dragged singly, with chains and oxen, to the river bank.

All through the short winter daylight they laboured desperately, haunted by the vision of those shivering women and children at Port Gambier. The cutting of logs was only part of their concern. The water-wheels of the crude little sawmills froze again and again; and they had recurrent battles with "a Stuff the Oldport Men call Anchor Frost, a strange thing, the Strangest I think in all this Strange Country," which curdled the mill-ponds from top to bottom and choked the wheel-pits until the clumsy wooden turbines refused to budge an inch.

The road from The Falls to Oldport town was nothing but a rough track by the river, impassable for loaded wagons, useless for sledding until there was snow deep enough to cover the stumps and boulders. The newly sawn boards and timbers had to be fastened together in rafts and floated downstream to the Oldport wharves, and there fished out—every board a glistening ice-wafer—and loaded into vessels for Port Gambier. And that was possible only while the river current and the heave of the tides prevented the water from freezing over. Sometimes on a still night of frost a thin sheet formed, and then men had to take boats and break a channel two miles from Oldport to The Falls.

In that way they managed until Christmas Eve, when the cold sharpened suddenly and the river froze hard all the way down to Justice Bunt's wharf in the harbour—froze beyond all breaking, not to open again until April. But then they were able to haul with sleds on the ice itself.

Around the cape at Port Gambier the boards had to be rafted again between ship and beach, where those anxious soldier-carpenters were waiting. Slowly the huts rose in the snow.

They built some shacks of logs, but as the clearings widened that became too slow and arduous, for every log had to be rolled over the rocks and stumps to the site—they had no oxen at

Port Gambier, and the few cavalry horses they had managed to bring with them were "to full of Sperrit for this Work."

Meanwhile the tents along the shore were banked with boughs of spruce and fir to hold the drifting snow and help keep out the wind. Great fires were kept roaring before the tent doors, and as the clearings grew they had to go farther for the fuel, carrying every stick on their backs, and more of the able-bodied men had to be kept at this one unending chore. The men had no greatcoats. Each cut holes in his old campaign blanket—the meagre shoddy blankets of the army contractors—and wore that and slept in it at night. The bedding put ashore from the ships was reserved for women and children and the sick.

It was past New Year, the stark cold New Year of 1784, when the last hut was finished and the new town stood amid the snow. They called it Guysborough after Sir Guy Carleton, who had commanded at New York and arranged the final evacuation of the loyalists. The chimneys, some of brick from Oldport, some of field stones and mortar, most of them mere swallow-nests of sticks and plastered clay, smoked blue against the snow on the hillside above. Before them the sands of the bay shone white as the snow behind, and beyond the twin humps of Spectacle Island and the long dark bulk of Mouton Island lay the wide sea, white-capped under a northwest wind blowing down from frozen Canada. In that sea and its fishery lay the only chance of a living at Port Gambier, but the men of Tarleton's Legion were not yet aware of it. They looked forward to spring and the raising of crops, for they were planters all, and the soil, the thin, stony soil of Port Gambier, was hidden by the snow.

The provisions landed from the transports lasted barely until the huts were finished, and Colonel Mollison sent an appeal to Halifax. Halifax was swamped with appeals just then—the migration of loyalists into Nova Scotia had out-run all calculations—but someone in the Commissary Office had a happy thought. The King's Orange Rangers, departing from Oldport in the summer of '83, had left some stores in charge of Justice Bunt. With a large-handed gesture the Commissary turned these stores over to Tarleton's Legion by letter to Mr. Bunt, and Colonel Larrabee went with Bunt to inspect them and effect the transfer.

The stuff was all there as listed—"pork, beef, flower, pease & Oatmeel"—old when the Rangers left it behind, and not improved by winter storage.

"Damme, the stuff is scarcely fit to eat, Bunt. Why should

I sign a receipt for pork and beef that was salted down, I wager, back in Queen Anne's time?"

"But I can't help that," stammered Mr. Bunt. "And I'm 'sponsible. The stuff was left in my charge. If I take a receipt for less than the whole, some quill-driver in the Halifax commissary'll have my scalp. Sorry to say it, sir, but ye must sign for all or none."

In the end Colonel Larrabee signed for the whole, but to ease his feelings he wrote a description of those stores on the back of the receipt. It must have been an interesting document. And on these provisions, and dried codfish purchased in Oldport, and a meagre supply of salt-junk and ship biscuit sent from Halifax toward spring, Tarleton's Legion existed during their first winter in the new land.

They sent out hunting-parties with the few muskets they had, but moose were scarce and the caribou had gone inland. In six months their only fresh food consisted of hares shot or snared in the barrens and quantities of clams dug out of the flats at low tide.

In mid-January they started to erect a building "for holding Worship & other Meetings." Sumter Larrabee and his men at The Falls had succeeded in running a sawmill through the bitter midwinter weather—a thing that no one in Oldport had believed possible—and somehow they got the timbers for the meeting-house shipped around to Port Gambier and landed there. Then a succession of gales and snowstorms interrupted all water communication for weeks. Nails and other ironwork had to be carried overland on the backs of men. Three Florida men were caught in a blizzard on one of these journeys and perished by the trail. Some Georgians, attempting an open-boat voyage to Oldport in weather no fisherman would face, were capsized off Topsail Point and drowned. At The Falls one of Sumter's Carolinians ventured too near the lip of ice at the lower edge of the mill-pond, and its breaking plunged him over the dam to a cold death where the river dropped into the tide.

But these were only the accidents. In the draughty huts at Port Gambier men died of old wounds and new exposures. Women perished. Children perished. Nothing was spared them. All the maledictions visited upon the loyalists by their late foes came to bitter fruit on Tarleton's men. Yet every Sunday they raised their voices in praise of the God who presumably had not forgotten them, and asked Him to save the gracious King whose ministers had signed away the loyalist homes and possessions in that feeble cynical "recommendation" to the several

States. History, most of it rebel-contemporary and bigoted, has said many things of Tarleton's men; but history has missed the story of their last and greatest battle together, where their courage, endurance, unselfishness, and discipline shine like stars.

In February Colonel Larrabee, seeing the uncertainty and danger of communication by sea in winter, arranged with Justice Bunt for the cutting of a proper wagon road through the woods. The Oldport men volunteered to cut part way, the Legion did the rest. They met on a snowy day at a stream the Indians called Wo-be-a-ga-de—place of the White Swans—a literal meeting of North and South.

"They talk like Yankees," said a Carolina sergeant.

"For that matter, son," grinned Sumter, "they reckon we talk like nigras."

On the whole they were favourably impressed with each other, and in their quiet Scots way the Highland emigrants who had flocked out of North Carolina to enlist with Tarleton now helped mightily to establish a solid friendship between the southern exiles and the Yankees of Nova Scotia. That friendship never wavered, though there was not much intermarriage until the second generation.

In April, when the snow had gone from the coastal slopes, Sumter went with four of his blacks to begin the clearing of his own grant at Port Gambier. He found all the men of the Legion so engaged; and as the clearings spread the whinstone and granite rocks stood forth in all their nakedness, and the thin sour soil was revealed at last, the men of the South cried aloud at its worthlessness.

Some began to talk of the West Indies, where the climate and soil were more to their custom; others favoured the Annapolis Valley; many favoured St. Croix, in the new province which another army of loyalists had carved out of Nova Scotia's sprawling flank and called New Brunswick. All this could only mean one thing—the final dispersal of the Legion, and Sumter Larrabee cried out against it. Disperse now, after sticking together through persecution and war and captivity and this last soul-wracking experience? Impossible!

Colonel Mollison made a last desperate attempt to keep them together. He went to Halifax and got a new grant for the corps at Chedabucto Bay, farther up the Nova Scotia coast, where the land was reputedly better and where in fact most of the Carolina troops had settled. He came back in triumph and the men cast out their other plans. It was all arranged. At the end of May they would take down their huts and remove "Guysborough" *en bloc* to Chedabucto Bay.

They were cheerful again. The hot May sunshine seemed to thaw the winter's frost from their souls. One day they noticed Indians busy with dip-nets in the small river at the head of the bay. Alewives were in the annual migration from salt water, pouring up the rivers to spawn as they do to this day. The Indians showed them how to make dip-nets and soon the banks were lined with shouting troopers, the long poles swinging back and forth and the ground alive with glittering fish. They had not looked for such bounty in this barren place. Fortune smiled on them at last.

But the smile was false. The crown of their misfortunes was descending on their heads at that very moment. No one ever knew quite how it started but it must have begun with one of the slash fires on the far side of the ridge, where some hopeful souls were still clearing that hopeless land. The woods were like tinder, for it was that dangerous time of year when last fall's leaves were dry and rustling under foot and the shrubs and hardwoods had not yet broken into green.

Nobody worried about the smoke at first. It was rising well to the north of the wooden town and the breeze was light and from the sea. They went on dipping fish. And suddenly the wind shifted to the west, blowing a gale, and the fire came leaping over the ridge like a charge of red-hot cavalry, with a front a mile long and a blast of heat that shrivelled everything before it.

They ran for the houses then and snatched up buckets and formed lines, men, women, and the older children, passing water from the sea, in the atmosphere of hell itself, in a tremendous hiss and crackle that drowned all their voices together, in a choking darkness where none could see more than ten feet and dead leaves whirled, burning like comets. And the little ones and the sick and old stood in the chill sea water at the foot of the slope, whimpering with fright and pain. Mercifully, the final struggle was short. The dribbles of water flung over those crisp wooden roofs and walls were pathetically useless. The western-most street burst into flame all at once, and as the flames came on those struggling people were forced back, down the slope, down the beach, and into the water.

Yes, after all their hope and labour and their long enduring they found themselves driven into the sea from which they had landed seven months before. And as the fire died at last for lack of fresh fuel and the smoke thinned, they saw the blackened hillside and the rows of naked chimneys standing like tomb-stones over the ashes of their homes and hopes. Sumter Larrabee, badly burned about the hands, stood there with the rest, the tide lapping about his boots. To his dying day he never forgot that moment, the silence, the smoulder, the gaunt tottering chimneys, and never spoke of it but in a hushed voice.

It was the end, of course. There was nothing for it now but to scatter and find homes where they could. And there was no time to be lost. Mollison went off to Oldport and Halifax to get ships for the removal. Some of the men were for Jamaica, some for Upper Canada. Mollison persuaded two hundred or so to accompany him to Chedabucto Bay, where they could (and did) raise a new Guysborough. The largest group crossed the Bay of Fundy to St. Croix, where they settled and prospered and long called themselves the Port Gambier Associates in memory of that final tribulation.

Sumter Larrabee was impressed with the possibilities of a timber trade with the West Indies and resolved to stay in Old-port, and a number of his South Carolinians chose to settle there with him. And a few, impressed perhaps by that miracle of fish, actually stayed on at Port Gambier, where their descendants are fishermen today.

On the last day, with an assortment of shipping lying in the bay and the ships' boats taking off women and children, the men of Tarleton's Legion formed up on the beach for their last parade, in orderly ranks, in their separate units, cavalry and infantry, the caricature of a once-smart corps with their ragged and patched green uniforms, their broken boots, their scorched beards and haggard faces. Their backs were to the sea, their eyes toward the black desert of the hillside and the mute rows of chimneys.

After roll-call devout Colonel Mollison asked the chaplain for a short reading of Scripture, and the man of God mounted a charred stump turning the leaves of his Bible. He chose Psalm 137 of course—what else could he choose amongst those men, in that place, in the light of all that had passed? But when he came to the eighth verse, with its harsh and strangely prophetic curse upon those who drove them into exile, his voice choked and his mind refused the words. He said "Amen" in a strong voice without going further, and closed the book. There was a silence. Then Colonel Mollison pulled off his hat and called a hurrah for the King. They gave it, a shout that rang around the bay. And they gave a cheer for Mollison himself, and another for Banastre Tarleton, across the sea in England. Then Mollison turned to Sumter saying, "I think the men 'ud appreciate a few words from ye, Colonel Larrabee. Ye've been wi' the corps all through."

Sumter stepped upon the stump, very tall and stern. "Boys," he said slowly, "we've come a long way together. Looking over your faces there's some I know for Florida boys and Georgia boys, and more than one that came to us on the march through Virginia, but most of you are from Ca'lina like me. Back in that old time and those old pleasant homes we'll never see again I reckon we were all men of peace. But being men we held opinions; and when we were persecuted for those opinions, being men we took up arms to fight for 'em. We got licked more than once but we always came back fighting, and by and large we usually won—up to Yorktown.

"There's many of us think it was a mistake to march north, that we should ha' stayed in the South where we belong, where a good third of the people were strong for the King and another third suspicious of the Yankees, anyhow. But as soldiers that's not for us to say. 'If' is a terrible word, boys, that eats the soul out of a man. Forget it. What's done is done. We fought for the King, we fought a good fight and a long one, and we lost. Down south we were pretty much a people to ourselves and had no great affection for the people north-away. I still think Ca'lina will regret the day she placed her destiny in Yankee hands, and there'll be bloodshed again before the matter's settled for good and all; but that may not come in our time and there's no hope in it anyhow—for us or for Ca'lina.

"Fix your minds on the new homes you're going to make under the old flag. I've a feeling that we've reached the end of our troubles. It's a bad moment, this saying Goodbye, but it's natural after all. War gathers men together and peace scatters them again. That's been the story of every army since wars began. Some of my Ca'lina boys are coming to Oldport with me. I say to you all what I've said to them—that as long as I've a penny in purse or a scrap on the table my door's always open to a man of the Legion. Write to me if ye can, and think of me sometimes as I'll think of you. Don't brood on what's past but never forget it either. There are good things to remember, boys. If I had the past eight years to live again I'd choose the same course and the same men.

"And whenever three or four of you are gathered together, in your new homes wherever they may be, drink a toast to the King, to old Ca'lina, Geo'gia, Flo'da or V'ginia, and then drink to the old corps and sing our old song, the Major's song. That's all I have to say. The women and youngsters are aboard and I see the boatmen are waiting. It's time to go. But before we go, boys, a verse and chorus of the Major's song, for the last time together!"

And they sang it together, there on the sandy shore of Port Gambier, for the last time—

The rebel flag waved high in air above the ragged crew,
When Tarleton and his troopers came a-ridin'.
The Game-Cock dropped his rebel rag and off to Charlotte flew,
When Tarleton and the Legion came a-ridin'.
O, we clipt the Cock's tail feathers by the sweet Wateree,
With a Ho-ro-aha! By the cool Wateree,
From Camden to Catawba by the lovely Wateree—
With Tarleton and his loyal boys a-ridin'.

The Game-Cock—that was Thomas Sumter—a distant kinsman of Sumter Larrabee's, by the way. He commanded a light corps on the rebel side and beat the Legion more than once in that cut-and-dash fighting in the South. But Tarleton gave him a beautiful thrashing at Catawba Ford, although the Legion was outnumbered five to one, and that is what the song's about. A swaggering, boasting thing, isn't it? And not strictly accurate, for the river's not called the Wateree above Camden. But for those exiles in the desolate Nova Scotia bay it had in it somehow the smell of piney-wood fires in the Carolina mornings, and the air of evening bivouacs sweet with magnolia blossom, and the gritty taste of corn-pone and hominy bolted hastily on the march, the pulpy sweetness of peaches plucked in wayside orchards, the squeal of the lean shoat-pig under chase for the next day's rations; and it had in it the creak of saddles and girths, the clank of sables and clink of spurs, the clip-clop of hoofs on the dusty southern roads, and the quick drumming of worn shoe-leather as those hard-marching light infantry of the Legion moved up behind.

And it had in it the sweetness of victory at Camden, Catawba Ford and Guildford Courthouse, and the bitterness of defeats like the bloody rout at Cowpens, and the thrill of a hundred small hell-for-leather affairs like the time Tarleton and Larrabee and half a dozen troopers rode through the night and scared Jefferson out of his bed at Monticello. And it had in it, for all its cock-a-hoop words, the cold sinking of heart when the Legion lay before Gloucester, ready to hack a way out for Cornwallis, and their patrols looked across the river and saw the white flag over Yorktown. But more than all that it had in it the pathos of that exiled Israelite beside the waters of Babylon, and when they sang of the sweet, the cool, the lovely Wateree, the tears sprang in all their eyes.

And just before the broke their ranks a South Carolina corporal tore off his tattered hat and cried, "A last cheer, boys, for 'Sabre' Larrabee—the fightin'est so'ger of the fightin'est corps of the fightin'est army in the war!"

And they gave it; not the solemn hurrah they'd learned from the British regulars but the war-cry picked up by their fathers from the Indians in the South—"Yaaaaaah! Yai! Yai!" Behind that cry they had fought their way and buried their dead from '79 to '81, from Charleston to the Chesapeake. Seventy-seven years after that morning at Port Gambier, when all those men were dead and forgotten in exile, that sound would be heard again in the South they had loved, and Yankee newspapers by a curious inversion would call it "the terrible rebel yell."

But all that is past and done, and the memory all but lost, and looking back with our modern English-speaking notion of threshing things out over council tables we are inclined to wonder why it all happened. Yet who will deny that good came of it? Independent, the United States has become the richest and most powerful nation in the world. And that exodus of Loyalists after the lost cause was the making of Canada.

Loyalist blood—those are proud words still in Canada, nowhere more than in Nova Scotia. In our own Pine County to this day, in unexpected places you will hear that musical "heah," "theah," "anywheah," and "Yes, suh!" on the lips of people who never saw the South and never heard of Tarleton's Legion, although they are aware of their Loyalist descent. But if you hunt in the scrub spruce and wire-birch and poplar on the low ridge facing the head of Port Gambier you will find, untouched since 1784, the shallow cedars, the tumbled stone foundations of the huts, the long low boulder walls that Tarleton's Legion built to mark their pitiful "garden plots." In 1904 the railway dug a cutting where the main street must have been, otherwise the ghost-town of Guysborough lies undisturbed. The modern village of Port Gambier is built along the shore, where Tarleton's Legion held its last parade.

"Years ago," Miss Letty mused, "when I was young and sentimental, I went to Port Gambier one day in the buggy with my brother Lawrence—he was killed soon after in the Boer War, when the Royal Canadians tried to rush Cronje on the last morning of Paardeberg—and we dug in one of the old cellars. I don't know what we expected to find. There was nothing but a heap of burned clam-shells and a broken quern-stone fashioned out of local granite. But the tale of the settlement was in those things—the shortage of food which drove them to digging in the clam flats like Indians, the high hopes for a crop in that barren land which led some diligent soul to shape and pierce that stone in the light of winter fires, and the final disaster that consumed the shack and broke the stone with its heat.

"But the thing that wrings your heart at Port Gambier is the cemetery they left behind, a pathetic group of low mounds in the pasture-land between the railway and the road. They're marked with chunks of field-stone, all unlettered but one, a polished slate slab brought from a distance—Halifax perhaps— and the epitaph all gone but 'Born 1758' and at the bottom 'A True Friend Lies Buried Here'—as if Britannia herself had put it there, purposely without a name, to mark them all. Most of those nameless stones are buried in moss, and the sunken mounds can barely be distinguished in the pasture all about; but there are fifty at the very least, and probably two hundred or more, neglected and trod by the village cows.

"You might say Tarleton's Legion left nothing behind but these and a ghost of an accent. For nobody reads history nowadays, and the old names have died away as the Larrabee name in Oldport dies with me. But they left something else after all, their loyalty, their courage, their endurance, the spirit that never dies—the spirit of that old brave boast of theirs, 'A corps, suh, that fears no venture, asks no quarter and takes no nonsense.'

"*Asks no quarter*—d'you hear me, Obie Callatt?"

But Obie was asleep.

ENTERTAINMENT was rare in Oldport in the olden days. Perhaps the times were entertainment enough after the wars began in 1793, and the West Indian trade was ruined by French privateers, and Oldport ship-owners turned to privateering on their own account, and our sailors, fishermen, townsmen, woodsmen, found new and exciting occupations in the Caribbean. Scarcely a fortnight passed without a privateer sailing over the bar, or another returning scarred with weather and battle in the southern seas, or a prize of some queer foreign rig tacking up the estuary and giving a gun and three cheers as she crossed the bar, or a recruiting parade for the latest letter-of-marque, with the enlisted seamen marching up and down Fore Street, ribbons fluttering, cutlasses swinging at the belts, the red jack flaming on a pole at their head, a powder-boy rattling the big painted side-drum, and a rabble of dogs and urchins bringing up the rear.

Prisoners from the Caribbees, strange, sad, swarthy men in outlandish garments, wandered freely about the narrow wooden streets of our northern town catching the bright curious glances of the healthy Bluenose girls. In the taverns bearded and ear-ringed seamen drank their ale and spun long yarns of hurricane and the yellow jack, of sea sharks and land sharks and the busy ship-worm of the warm seas that broke men's hearts at the pumps, of fights ashore and afloat under a burning sun, and the lotus life of the islands where rum flowed like water and every night was Midsummer's Eve and none of the girls was shy.

One consequence of all this was a constant chaffer in Oldport counting-houses and auctions of captured ships and goods— cacao and sugar and indigo, boots and hats and fancy silk waistcoats, rum and logwood and casks of oranges. The town waxed fat. For the first time in Oldport history cash was plentiful, and very strange cash it was. Though merchants kept their accounts in pounds, shillings and pence, the standard of currency was the Spanish dollar, the famous old piece of eight *reals*, and about it, at fixed rates of exchange that were posted on every merchant's door, circulated coinage from half the world.

Strangers came to fish in this glittering stream—pedlars and trollops and a slick gentleman with three thimbles and a vanishing button—but entertainers, proper, were few. Perhaps the little Nova Scotia seaport lay too far from the gay world. Perhaps it was known how Cape Cod conscience of its founders still lay like ice beneath the froth. Those who came were recorded carefully in Colonel Larrabee's diary.

There were Swiss bell-ringers, "decent People & a verry Eligant Performance." There were rope-dancers who for want of room performed in James Gow's sail loft—but the young woman of the troupe scandalized the elders with her long cotton-stockinged legs, and Magistrate Larrabee ordered the show out of town. There was the singular affair of Mr. Harrap and the Learnèd Pig, which told fortunes by placing her neat polished hooves upon lettered cards, and came to a sad end—kidnapped, no less, by a party of rollicking tars from H.M.S. *Bream*. ("Where is my Learnèd Pig?" demanded outraged Mr. Harrap of the town's chief magistrate. "I suspect," replied Sumter with immense gravity and no less truth, "she is now His Majesty's boilèd pork.")

But clearest of all to posterity are Signor Malatesta and his waxworks, a Larrabee legend, handed down in all detail from generation to generation in the tall-pillared mansion where the Larrabees had their Oldport being for a century and a half. Sumter's diary makes only a passing note of the signor's arrival—

"Sunday, Jan. 5th, 1800—Cold wether & good Slaying. I ride in my new Slay to the Methodist Meeting & hear a Tolerable good Sermon. Brig. Betsey, Rington master, returns from Boston, reports Fish in poor Demmand & prices low. Brings a littel Corn, some salt Pork, Cyder & Apples. One Mallatesti comes with Rington & has some Wax Works, some kind of Raree Show as I understand."

He was in his store, in the counting-room, next morning when Signor Malatesta called. It was cold. A chill vapour arose from the harbour, coating the rigging of the ships with white hoar and spreading a shroud about the waterfront. The snow had a shrill whine underfoot and the planks of the stoop crackled as Signor Malatesta approached the door. The store of Larrabee & Son was an unpretentious affair of pine boards and hand-split shingles, two narrow storeys and a garret, running beside a lane toward the wharf, with an end facing Fore Street.

A squat brick chimney sent up a column of blue wood-smoke toward the canopy of frost vapour that hung over the town in the bitter January morning. Malatesta, not used to such temperatures, flung himself inside and slammed the door as if pursued by wolves. The interior was dim after the white glare of the street. A meagre gleam of daylight entered a pair of windows flanking the front door and two other windows, small and obscured with frost, near the rear of the long wooden cavern in which he stood. A vague multitude of bins, barrels, and shelves loomed in the twilight, and a strong mingled smell of molasses, vinegar, Jamaica spirits, leather, drapery goods, paint, tea, coffee, and spices floated about him with an illusion of warmth, though he could see his own breath rising in little clouds.

Out of this scented murk swam the face of young Johnnie Hampton, apprenticed to Colonel Larrabee by the overseers of the poor, a lank orphan of fifteen with bony red wrists protruding out of his jacket sleeves, and wearing a pair of thick homespun long-togs that came to an end abruptly, sailor-fashion, halfway up his grey woollen calves. He snuffled a long red nose and regarded Signor Malatesta with astonishment. Customers were unusual at that hour of a winter morning. A customer like Malatesta was unusual any time.

The signor had hidden himself from the weather in a capacious black cloak, with a broad red woollen muffler wound about his throat and across his mouth. A Barcelona handkerchief bound his glossy black hair, and over the handkerchief a little old cocked hat was jammed as far as it would go. Between muffler and handkerchief Johnnie could see a nose longer and sharper and redder than his own, and a pair of small round black eyes that glittered like jet-stones. Behind the muffler sounded a continuous rattle of teeth.

"The Colonel Larrabee ees een, no?" gibbered Signor Malatesta.

The bemused apprentice waved toward the counting-room door and watched the signor step inside on a pair of thin black-stockinged legs.

"Furriner!" muttered Johnnie. His mind was stuffed with tales of war and the sea and he beheld Oldport as a kind of oasis in a desert of hostile furriners like this mincing little man in the cloak. Of course most of the furriners lived far to the south, where the palm trees grew and the rum came from, and where the men of Oldport went to drub them for pieces of eight, not to mention *eagles* and *crowns* and *joes* and *half-joes* and *doubloons*. Sometimes the furriners spoke French, and you called them Johnnie Crapaw. The rest were Spanyers, who lived on the Spanish Main, where *doubloons* grew on the bushes and the Oldport privateers had a thriving trade. As for the rest of the world, there was the King, who lived in England (a legendary country on the other side of the world), a personage remote and magnificent like God in Heaven; and nearer to home the Americans, who had fought against the King upon a time and therefore were furriners the same as the Crapaws and Spanyers.

The queer thing was that Americans looked and talked exactly like Oldport folk. When American skippers came to do business the Colonel addressed them as "you Yankees." It had a stinging sound, though the Colonel said it pleasantly, and the Yankees seemed to like it, just as Colonel Larrabee never minded being called " a rale old high-tory Carolinian, dyed in the wool." But when an old loyalist soldier came to the store for a yarn or a shilling or both, and the Colonel called for tobacco and glasses and a pair of new clays and a bottle of peach brandy from the last Savannah voyage—then the Yankees became "the rebels," and there was a great pounding of fists on the counting-room table, and tales of old battles, and toasts to The King; and the visit ended always with a song, a queer leaping sort of song that always made Johnnie's feet itch for the road, with a line about *Tarleton and his loyal boys a-riding* that weaved in and out of the verses and chorus. Whenever that song drifted out of the counting-room young Johnnie Hampton sat on one of the sugar casks and grinned and marvelled. It was the only time that Colonel Larrabee ever seemed quite human.

Signor Malatesta found himself in the presence of a tall spare man of fifty, with a dark aquiline face clean-shaven to a point just short of the cheekbones, where the black hair began. His coat, stock, breeches, and stockings were black, too, but these sombre garments were offset by a bright scarlet waistcoat which gave Colonel Larrabee, in Malatesta's eyes, the look of one of those preposterous American robins. At the moment Sumter's bony fingers held a pewter inkpot, which he was thawing in the heat thrown out by a blazing Franklin stove.

Three walls were hung with nautical prints. Upon the fourth, drooping from ceiling to floor, hung the ragged tricolour of the *Renard*, store-ship, captured off Guadeloupe by an Oldport privateer the previous year.

The softwood floor was bare and worn, so that the tough spruce knots stood out like warts. Two or three chairs stood about a long oak table. A wooden clock ticked on the mantelpiece. The windows were clouded with intricate frost patterns, but the upper panes were beginning to thaw a little in the warmth flung upward by the stove.

"Signor Larrabee?" murmured the visitor, prying off his hat.

"At your service," Colonel Larrabee said, turning and straightening up.

"I am Mario Malatesta, signor, a citizen of the keengdom of Napoli."

Sumter examined him with a cold eye. The fellow spoke English fluently enough but a strong foreign accent crept in and out of it. Sumter was distrustful of foreigners and he did not like that glib word citizen. It had a republican sound.

"And your business, sir?"

"Signor, I am the creator and owner of Malatesta's Celebrated Waxworks, education - to - young - and - old, warranted - not - to breeng-a-blosh-to-the-mos'-delicat-cheek."

He paused for breath and caressed a drooping and beautiful moustache.

"I am eenform, signor, I must 'ave first a permission of the chiff magistrate. Ees you, no?"

"Yes," Sumter said. "Sit down, sir. What is the nature of these—ah—waxworks? I confess I've never seen such a thing."

The visitor opened his cloak and made elliptical movements of his hands.

"Waxwork, signor, ees an image of the hooman form, but of wax."

"I trust these—ah—images are decently clothed?" said the Colonel darkly, remembering the rope-dancers.

"Ah yes, indeed. Clo'es, yes, signor. Beautyfool."

"And what human forms do they represent, sir?"

Signor Malatesta swelled. "Julius Caesar, the gret hemperor of Rome!"

"Um!"

"Brit-hanya, the Quin of the Sea!"

"Ah!"

"Ees Majesty Keeng Chortch of Engelland!"

"Well!" Sumter warmed. He had feared something outlandish and perhaps immoral. Shrewdly he said, "Perhaps I'd better see for myself first—a formality, you understand, sir, a natural pre-caution—"

Malatesta spread his hands in the manner of one who has nothing to conceal. A delighted smile shone in the room like a Neapolitan sun.

"Come! Come signor! At the tavern of Signor Falp. I am honour — we — Malatesta's Celebrated Waxworks are honour—"

"This afternoon," murmured Sumter, a little overwhelmed, "at three of the clock."

Signor Malatesta arose and swept the little cocked hat to his breast.

"Breeng your family, signor, your frands! To a frand of the good Colonel Larrabee"—he laid a long unclean finger against his carrot nose—"costs eb-so-lute-ly notting! Notting!"

They were quite a show in themselves, going down from Larrabee House to Phelps' Tavern—Sumter in black velvet gaiters buttoned to the thigh, his favourite blue cloak, his best London hat cocked with gilt buttons; young Allan with a thick seajacket over his broadcloth; and the handsome Larrabee daughters Arabella, Flora, Catherine, Priscilla, all four in new green pelisses of "imported English Lady's Cloath"; and Black Hagar bringing up the rear in her thick homespun gown, a pair of thick cow-hide boots and an old army greatcoat.

As they gained the town pump at the foot of the hill Sumter paused in the trampled ice-spattered snow and sent a thoughtful glance toward his store.

"Allan, go down to the store and take young Johnnie's place for half an hour. He'll never get a chance like this."

Allan gazed longingly toward the snowy roof of the tavern down the street.

"You shall see the show tonight with the townspeople," Sumter declared firmly, "and pay your way like any other, for the look of the thing if nothing else."

Johnnie Hampton came on the run, eyes wide and shining, and fell in at the rear beside the negro womanservant. The afternoon sun was without warmth, though the snow had lost some of the morning's crispness and the harbour no longer smoked. A few sleighs were abroad, harness bells a-jingle, drivers well muffled in furs, and a number of ox-sleds creaked slowly along with firewood from up-river.

Phelps, late sergeant in the King's Orange Rangers, that celebrated loyalist corps, kept the chief tavern of the day, two storeys of brown-painted clapboards with a gambrel roof. The surface of his big oak door was a quilt of tattered paper notices, advertisements of Oldport merchants for the most part, and a bold new sheet which declared—

ALL TIGHT LADS

Who wish to serve His Majesty and their Own Fortune can do so by Applying Within or on board that Good Fast-Sailing and well found Brig, the VENTURE private ship of war, Jonas Follard master, now Fitting for Another Cruize against the French & Spanish in Southern Waters. Capt. Follard wants a few more Jolly Spirited Lads to compleat her Compliment & will Sail at Once. All who Apply Within may expect the Finest Treatment, with grog & Cherry Tod for All!

Sumter paused a moment in the tobacco-stained snow before this masterpiece and surveyed it with satisfaction. The penmanship was his own (and who in Oldport, barring the schoolmaster, wrote a better hand?) and so was the *Venture*. He threw open the door, and a tide of warm air poured out over them, heavy with grog and tobacco and human breath, a smell of damp cloth, and a reek of sea-boots waterproofed with fish-oil. The big keeping-room really ran the full length of the tavern, but it was divided halfway by a folding wooden partition which could be opened for dances and other spacious affairs. Common folk used the first half, which was in fact the taproom; the inner chamber was reserved for merchants and captains. Half the business of Oldport was done in that inner room, a Lloyd's in miniature.

The partition was closed now but the business inside was Malatesta's Celebrated Waxworks, and the door in the central panel was guarded by a huge negro of an unfamiliar cast, clad in scarlet and gold (the scarlet shabby, Flora noted aloud, and the gold badly frayed) with a white-plumed shako on his woolly head and its glittering chain-metal strap caught under a flat black nose. A dozen seamen in red nightcaps and blue fearnaught jackets lounged against the bar, and Captain Jonas Follard sat at a small table by the fire with ink-horn, muster-roll and a steaming bowl of cherry-tod at his elbow. Between fireplace and main door clustered a little throng of townsfolk, of both sexes and all ages, with eyes for no one but the astonishing negro tyler. Evidently Signor Malatesta had lost no time in advertisement.

There was a murmur of "Here's the Colonel!" and the Larrabees trooped in under a massed stare that could be felt. Seamen pulled forelocks, Phelps drew a smart veteran hand to his broad red forehead, and Captain Follard arose and kicked back his chair and took off his hat. Sumter gave him a nod and in turning somehow bestowed the nod upon them all. The big black opened the partition door and whispered inside, and out popped Signor Malatesta bowing and smiling and making washing movements with his hands. Hagar giggled and nudged the big buck at the door as she passed inside.

It was not much of a show after all. A dozen costumed figures stood stiff and corpselike at the end of the chamber, well removed from a blazing fire. Subtle Malatesta had closed the window drapes and lit a few candles to heighten the show's pretentions—or to obscure the shabby costumes. Each figure held in its waxen hand a card printed in bold black letters, but the signor introduced them with separate oral flourishes, as if they were alive.

"First"—grandly—"we 'ave Louis the Seexteent," adding in a hushed voice, "the martyred keeng of the Fransh."

Sumter surveyed Louis Seexteent with contempt. "Martyred, bah! Sent his troops to play at revolution with the Yankees—reaped the whirlwind—serve him right! Why, sir, it was that fellow's fleet shut us up in Yorktown; shut us up, damme, like rats in a hole, with no choice but surrender!"

Signor Malatesta moved on hastily to Admiral Rodney, an unfortunate choice, for Rodney was in the same boat, so to speak—"Rodney, umph! A pity he couldn't ha' drubbed De Grasse a year before he did, sir!"

Malatesta began to perspire, though the big drafty room was frigid away from the fire. The young women had gathered themselves about Marie Antoinette, discussing her tawdry magnificence in the musical but merciless Larrabee voices. Young Johnnie was rummaging amongst the shadowy dummies, touching each chilly wax hand, drawing the swords of Rodney and General Wolfe an inch or two to see if they were real, peering indelicately under Britannia's flowing robe. Black Hagar hung in the offing, eyes all whites, awed out of speech by the uncanny wax company.

Nobody was paying attention to the proprietor of Malatesta's Celebrated Waxworks but Colonel Larrabee—who was paying a little too much. Malatesta wondered if the Larrabees were a sample of an Oldport audience. In desperation he drew attention to his *pièce de résistance*—"Ees royal majesty Keeng Chortch! Our grrraciose Soverain!"

The effect was magical. In a little rush the Larrabees gathered loyally to their King.

"He really looks like this?" Sumter murmured in a subdued

tone—it seemed a little indecent to be discussing His Majesty before His Majesty's face in this way.

"Malatesta's Celebrated Waxwork," said the signor proudly, "ees model from life."

"Taller than me, begad—and me six foot if an inch!"

"Yes, signor. Verree tall. Verree grrrand."

"A little mad, they say," observed Arabella coolly.

"Bella!" chorused her sisters, a little harmony of disapproving notes.

Sumter examined the large calm face. "I see no madness there," he observed with the air of a physician. "Strength rather —strength in every line. And courage, my dear. No man, that, to be ruffled by a passing storm. Fit head of a great nation, begad, with that face and build. Look closely, now. Ye may never have the chance again in a lifetime—as good as seeing the King himself. Something to tell your grandchildren!" And to the proprietor, kindly, "The show's an education, sir, and a credit to you."

The delighted Malatesta bowed, and bowed again. He motioned gracefully toward Julius Caesar, but Sumter, fierce old loyalist, was not to be moved so easily from his King.

"A good face," he went on, nodding amiably to King George. "A firm face. Resolution's the word—resolution all over the face."

"Eh?" squeaked Signor Malatesta sharply.

"Resolution, sir! All over the face!"

"Ah! Yes, yes, signor. Sooblime!" something—was it relief? —passed over the proprietor's face, but his olive countenance retained a tallowy tinge and Sumter's daughters regarded him curiously for a moment.

"I fought hard and long for him, sir!" Sumter declared, his keen black eyes fixed on the royal face as if he half hoped the King might hear. 'Gave up home, fortune, friends, everything for him. Suffered persecution. Shed my blood. Never regretted it. Proud of it. Look at him! A man, sir, a man! D'ye know, I'd always pictured somehow a Germanish sort of person on the fat side."

At last he permitted himself to be diverted to Britannia—"a true copy, signor and yong leddies and you too, leetle boy over there—a true copy of the Brit-hanya made by the beautyfool Lady 'Amilton when she welcomes back the gret hadmiral Nelson to Napoli from hees gloriose veectory on the reever Nile!"

"Humph!" said Arabella tartly. "Wonder which the 'gret hadmiral' embraces most—the lady or Britannia?"

"Nelson?" snorted Sumter, surprised.

"All the fleet knows—all the world. It's the talk of Halifax."

"Nasty idle gossip! Let's have no more of it. Who's that over there?"

Malatesta led the way with his sidelong bow and splendid gestures, but there was an interruption. Young Johnnie Hampton appeared from behind one of the figures waving a card.

"Hi! Colonel Larrabee, sir! Here's furrin writin's!"

Signor Malatesta moved swiftly, but Flora's hand was quicker.

"Jeanne d'Arc, she read aloud. "That's French, Johnnie."

"Ah!" roared the apprentice, dancing all about the flustered Malatesta and pointing an accusing finger. "He's a spy, that's what. He's a bloody Crapaw!"

"Give me the thing," demanded Sumter. "And you, John Hampton, mind your language. Now, what have we here?" He examined the card.

"Jeanne d'Arc, signor. Means notting, signor, eb-so-lute-ly notting!"

"That may be. Where'd ye find it, Johnnie?"

"Stuck under the tail o' her grown—that 'un there, the lady wi' the yeller nightcap an' the hay-fork."

"That's Britannia, idiot! Kate, see what General Wolfe's got under his coat."

Catherine fumbled, and drew forth a card like the one in Sumter's hand, except that it read "Marquis de Lafayette." The girls could see the Colonel's hackles rising.

"Priscilla—you're nearest—see about Admiral Rodney."

Priscilla, most prim of the Larrabee daughters, rummaged in the admiral's coat-skirts with obvious distaste. She held a card to the candlelight.

"Admiral John Paul Jones."

Thunder loomed in Sumter's face. Signor Malatesta closed his eyes.

"Well, sir," uttered Colonel Larrabee grimly, "what's the meaning of all this?"

Signor Malatesta dropped his glance to the strong fingers twitching on the stout ash stick. For a moment he hesitated, then, his narrow shoulders rose to his ears and fell hopelessly. In a thin toneless voice he began :

"I geev you the truth, signor. I model the waxwork. Ees true, signor. Een Pareés when comes the Revolution I 'ave some wax-work I show for a few sous—King Louis, Quin Marie-Antoinette,

Jeanne d'Arc, the Cardinal Richelieu. Een the Revolution, ees no good, eh? I lose my 'ead, eh? So! I change, signor, the card, the clo'es. I make a wooden guillotine, I put Louis Capet in there and Marie Capet waiting 'er turn. The people of Parees like that, eh? The Cardinal, 'e becomes Citizen Robespierre. One mus' leev, signor. But soon ees no monney een Parees any more. I go 'ome to Napoli. Bimeby ees no good there. So—I come to Amereeca. Eees good there. But Robespierre—no, no! An' Jeanne d'Arc—'oo ees she? So I change 'er clo'es, I call 'er Leeberty. Robespierre, I chenge eem to the great Benjameen Frankleen. People come to see. Good! I get more wax, make more figure."

"Ha! And when ye come to His Majesty's provinces, sir, what becomes of the citizen Robespierre-Franklin.

Silently, Malatesta pointed to Julius Caesar.

"Egad! And Liberty's now Britannia?"

"Yes, signor. I am sorree."

"And Lafayette's become General Wolfe?"

"One must eat, signor."

"And Paul Jones—Admiral Rodney?"

"Life ees very 'ard, signor."

"Damme," Sumter said, "it's ingenious."

He noticed a profound silence and found them all watching him carefully—Malatesta, the girls, Johnnie Hampton and Black Hagar. Then it dawned on him. Out he strode and confronted the waxen ranks like a sergeant-major addressing defaulters. He indicated King George with his stick, and the stick shook.

"And who, sir—don't lie to me, damme!—who's that?"

"Signor!" faltered Mario Malatesta.

"Out with it!"

"Ah, signor, signor!"

"The truth, or begad, sir, I'll—"

It was King George whom Sumter menaced with the uplifted stick, but Signor Malatesta cringed and his hands fluttered.

"Chortch" he choked on the fatal name—"Chortch Vashington, signor."

"What!"

"From life, signor, een Pheeladelphia." .

The young women fled to the fireplace and opened their cloaks, glad to turn their backs upon the chilly room and this uncomfortable tableau. Black Hagar and Johnnie stared, and Malatesta gibbered when the Colonel raised his stick—as he might have raised his sabre twenty years before and praised God for the chance. But he paused, with his black eyes ablaze.

and was heard to say, "Pshaw! Pshaw! A lump of wax!" and he began to pace the floor in great strides, the cloak flapping about like a spilled sail, the stick striking hollow thunder from the boards at every step. The door in the partition opened at the sound, and the foreign negro put a curious head inside. Sumter marked the intrusion with a flourish of the ash.

"Tell that blackamoor to keep his nose out o' this!"

Malatesta yapped something in falsetto Italian, and the head vanished.

Sumter resumed his tramp from Washington to the door, from the back door to Washington, and on each journey down the floor his eyes fastened upon the calm wax face as if to shrivel the thing with a look. Once he glanced at his girls; but they had found a Boston newspaper, weeks old, brought in the *Betsey* along with the "Raree show," and were clustered about it, four charming faces together in the light of the mantelpiece candles. Suddenly he paused and demanded, "Why, man, did you bring this—this treasonable sham, this waxen swindle, to Oldport of all places?"

Huskily Signor Malatesta murmured, "Een Boston, signor, ees 'ard een the winter. People say to me, Go to 'Allefax, where ees the Englees preence Eduard, many soldir, good Engleesh guinea, good times. So, signor, I come. The capitan Rington brings me 'ere on the way. Signor, I am a peaceful man, I no weesh to offend the good people of Keeng Chortch, so I chenge the card. Ecco! I am a poor man and mus' leev, Signor."

"False pretences, damme!"

Malatesta did not know what pretences were, but in Colonel Larrabee's tones they had a jail-door sound. He fell upon his shaking knees and washed his hands upward in great fear. But the Colonel had resumed his march. The truth was that Colonel Larrabee burned not so much with the old bitterness—sixteen busy years in Nova Scotia had mellowed that—as a strong suspicion that he had made himself ridiculous in the eyes of a foreigner. He was not a man who could laugh that off, his sense of humour was not geared to such strains. And because Signor Malatesta was the cause of his embarrassment it seemed just that Signor Malatesta should suffer for it.

"Give me a reason—one, sir!—why I shouldn't call in my privateersmen and have you and your fraudulent graven images thrown out in the snow!"

The proprietor of the waxworks answered with a thin wail. The group by the fire opened suddenly, crying "Father!" indignantly, and Arabella—the Colonel's favourite—swept toward him with the newspaper in one hand and a candlestick in the other. She had an instinct for dramatics and she used it now.

"Since when," demanded Arabella, "has a gentleman from Carolina demeaned himself and his King by insulting a dead enemy?"

"Eh? Pooh! Nonsense!"

"Dead! At Mount Vernon, three weeks ago." She thrust the rolled newspaper like a pistol under Sumter's nose and held the candle for his reading.

There was a tremendous silence. The paper crackled in the tense grip of his fingers. He stared at the print for a long time, an hour according to the family legend, but that has an excessive sound; no doubt it seemed so long to Arabella, holding the candle, and to the other young women who passed the tale to posterity. At last he exclaimed, "So! It's true! He's gone! That man!" And in a lower tone, "As we must all go, I suppose, and take our quarrels with us." Then, jerkily, but in the subdued voice, "I'd no love for him—not I, damme!—but I take back nothing I said of that image yonder. Resolution he had, and courage, yes, and faith, the faith that moves mountains according to the Scriptures. He needed it—the rebel congress was mountain enough to break any man's heart. He was proud, they say, proud as a king—a bit too proud for some of 'em. But then the mantle of the levellers never did sit well on a Virginian. And now he's gone! 'Died hard', it says, as if that were something strange. Lived hard, didn't he? So lived we all. Fighting times! Fighting times! Well, here's an end to the chapter, and what's left? Wax, wax, to be changed by the scrawl of a card. There were men in those days. So it goes."

He addressed this to nobody in particular, unless it were General Washington, tall and impassive before him. The news had thrown Sumter into what Flora always called his graveyard mood, when doubt of the rising generation rose bitter as bile to his tongue. But in the end, in a voice cold as the weather outside, he announced, "You may show these things to our people, sir."

"Signor!"

"But no more humbug! Let 'em be seen for what they are. We live, sir, in an age of enlightenment, and a free country."

"Ah, signor!"

"The charge not to exceed sixpence a head, lawful money."

"Each afternoon and evening," suggested the joyful Malatesta, riding the tide.

"Bar Sunday. But I'll have no interference with the working habits of our people, sir. Let's see—gets dusk at four. dark at five—um!—you may exhibit your images between the hours of four in the afternoon and eight in the evening, no sooner, no later. Any disorder, for whatever cause, will be upon your head. Is that clear?"

"I understand, signor," whispered Malatesta, wondering when the packet schooner left for Halifax.

Beyond the partition door Sumter crooked a finger, and Captain Follard came.

"You will kindly hoist your flag at half-mast on the *Venture*, Follard, and notify the other ships in port. I am sending word to the battery."

"Very good, sir," answered Follard; and diffidently, "Who's dead?"

Sumter threw his head up and squared his shoulders, as if to challenge all argument.

"General Washington—the late president of the United States."

With that he turned, and the Larrabees marched out in a stark silence that chilled the eager taproom like a frost. Behind them, as young Johnnie closed the door, they heard the rush of feet toward the gaudy negro and his guarded mysteries.

But Captain Follard did not move. His bearded mouth was open still. He was stunned by an incredible fact. It was not that an elderly American soldier lay dead in far-away Virginia. It was that Colonel Larrabee—"Sabre" Larrabee of Tarleton's Legion—had recognized at last, by act official, the existence of the United States.

It is all there in old Sumter's diary, in two prosaic entries in the early winter of the year 1800, sandwiched amongst items of sawmill business, the final accounts of the season's codfishery, the salmon-netting in the Labrador rivers, the trading-voyages to New England, Carolina, and the West Indies, and the news of his privateers harrying the French and Spanish trade in the Caribbean.

Nowadays the story of Flora Larrabee reads like a bad melo-drama in one or two acts, but the art of the play was far from old Sumter's mind when he sat down one bleak night of early winter and wrote—

> Nov. 3, 1800. Wind N.W. and cold. Mr. Bolger's Schooner gets in from Halifax this evening's Tide. Lieutenant Rich'd. Green is come in her with a Military Party seeking a Deserter from the Nova Scotia Fencibles. At his request I sent out Notices by Black Philip to be Posted on the door of the Church and the Methodist meetinghouse and the Bridge towards the Falls, but I judge the Man has gone to the Westward in one of the fishing Shallops. This after-noon my daughter Flora rode Manners to the Falls, Abi-gail Fisher & Mary Gidner went with her, all on Horse Back, and returned at Sunsett. Squally and spitting Snow.

At that time our town of Oldport was still no more than a colonial outpost, settled barely forty years on a lonely coast, drawing its life from the sea by way of fishery, the West India trade and the lucrative business of privateering; knowing little and caring nothing of the still mysterious interior that came down to the skirts of the town in a forest of pine, hemlock, and spruce.

The river that fed the Larrabee sawmill came out of a wilder-ness traversed by a few trappers and woodsmen and by wander-ing bands of Micmacs, no longer warlike. A government sur-veyor had blazed a trail across the province to the Bay of Fundy in '98, but little had been done to make a road of it and his blazes had turned grey on the hardwoods and filled with gum on the softwoods, and soon would be healed over and forgotten.

It is a curious commentary on the life of a seafaring community of the time that nearly two hundred men and boys in Oldport could speak familiarly of Labrador, Madeira, New York, or "Curassow," while those who had seen the first lake on the river, twenty miles upstream from the town, could be numbered on a pair of hands. A track straggled down the coast from Halifax, barely passable on horseback as far as the German settlements, but there it ended.

For the Oldport women who lived and toiled in frugal isolation on the stony shelf between the forest and the sea it must have been one long monotony. Most of them died young, worn out by the endless labour and repeated childbirth and it seems to me the sheer lack of interest in life. The Old Burying Ground, enclosed now in an iron fence and open to visitors in the summer season, is full of pathetic little monuments. If you demand a clue to the strange affair of Flora Larrabee I think you must seek it ultimately in that mute but eloquent spectacle, which confronted her every time she went down into the town.

Colonel Larrabee had a sawmill at The Falls, two miles or so above Oldport, where the river dropped in to the long tidal estuary. The boards and ship-timber from the mill were floated down to Oldport in great clumsy rafts, for the road up-river was impassable to a loaded wagon and barely tolerable on horseback. The sawmill hands lived with their families in a little scatter of houses about the falls, and Flora Larrabee went there frequently, sometimes with a message from her father, often merely for the ride.

She was a small girl of twenty-two, finely made, with her father's glowing black eyes and a lively manner that came through her mother from the Nesbits of Savannah; and if you wish to read between the lines of Sumter's diary you must see her now, riding up the river road from Oldport with a pair of boon companions on that bleak November day so very long ago.

The three girls jogged along the narrow track in file, letting the horses pick their own way amongst the stumps and boulders. Each held the reins in one cold hand and warmed the other in her muff. There was shelter wherever the road crossed a bend in the river, with dense walls of pine and spruce on either hand, but where it came out on the bank the wind rose off the grey water in icy gusts, flinging itself in their faces.

In one of these comfortless places they came upon a man

footing it briskly toward the falls. The raw wind carried the sound of their approaching cavalcade away from him until Manners clattered a hoof at his very back. The man's response was prompt. He leaped aside and opened a large clasp-knife in a single movement, a swift instinctive movement, as if he had done it a good many times before with as little notice. The girls pulled up at once. For a moment they stared at the man, and a pair of desperate blue eyes stared back at them, roving from face to face.

"The deserter, I presume," said Flora, sitting up very straight.

"You presume too much," said the man shortly. He shut the knife and put it in his pocket.

"Don't lie, my good man. The description's out and everybody's seen it by this time—'Age 28, light brown hair, sharp visage, blue eyes, wearing the uniform of the Nova Scotia Fencible Regiment, grey jacket, yellow facings, pantaloons a shade darker grey. Name Aquila Denby. Has been a seaman.' That's you. Don't deny it." She might have been Colonel Larrabee himself.

"It's past denying," murmured Aquila Denby. "They've been devilish quick."

"I think," said Abigail faintly, "we'd better be going."

"Hush up, Nabby, do! You're a foolish young man, Aquila Denby—foolish to run away in the first place and foolish to come this way in the second. Why didn't you keep along the coast?"

"Because that's the way they'll expect me to go. Who is it? Old Wollenhaupt?"

"It's a Lieutenant Green with four soldiers."

"Whew! Want me badly, don't they?"

Flora let the reins drop and thrust both hands into her muff, completely mistress of the situation. "They'll get you, too."

Aquila Denby looked up and down the lonely road. The long reach of the river lay ahead but the distant sawmill and houses were hidden by a wooded island below the falls. Oldport was lost in the woods behind the three young women.

"Not if I have your horse," he said coolly. He stepped up to Manners and seized the idle reins. Mary Gidner dropped her muff and jerked her horse about, squealing absurdly, "I'll—I'll rouse the town!"

"You'll do no such thing," Flora snapped. "There's no harm in the man. He's an idiot. Where would you go with my horse, idiot? The road ends at the falls, a mile ahead."

The man read truth in her confident black eyes and dropped the reins.

"I could take to the woods," he said stubbornly.

"In November? Without an axe and gun? You *are* an idiot!"

Aquila Denby folded his ragged arms. "I'm none of your blessed town-bred regulars, ma'am, that's lost outside a barrack-yard. I'm country-born, and lived in the woods before this. I'd shift somehow, I guess. There's Indians. Hunt up a band o' Micmacs somewhere and pass the winter with 'em. Then pull foot in the spring, when the regiment's written me off the muster roll."

He went over the prospects aloud, as if the girls were not there at all.

"Indians!" Flora cried. "Always begging for bread about the settlements in winter time—too shiftless to hunt. You'd starve. Better give yourself up."

The deserter looked up with a wry face. "What for?"

"Four or five hundred lashes," chirped Abigail suddenly. "And serve you right."

"That comes off your lips very easy, ma'am. There's hanging, too—have ye considered that? Only a few months back there was a fine hanging of deserters at Halifax, with all the towns-folk there to see, and the garrison drawn up in square—on the town common 'twas—and eleven poor devils rigged out in white for the great occasion, and the garrison chaplain and Father Burke to give 'em a word in the passing. I was there, ma'am, on the flank of my company, with my hands dead cold on the musket muzzle, though it was summer weather. But the Duke of Kent, that ordered the execution, *he* wasn't there—he was off for England with his little French mistress, three days before. 'Twas nice of him, wasn't it, to leave us that little rope-dancing show to remember him by? All soldier, he is, and that's a fact. You should have been there, ma'am, you'd have enjoyed it—the sun just up over Citadel Hill, and all the pretty uniforms and buttons and epaulettes a-shining in the glint of it, and those eleven runaway scoundrels in their nice white grave-clothes, and eleven new black coffins in the cart before 'em, and eleven gallows all in a row with the hang-ropes swaying just a little in the first breath o' the morning...."

"Stop!" cried Flora, very white. "I've said nothing of giving you up. Be still, do, Nabby!"

The deserter looked up and down the road again. "Then why, ma'am, do you suggest I head back toward the town?"

"So you can hide in my father's store-loft, idiot!"

Abigail and Mary sang "Flora Lar-ra-bee!" in a horrified duet.

"Yes!" Her black eyes were dancing with excitement. "It's the last place they'd look for him. I'd love to see the face of that pompous young lieutenant if he knew."

"Or your father's," suggested Abigail Fisher pointedly.

"That's my affair, Nabby Fisher. If you or Mary breathe a word, I'll—I'll scratch your eyes out." She turned to the man eagerly. "Keep off the road, you understand? There's a bridge where the road crosses the grist-mill brook on the edge of the town; make your way there through the woods. I'll meet you at the bridge tonight, after dark."

She found him lurking under the timbers of the bridge itself, his teeth rattling in the cold draft down the stream.

"You picked a good place for me, ma'am. A corpse would keep there a twelve-month."

"You're not dead yet, idiot. Put this on and take care of it—it's a cloak that belonged to my poor Mamma. And here's a calash to hide your head."

"No!" He had a sudden sharp suspicion that this madcap girl was out to play a prank. His impulse was to dash back into the woods.

"Put them on! If I'm seen with a man after dark there'll be tongues to wag and ears to hear—my father's, 'specially."

He tried to step into the gown as if it were a pair of breeches, and the girl gave an impatient cluck, snatching it up and dropping it over his head. He was lean and it fitted where it touched. The calash was a stroke of genius, for his face was completely lost in its shadow. It billowed and settled uneasily as he walked; the deep hood caught the air like a wind-scoop.

In the outskirts of the town most of the homes were simple log shanties, and because the poor could not afford candles and went to bed at nightfall the street was dark and silent like a double row of tombs; but toward Shipyard Point and the militia parade-ground, the heart of the town, the tall frame houses of merchants and ship captains stood lit at what seemed every pane with the yellow glow of tallow and spermaceti and the flicker of comfortable hearths. The street itself was a quagmire after the autumn rains, but the sharp frost of the November night had given it a thin crust through which Flora's pattens sank at every step.

At last there was a pattern of masts and spars against the starlight to the left, and the girl jerked his arm that way. So far they had not met a soul, but now a door opened suddenly and there was a shadowy play of figures in a rectangle of light, and voices calling Goodnight and complaining of the cold.

"Run!" whispered Flora Larrabee. They ran, past a number of silent houses in a lane, past a dark forge with its great cooling-tub and smell of Cape Breton coals, past a succession of looming sheds. There was a whiff of salt and a reek of dried codfish stored in the lofts.

The girl halted at a dim door, rattled a key, pulled him into a black cavern full of the smell of tar and gun-grease, and another scent, faint but pungent.

"Take my hand," she whispered. "We daresn't strike a light."

"Who's to see?" grumbled Aquila Denby, blundering against hard and bulky objects.

"Nobody, idiot. It's the powder."

She felt for the loft stairs with a foot and led him upward, her iron-shod pattens clinking on the steps.

"Powder?" he repeated, sniffing.

"Yes. And the King's powder at that. Father's commander of the town militia."

They were in the loft, and paused in silence, their hearts beating quickly—from the run, no doubt. The deserter retained Flora's hand in his strong fingers.

"Who are you, ma'am, if I may be so bold?"

"I'm Flora Larrabee. My father's colonel of the militia, and chief magistrate, and Deputy Registrar of the Vice-Admiralty Court, and representative in the assembly and a lot of other things. They'll never look for you here."

"Flora! Um! A good name—a pretty name, like the one that wears it. And wasn't it the name of the goddess of flowers in my schoolbooks? So I must thank a goddess, not the gods."

"Thank your stars, Aquila Denby,"—a little tartly. She pulled her hand away and put a small bundle in his arms. "There's bread and cheese, and corn-cake, and a bottle of father's Madeira. Keep quiet and don't stir from this loft. I'll come again tomorrow night."

The deserter took the package absently.

"One moment, Flora, ma'am. Why are you doing all this?"

"You wouldn't believe me if I told you."

"I'll believe anything you say, ma'am."

"Well, you looked hungry and—and hunted. And young. And brave, in a desperate fashion. It seemed to me that you were like Prince Charlie in the Highlands—and, you see, I was named for the woman who saved Prince Charlie's life. My parents knew Flora Macdonald in Carolina. She and her husband

and sons and my father and mother were loyalists together in the American Revolution. My mother told me the story many a time. It was that, and—well, I thought it would be exciting. Now that you're here, I'm a little afraid. You must stay here till Green and his soldiers are gone."

"And then?"

"That's for you to decide. Why did you run away?"

The deserter shrugged in the darkness. "For the same reason I enlisted—a whim. Oh, I was ripe for it. I wouldn't have minded fighting; I've done a bit of that, and in some queer corners. But garrison duty in peacetime—that only eats out a man's heart and brains."

The phrase reminded him of his empty stomach. He tore open the package and gnawed at the great country loaf.

When the girl had gone he fumbled his way about the loft and found a bundle of old herring-net stowed upon a rafter. He pulled it down for a bed, and discovered with a whimsical grin in the morning that his pillow was a little heap of long flannel powder-cartridges for cannon. As the grey morning light struggled through the single dusty window he saw that the storehouse was a stout affair of massive hewn pine beams and posts, with oak treenails running through tenon and mortice, the work of men whose chief trade was the building of ships.

There were many squat kegs with the government crow-foot burnt in the wood. There were two open barrels of musket cartridges, some of which had the paper broken and the powder spilled. He thought of rats.

Over all was a thin film of dust. Evidently the militia had not been mustered in some months. Their muskets, a hundred perhaps, stood in racks along both walls of the loft, and above them hung the worms, rammers, and sponges for the cannon on Fort Point. Rubbing his finger in the dust that clung to the oil of the muskets he decided there had been no muster since early summer, probably the celebration of the King's birthday in June.

He called up a picture of the militia company forming up awkwardly on the rough parade-ground, amongst the scattered chips and sawdust from the shipyard, with cross-belts slung over homespun jackets to support their bayonet sheaths and cartridge boxes, and all these muskets polished under the critical eye of Colonel Larrabee—a fat and pompous little merchant surely—and then the ragged march along the town street toward Fort Point where three or four long eighteens commanded the river entrance; drum rattling furiously, colours tossing on a pike, a patter of urchins alongside, all the women running to the doors; the flag run up at the Point, the crash of a salute—with His Majesty's powder—from the long eighteens, the more modest salute—owners' powder—fired by the privateers lying in the river; and then nightfall, and the houses of merchants and ship-owners and the more prosperous captains lit from cellar to garret with candles in every window, and poor folk and sailors wandering along the street to gaze at the "illumination," and twenty or thirty gentlemen sitting down to a dinner at Boyle's Tavern and toasting The King, The Governor, Our Fair Province, Success to the Forces, and so on far into the night.

Aquila Denby's refuge (always described in the Larrabee diary as the King's Store, to mark it from the building farther up the lane in which the Colonel conducted his own business) lay at the head of the Larrabee wharf, and all day long the deserter listened to passing feet and voices. There was no window on the river side but he guessed that a ship of some importance lay at the wharf and that she was fitting out for a voyage. An ox-cart made regular trips down the lane and back, and there was a constant rattle of wheelbarrows.

Each night the girl came like a ghost with her key and with food and drink—sometimes wine, sometimes beer, often merely water.

"I daresn't take too much from father's cellar," she whispered ruefully on the fourth visit. "Are you all right?"

"You're taking too much risk for me," said Denby gravely. "Clear of anything else I'm afraid for you in this dark lane. Wenches that hang about the wharves o' nights are considered fair game all round, and a seaman full of hot flip's no gentleman."

"Pooh! That's only if the wench is looking to be caught."

"Where's the lieutenant?"

"Staying at our house, if you please. The soldiers bed in the garret. They went down to Gun Cove in a sloop yesterday to search the fishing-vessels there, and found a pair of deserters from the Royal Artillery at Halifax—at least that's what Lieutenant Green says. He's lodged them in the town gaol. The men insist they're fishermen lately come from the eastward. How do you get along?"

"Well enough," Denby said; and then in a passionate voice, "If only you could come by day, so I could see your face, the look in your eyes, the way your lips move when you speak . . . but that's not to be thought of, of course. I lie here like a bear denned-up for winter, and peer through that filthy little window from morn to night. There's an opening between the sheds and lofts where I can see a bit, a fathom or so, of the town street, and I watch there, hoping to see you pass, to see you turn your face my way and smile a bit, perhaps—go on, call me an idiot if you like. Even idiots can be lonely for a look or a smile. Wishful, that's the word. But it's just as well you come by night. A look at me would frighten you—dirt from head to foot, and a beard like a handful of oakum."

Flora Larrabee put out a hand and touched his face. She laughed softly.

"You'd be better for a shave, Aquila Denby, that's the truth. I'll bring soap and razor tomorrow."

He caught her hands and pressed them against his stubbled cheeks, like a small boy seeking comfort in the darkness. She resisted a little and then her fingers relaxed in his grasp as if she had decided to be merciful.

"Flora, ma'am," he said huskily.

"Yes—Aquila?"

"D'you think, just for once, just out o' kindliness, you'd let me kiss your lips?"

He felt the slim hands go rigid in his.

"I'm sorry—ma'am."

It was a long time before she said anything. Then, with a resolute intake of breath, "You may kiss me, Aquila, if you want."

He drew her against him gently and his lips brushed her face high on the cheek. She fled, but called up to him shakily from the dark foot of the stairs, "Is your aim as poor with a musket, soldier?"

Two nights later she let herself into the store and walked blindly into a pair of ready arms and found a clean-shaven cheek against her own. Aquila Denby kissed her very accurately.

"Aquila! You frightened me out of my wits!"

"My dear, I'm nothing frightful, I assure you. I wish you could see me in these homespuns—where did you get 'em?"

"Do they fit? Nabby Fisher got them for me. I daresn't steal anything of father's or Allan's. There's a bottle of Malmsey this time, and some roast beef—Miles Ferguson killed his fat ox yesterday and father bought a quarter. What have you been doing today?"

"Thinking of you, my dear, as I do always." He laughed, and it was good to hear the new ring in his laughter. "But I must confess, Ma'am, I was abroad last night, airing my new clothes."

"Aquila!"

"I climbed out of the lower window and tramped up and down the wharf in the dark. Quite safe, I assure you. Midnight, snow flying, and nobody about. That's a fine brig at the wharf."

"The *Nymph*? Yes. She's fitting for a cruise against the French and Spanish in the Caribbees. The Governor's encouraging our merchants to fit privateers against the King's enemies, and father's got a letter-of-marque. That reminds me, Aquila, you must lie very still in the loft tomorrow. They're shipping the brig's guns out of the store downstairs."

He whistled. "So that's where they go! I've been wondering— I've been all over 'em. Two long eighteens, ten twelves, a long brass swivel—a beauty, that; a few carronades—twelves—all right for close work. She ought to give an account of herself. Is she coppered?"

Flora considered a moment. "No. She was built here this summer past. Our people can't afford coppering. They scorch the planking and then paint it with hot stuff—tar and sulphur, I think."

"Umph. That means pump-or-drown afore the cruise is up, I'll warrant. The ship-worms are bad where she'll be going. Has she a full crew?"

His arms were about her. She took off her bonnet, holding it by the strings and resting her head against his shoulder.

"Crew? Yes, I think. Captain Beddoes hoisted his colours at Mrs. Gallihew's tavern and opened a rendezvous five days ago. I heard father say that men were coming in well."

"And they ship the guns tomorrow. That means they'll be up here for powder and shot, my Flora."

A quick lift of her head, a sudden fear in her voice. "Oh, but they can't! I mean, it's government powder and shot. It's for the defence of the town."

"That! Who's to stop 'em borrowing the King's stuff to fire at His Majesty's enemies anywhere they choose—in the Caribbean, say. If they don't, my dear, then I don't know my privateersmen. All due respects to your father, of course."

There was a rattle below. They froze. The lower door opened and a crisp voice echoed in the hollow dark. "Go ahead with the lantern, Philip, and steady about it. There's powder enough here to blow us to the moon."

"Speak of the devil—" murmured Aquila Denby, drawing a great breath and squaring his shoulders. Black Philip came up the steps cautiously, an absurd figure in the glimmer of the lantern, his jet face beaded with unseasonable sweat, mouth open, eyes rolling and showing the whites. At sight of the silent pair at the end of the dusty musket rack he checked and drew back, gibbering.

Colonel Larrabee appeared at his heels, the black eyes glittering in his lean hawk face. Sumter Larrabee was fifty then, and a fine figure of a man. A resolute military air sat naturally upon his six-foot frame, although he had never been more than an amateur soldier and it was nineteen years since Yorktown, the last of Tarleton's Legion and the end of a world.

"Ha!" he uttered in an edged voice. "So this is where you go at night, Miss. And who the devil is that, may I ask?"

"Father, I—"

"Silence! Let the man speak for himself, if he's a man and can speak."

Aquila Denby took his arm from the girl's waist deliberately. He stepped forward as if to come to attention but thought better of it and hooked his thumbs in his belt.

"As a magistrate, sir, you ought to know my name," he said coolly.

"Eh? Hold the lantern closer, Philip, and stop shaking the thing. Aha! So! Brown hair, blue eyes, and a damned sharp visage—you're the deserter from the Fencibles."

"Visage no sharper than yours," retorted the younger man quickly. In truth they were much alike with their long jaws and beak noses.

"Insolent, too, I see. You'll sing a different tune at the triangles when the hide's half off your back. Philip, bring Lieutenant Green here at once."

"They'll not flog me again," Aquila Denby said, and snatched the lantern from Black Philip's uneasy hand. "Not while there's a barrel of broken musket cartridges at my elbow, and powder enough in the loft to blow us all—to the moon, did you say?—at the drop of a lantern."

Sumter bristled. "Damme, sir, you wouldn't dare!" The negro began to moan, a queer crooning sound.

"Oh yes, I'd dare. You're at a tactical disadvantage, Colonel Larrabee, if you know one when you see it. Take a hold on your sense of duty, sir, before something happens that we may not have time to regret, and listen to this. Your daughter is none the worse for her charity. She's sheltered and fed me here as she'd shelter and feed a sick dog—nothing more. If you've hard things to say, say 'em to me."

Sumter Larrabee turned to his daughter grimly. "And what's your story, Miss?"

Her eyes were shining and she had that proud tilt of the head that was so like her dead mother's.

"Nothing, father, except that I love him and he loves me." Sumter's handsome black brows shot up. His eyes blazed.

"Say that again, Miss!"

"I love him," Flora said.

The colonel's face went white to the lips. "Then by the eternal heavens, Miss, you shall have him."

"What?" Aquila Denby cried.

"Here, sir! Now! Tonight! She's made her bed and begad she shall lie in it. Off with you, Philip, and fetch the parson here at once. And another candle for the lantern."

The old negro's eyes were popping. He was in a convulsion of terror, partly for himself in this awesome place, partly for Miss Flora, on whose small head some unmentionable wrath seemed about to descend.

"Parson, he went to Hal'fax in d' packet, Cunnel Larby, sah. Monday, sah."

"Ah! Then it'll have to be that Methodist fellow. What's his name?"

"Oliphant," said Flora, very low. Black Philip stumbled away down the stairs.

"I'd rather the Established Church made an honest woman of you," Sumter said, "but it seems we must fall back on the Dissenters. As for you, sir, I doubt if the devil himself could do much for your honesty. Have you any accomplishments besides running away from your duty?"

"I'm a sailor, if that's what you mean," Aquila said, looking him in the eye. "I've quite a knowledge of mathematics and the art of navigation. I can hand, reef, and steer—and swing a cutlass if it comes to that. And I can play *The World Turned Upside Down* upon a fife."

"Eh? What's that?" Sumter said, throwing up his head like a stung horse.

"Ah, that tune fetches you, sir, don't it? That's the tune Cornwallis' men played, marching out of Yorktown to surrender, back in '81. And here you are in Nova Scotia—a good thousand miles. That's a longer run than mine."

Colonel Larrabee turned a rich plum colour. He threw aside the cape of his old blue cloak and brandished his ash stick fiercely.

"Confound you, sir, d'ye compare yourself with me? I never turned my back on a fight in my life."

"Fight?" Aquila said. "There's a word you didn't mention before. I've yet to run from a fight myself."

"You deserted the King's service in time of war," Sumter roared.

"I deserted an idle garrison that'll never see a shot fired in this war or the next. Are they the only patriots, those poor stupid lobster-backs at Halifax, drinking themselves to death in the Barrack Street groggeries for sheer want of excitement?"

The door below opened again, uncertainly, and a pair of feet made tentative sounds on the stairs. An uncocked hat rose into view, the brim drooping. The Reverend Mr. Oliphant was a little whisp of a man in black homespun small-clothes and thick grey wool stockings. The collar of his threadbare fly-coat was half up and half down. He had put it on in a hurry. A summons from Colonel Larrabee in the Oldport of that day was tantamount to a blast of celestial trumpets.

"Where's my nigra?" Sumter said.

The preacher blinked a pair of pale myopic eyes in the lantern light. "He accompanied me to the door of this place, thrust a candle in my hand, and told me to go upstairs. I think he ran off. I had no means of lighting the candle. It is all very strange, Colonel Larrabee, if I may say so."

"Humph. You're the Methodist preacher, eh?"

Mr. Oliphant took a prayer-book from under his arm and waved it slightly. He had a large voice for so small a man.

"It pleased God to call me here by the *Susan*, brig, from Connecticut two weeks back. You have a town full of iniquity, Colonel, but many poor souls seeking the light. At meeting last Sunday three men and nine women were moved with the spirit, and four of the women cried out aloud. There is a great work to be done."

"There's a bit of work to be done here tonight," said the Colonel dourly. "I wish you to marry my daughter to that fellow holding the lantern."

Mr. Oliphant turned his mild gaze upon Flora Larrabee, slim and pale at the deserter's shoulder, and then to Aquila Denby, who was staring straight into the darkness at the other end of the loft. The good man hesitated.

"This hardly seems the time or place—"

"Get on, man, the time's short," said Denby, listening for sounds in the lane.

"But the young people should be published first in the meeting-house."

"Published!" rapped Sumter with a fierce twist of his long

lips. "I tell you, parson, we're a lot nearer heaven here than we'd ever be in your meeting-house. If this hot-headed fool should drop the lantern—"

The little preacher shrugged in a mystified way and pulled at the stock about his scrawny neck. "Very well then, Colonel. I daresay the Lord's work may be done in a fish-loft as well as in the meeting-house, though it seems strange at this time of night. Um! Well—" He opened the worn book and thrust it toward the lantern for better light. The ceremony was short. The bridegroom looked grim. Flora sobbed once or twice, and the preacher stopped and looked at her with kindly eyes, but she kept her gaze on her lover and the voice went booming on.

"Have you a ring?" asked Mr. Oliphant at last.

The deserter hesitated, then on an inspiration delved into his pocket and produced a small crude hoop of silver.

"An heirloom?" Sumter asked acidly.

"Hammered out of a shilling by a French prisoner at Melville Island—I did guard duty there."

"Ha! You'd no respect for the King's shilling one way or the other, it seems to me. Get on with the business, parson."

The preacher paused. "There should be witnesses."

"I'm witness enough," Sumter said.

Aquila Denby smiled faintly. "Here come witnesses a-plenty, sir."

The door flew open again, this time with a sound of several feet, and Black Philip chattering, and a rattle of trailed muskets against the door-posts. Colonel Larrabee strode to the head of the stairs, roaring down into the blackness. "Don't strike a light as ye value your life. Who's there?"

The torso of a man swam into the lantern light from the murky stair-hole, a young man of twenty or so with a grey uniform and astonished brown eyes. A dark and curly fuzz flowed down his cheeks from under a round black leather shako. He stood there blinking rapidly in the edge of the light with a pistol in each hand.

"Well!" he announced in a high voice. "So you've got the rascal, Colonel."

"I don't know what you're talking about!" Sumter snapped. "And stop this play-acting, sir—d'ye think I lent you my best pair of pistols to point at my own son-in-law?"

Lieutenant Green's mouth opened and closed several times like that of a stranded tom-cod. Then, swallowing violently, "This is a dem poor jest, Colonel. That's my man. A. Denby.

private, Royal Nova Scotia Fencibles. What's he done with his uniform?"

"Uniform! What should he wear but the clothes he's got, eh?"

"I know this," Green said stubbornly. "He was wearing boots, pantaloons, and jacket when last seen, the property of His Majesty and the Province of Nova Scotia."

"Last seen, bah! You see the man now, don't you? You see what he's wearing? Check shirt, homespun trousers, fear-naught jacket. That's the uniform of a privateersman hereabouts." Sumter turned to the bridegroom magnificently.

"Speak up, sir. You're my daughter's husband, are you not?"

"Ay, sir."

"And master's mate of the *Nymph*, privateer?"

"As you say, sir."

The lieutenant's eyes, bright with suspicion, went from face to face, lingered to inspect Flora with a certain resentful curiosity. He had nourished a conviction that all females under fifty were susceptible to a uniform, especially one with a gold swab on the shoulder and worn with a dashing air copied carefully from Prince Edward's young gentlemen at Halifax. He had lived under the same roof with this dark intense girl for a week, had flattered himself on a conquest, seeing the way she hung on his every word; his self-esteem was bruised.

"This is all dem queer. I'll swear this man's a runaway private of the Fencibles. May I call to your mind, Colonel Larrabee, a proclamation issued by the governor last summer, demanding that provincial magistrates and all other civil officers use diligence to seize and return deserters from His Majesty's forces?"

"Bah! Am I to be told my duty by a half-grown subaltern of Fencibles? You give yourself airs, sir, that'd sit badly on a major of the line."

The young officer stiffened. "You're entitled to your opinion, sir. I arrest this man in the name of the King!"

Flora threw her arms about Aquila's neck and burst into tears.

Sumter barked, "Put down my pistols, sir! The King's name indeed! If there's pistol play here we'll be blown sky-high with the King's powder, and His Majesty will be rid of a fool and a rogue, not to mention me and my daughter."

"And me," suggested Mr. Oliphant, vaguely alarmed.

Lieutenant Green looked at the stacked kegs for the first time, and stared hard at the broken paper cartridges in the open barrel, his brown eyes growing very large and round.

"You quote the governor—let me quote him, too," Sumter

went on harshly. "I've a commission from Sir John permitting me to recruit seventy-five men of the county militia for the crew of my new privateer. I count this man one."

"A demmed quibble, Colonel Larrabee—merely a protection against impressment by His Majesty's ships at sea. Your crew no more belong to the militia than Denby, there, belongs to your crew."

"Hang me, sir, d'ye dare say quibble to a document signed by Sir John Wentworth? What's good enough for a man-hunting frigate captain ought to be final to a—"

"I object to this violent language," boomed the little preacher suddenly. "Consider, if you please, the presence of this young lady and myself."

A pause. They could hear the soldiers muttering below-stairs. Lieutenant Green came to a decision.

"Very well, Colonel—here are your pistols. I shall return to Halifax and lay a full report of this extraordianry affair before my superiors. Sir John—"

"Is an old loyalist like myself," Sumter said with a thin smile.

Green clutched the rags of his dignity about him. "I must in all conscience refuse to consider myself a guest in your house the past week. That applies also to my men. You will kindly draw on the regimental paymaster for billet-money as the regulations provide. I think there is nothing more to be said. Goodnight, sir. Goodnight, madam." He ignored Denby and the parson and marched austerely toward the stairs. The dignity of his exit was marred on the dark steps by a stumble and a thundering descent into the arms of a surprised corporal below. The door closed with a hollow slam.

"Strange. All very strange," murmured Mr. Oliphant, making for the stairs himself.

Flora Denby moved with a sudden impulse toward her father but Sumpter stopped her with an imperative gesture. "I'm in no forgiving mood, Miss. You've disgraced an honest name by your own choice and now you have another by mine—and you shall wear it. But you'll return with me to Larrabee House. As for you, sir, you'll sail in the *Nymph* tomorrow, and a good riddance. We shall see if you fight as well as you talk. There'll be fighting, and there'll be yellow jack; and I for one will shed no tears if you come to a shotted hammock somewhere south of Cuba. On the other hand, if you return you shall claim your wife—and I'll not say a word. And now, Miss, I'll give you three minutes by the watch. I'll wait below."

He turned his back on them abruptly and went down the

stairs into the murk, a sombre figure of parental justice, all
the relentlessness of the Larrabees in the rigid set of his fine
shoulders, all the quixotic humour of the Sumters in the twist
of his long thin lips.

And later, at his cherry-wood escritoire in the long parlour at
Larrabee House—the same parlour in which, after one hundred
and thirty years, Miss Letty showed me the logbook of the
Nymph, the pistols Lieutenant Green borrowed, and told me
this story—Colonel Larrabee sat and completed the papers of
his privateer. It must have been very late when he took a new
quill and addressed his now famous diary, but the handwriting
is steady and the capitals lack none of his usual flourish.

> November 10, 1800—Wind North. Looks fair for Tomor-
> row, the *Nymph* being ready for Sea and a Good Tide to
> get over the Bar. I write John Robinson, my agent at Saint
> Kitts, to look out for her and keep her Account sepperate
> from the *Dolphin's and Venture's*. This evening my
> daughter Flora is married Quietly to one Denby, priva-
> teersman. I write a note to Capt. Beddoes desiring him to
> shew Denby no Favours except upon his Merrits. Seems
> to be a fellow of Spirrit and some learning and may Turn
> Out Well. The Paymaster of the N.S. Fencibles owes me
> 36 shillings Billet Money

THE tale of that winter siege of our town deserves a better pen than mine. Poe—Poe alone could have done justice to its stark and lonely horror, although Stevenson could have given it a most dreadful fascination, and Doctor Jenner, had he known, could have left the world a discerning account of the early practice of his principles in a remote colonial settlement.

But you and I, who remember the strange wedding of Flora Larrabee and Aquila Denby in the powder loft—we shall sup light of horrors, whet merely the historical appetite of the doctors, and see that siege of Oldport in the light of romance, the romance of poor Flora, secluded and lonely in Larrabee House, and her husband of half an hour, Aquila Denby, master's mate of the privateer brig *Nymph*, somewhere in West Indian waters.

Just a month after those queer nuptials in the King's Store, surrounded by the materials of war, there came to our town an enemy against whom His Majesty's powder and shot, the muskets of the militia, the three long eighteen-pounders in the town battery, all were futile. Colonel Larrabee records it in his diary, but there exists a better account in the letters Flora wrote her sister Arabella, spending the winter in Halifax.

Flora wrote a good hand, rather like her father's, with somewhat more uniform spelling perhaps but the same weakness for capital letters and flourishes. The epistles are before me now, yellow and tattered. There were no envelopes in those days. Flora folded her sheets twice, sealed the last fold with a generous splatter of red wax, and wrote the address in a bold hand upon the exposed back of the letter itself. They were carried to Halifax by coasting skippers and merchants going up to the capital on business, and the exposed parts bear thumbprints made, I like to suppose, nearly 140 years ago. They are generous thumbs, with a suggestion of tar about most of them, the tarry thumbs of Nelson's day, when Halifax was enlivened by a large garrison and the fleet and a handsome prince of the blood, when the war with France and Spain was in full swing, and Nova Scotia privateersmen went a-ferreting for prizes in the Caribbean Sea.

With his customary simplicity Sumter records the beginning of the siege thus :

> Wednesday, Dec. 10th, 1800. The Small Pox is Broke Out among us. Two black women, one the wife of Prince Davis, mulattoe, and a girl named Salomy. Also a seaman named Kellaher lately from Halifax where they have Considerable of the Disease. Our people much Alarmed. I ride with the Sheriff to inspect a small hutt upon Simon Fraser's fish-lot near the Battery & conclude to Have the Sick removed Thither.

It was a strange thing that Oldport had escaped so long. The settlements in Upper Canada had never been quite free of smallpox from the earliest times, and in Nova Scotia, especially in Halifax, there had been frequent epidemics. And for forty years our town had carried on a brisk trade with the West Indies and the Spanish Main, where all manner of ills abounded. Port regulations, when carried out at all, were sketchy to say the least. A ship suspected of infectious disease was required to anchor in the bay and segregate her sick, of course. And the sheriff or his deputy went on board to pledge the health of the crew in the captain's best brandy, and incidentally to see that a small mixture of tar and brimstone was burned in the 'tween-decks and all suspect woodwork swabbed down with vinegar and water. The good ship was then permitted to enter the river and pursue her normal business in the town.

There had been no competent doctor in Oldport since the able though drunken Furbish, late surgeon of the Loyal South Carolina Regiment and Tarleton's Legion, died in '87 in a back room of Japhet Corby's tavern "after drinking Four bottels of Madeira & a quart of Cherry Rum, a mellancolly affair & a Great Loss to the Town." For the rest, our Oldport ancestors were at the mercy of quacks who wandered up and down the coast in trading-vessels. These divided all bodily ills into three simple classes—consumption, fever, and "Inflammation of the Bowels" and dispensed nostrums of their own or other dubious manufacture.

The poorer folk—and our town was very poor in those days—put their faith in herbal remedies and queer witch-doctorish beliefs acquired partly from the Indians but chiefly from an inheritance going back to mediæval Europe. Into this welter of ignorance and superstition, in that severe winter of 1800-1801, came the smallpox and Doctor Phineas Bartelo.

Bartelo remains a mysterious figure in our history. Like so many of those itinerant medicos he came to town aboard a coaster, and after a grim winter wrestling with the smallpox he departed in the same way. One hopes he was well paid, but I suspect he left as penniless as he came. Sumter does not say.

On that December day in the year 1800 Bartelo came up the steep road to Larrabee House wearing a brown fly-coat, a pair of black broadcloth trousers—unusual in the Oldport of that day, when homespun breeches and long woollen stockings were considered the only possible winter wear for gentleman and commoner—a waistcoat whose stiff collar reached his ears, a stiffer shirt-collar that came little short of them, a huge red cravat and a tall beaver hat—the first top-hat ever seen in our town. He wore as a concession to the climate a pair of country-knit red mittens, and there was a rectangular brown leather case slung from his shoulder by a strap.

Flora saw him coming through the gateway and flew to the door, forestalling Black Philip the manservant. She was still in disgrace, forbidden to leave the house except in the company of her sisters, but daily hoping for a word from her husband by some north-bound vessel. The appearance of this remarkable stranger filled her with wild hopes. She let him give a polite summons on the great brass knocker and flung open the door, smiling eagerly.

"Colonel Larrabee—is he in?" asked the stranger. He was a dark man with a sallow clean-shaven face and shrewd grey eyes, a lock of black hair drooping.

"Come in, please," murmured Flora in a small choked voice. She walked before him along the hall with that straight-backed carriage of the Larrabee women and ushered him into the presence.

Sumter was in the long parlour writing at his rosewood escritoire. Bartelo, hat in hand, regarded a tall man in black small-clothes and stockings and silver-buckled shoes, with a waistcoat of some light-coloured mixture, a black stock, and a blue coat with brass buttons and long tails that drooped over the chair to the floor. There were a few threads of silver in Sumter's thick black hair, and a pair of spectacles sat mildly on his raptorial nose.

For a moment he sat absorbed in contemplation of his quill; then deliberately he dipped it in the silver inkpot, flourished a bit, scratched for a few seconds with flowing gestures over the paper, laid the quill aside, inspected his penmanship, dusted it from the sandbox, and looked up. Seeing a visitor, and a man at that, he rose swiftly, tearing off the spectacles, which he hated and considered womanish and wore only in the solitude of the parlour or the privacy of his counting-house.

"Colonel Larrabee, I believe," Bartelo said.

"Late," Sumter declared from his full height, "of the British Legion, sometimes known as Tarleton's Legion." When strangers addressed him by his old rank he said this always; first, because they might be Yankees, and he felt they should know who he was and what he represented; and second, because the provincial militia nowadays contained an astonishing number of colonels, most of whom had never smelt powder in action.

"A very fine corps, I have no doubt," said Bartelo politely. "My name's Bartelo, sir, Phineas Bartelo. A physician and surgeon, and seeking a place for the practice of my profession. At the wharf they told me to see you."

"Um!" grunted Sumter, distrusting all coasting doctors. Then, remembering the scarce-dry entry in his diary, he said with a sardonic smile, "As it happens, sir, you've come at a good time."

"Aha!"

"We've an outbreak of the smallpock."

"Oho!"

"Three sick with it. Had 'em removed to a hut east of the town, and engaged a black man that's had the disease to look after 'em."

"Your promptness is most commendable, sir."

"As an old soldier—be seated, man, be seated—I believe in prompt measures when danger's abroad."

"Have you—ah—taken any other measures, Colonel?"

"What others might we take, eh?"

"There's inoculation."

"Eh? What's that?"

"They're inoculating everyone in Halifax, where there's now a serious outbreak."

Sumter regarded the doctor with a beady black eye. A quacksalver, begad! Hoping to drum up business in a country town with this high-sounding word! Damn the fellow's impudence!

"What is it—this thing—whatever you call it?"

"Nothing very new," Bartelo said. "Known for a century, I s'pose. Two or three years ago one Jenner published some remarkable discoveries about it. That's what I have in mind, chiefly." He leaned forward earnestly. "You infect a well person with virus from a sick one—"

"In God's name, what for?"

"—Or with the kine-pox if you can get the stuff."

"Damme! From a sick cow?"

"The person so treated suffers the disease in a milder form and is thereafter immune; or if he should contract the disease later it'll run a light course in him."

"I never heard anything so filthy in my life!"

Bartelo could not help smiling, and Sumter was enraged.

"I assure you, sir, our people will submit to no such dangerous nonsense, and a very good day to you!"

Doctor Bartelo picked up his beaver hat. "When the contagion's spread a bit—as it will, Colonel Larrabee, as it will—they'll submit readily enough. In the meantime—I understand you're the chief magistrate—have I your permission to engage in the—ah—ordinary practice of my profession in Oldport?"

"You have, sir," Sumter granted curtly. "But no humbug, you understand? I'll have no humbug, sir, in this matter of smallpock. Sell your pills and powders as ye like but, damme, no humbug!"

He regarded the departing form of Bartelo with extreme distaste.

On Christmas morning Sumter rode down to the fish-lots and sat in the saddle hailing a lonely hut beside the water. Black Boston came to the door, his dark face pitted from an old acquaintance with the "smallpock."

"How're your people, Boston?"

The negro closed the door behind him and stood on the rotten step rolling his eyes.

"Dem nigger womens ain' so bad, Cunnel. But Mistah Kellaher, he all choked up an' got a belly pain an' he's face all swole up purple, sah. Doctah say he gwine die."

"Um. Anything you want?"

"No, sah, Cunnel. Doctah, he lef' some stuff."

Sumter rode back thoughtfully. Mahon, the sheriff, was waiting for him at the town pump, where the road turned off toward Larrabee House.

"There's four more got the pock," Mahon said grimly. He named them, one in each quarter of the town, as if Death had made a careful sowing for the harvest.

"There's a lot o' talk amongst the people, sir. The new doctor says there's a thing called—"

"Bah!" shouted Colonel Larrabee.

"I was thinkin'—"

"Keep your thoughts to yourself, Mahon, and let's have no more of this nonsense. The disease'll spread fast enough without spreading it ourselves."

"Very good, sir."

Next day the sailor Kellaher died, and the black girl Salome was very low. And six new cases were reported. The hut in the fish-lots was too small for this increase. Sumter despatched a message to the magistrates and principal merchants, and they came to Larrabee House for a conference, with the new word on all their lips. But the Colonel resisted firmly, and finally they agreed to erect a new pest-house, a long single-storey building of logs, on the river bank half a mile above the town—"to be in the care of the Overseers of the Poor."

While it was a-building, Sumter's old comrade-in-arms Major Blount rode down from his home at The Falls, two miles above the town. He was a thickset man with serious blue eyes.

"Sumter," he announced abruptly, "I want inoculation for me and my family."

"Not you, Blount! You? Nunno! You've too much good sense for that. Besides, your neighbours at The Falls have sent a petition to the magistrates praying them to forbid anyone bringing the pox into their midst by inoculation."

"Petition or no, sir, I'm determined on it."

"And if the magistrates forbid?"

"They can forbid and be damned. Call it mutiny if ye like."

"Begad, I'll order this man Bartelo out of town!"

"The only doctor we have?"

Sumter considered a minute. "Blount, old friend, if you persist in this folly—very well. But you must remove your family from the settlement—to the pest-house if you like, or you may build one for yourself."

Blount rode off, a sturdy determined figure, and built a log hut on the river bank opposite Birch Point, where the doctor could cross on the ice.

The town pest-house was completed in mid-January, 1801. By that time there were nearly fifty cases and the place was at once a crowded horror. The weather was bitter. The river was frozen right down to Colonel Larrabee's wharf. There was a scarcity of firewood, for most of the men were away in the privateers, and sickness lay heavy on the rest. Each afternoon small parties of women and boys trudged off to the forest with axe and hand-sled for the next day's wood.

Through all these trying days Sumter planned and laboured like ten men, seeing that his own and other available horses and oxen hauled wood to the neediest families, making a daily round of the town on horseback, dealing faithfully (though not always patiently) with people who flocked to his door to heap their troubles on his erect shoulders. He spent hours at his quill, for there was a tremendous amount of correspondence regarding such matters as the militia in this busy time of war, and the various business of the town, not to mention his three privateers abroad and the trading-vessels that, pox or no pox, flitted in and out of the harbour. As notary he went on preparing deeds and contracts, and never hesitated to visit and write a will for someone dying of the disease.

The parson of the established church had gone away for the winter, and so Sumter attended the Methodist meeting-house, for he firmly believed in a just balance between God and Caesar. The meeting-house was a bleak place without a stove, where the preacher often wore mittens in the pulpit and the spartan congregation sat rigid in coats and shawls through long austere sermons, and at evening service the very candles made winding-sheets for themselves and required constant attention. Yet the people flocked there, confident in the immunity of godliness.

Sumter attended the funeral of a child dead of the contagion —"carried to the Grave by six Young Girls in White, a very Pathettick Scene." His own daughter, Flora, eager to break the bonds of her imprisonment, begged his permission to serve as a nurse at the pest-house. He refused, but in the town where his word had been law for so long something strange was happening—the people were clamouring for inoculation so loudly that defiant Doctor Bartelo began to administer it, using "kine-pox matter" obtained from somewhere to the westward—probably Boston. Sumter and his magistrates were obliged to recognize the fact by naming certain private homes as additional pest-houses "where Inocculated People might Stay and have their Illness." The town pest-house was full.

On the 25th of January Catherine, youngest of the Larabee daughters, complained of headache and pains in her back, and "fitts of Feaver with shivering Spells & a Sinking Sensation of the Stommach." Three days later the ominous spots appeared, and Sumter despatched Black Philip for Phineas Bartelo. That sardonic man confirmed Sumter's worst fear.

"And shall I remove her to the pest-house proper, sir? A fine place, that. A jolly company, and the wind whistling *Down Among The Dead Men* through the logs—ventilation, sir, and—"

"Enough!" said Sumter grimly. "I'll declare this house a pest-house. We're alone here in the edge of the woods above the town."

"And your family?"

Sumter swallowed his pride with an audible gulp. "We'll have the inoculation, sir."

"Then why can't other townsmen be inoculated in their homes?"

"They shall. I've talked with the other magistrates and they agree on it. There's one regulation. Every house infected, whether by the natural disease or by inoculation, must hang out a white flag of some kind. Those who wish to enter an infected house may do so at their own risk—I see no way we can stop 'em now—but those who wish to avoid the disease must have some way of knowing the—um—sheep from the goats."

"I'll instruct my sick," replied Bartelo gravely. He had gained his point but there was no triumph in his sallow face. He pointed a finger at the flagstaff before Larrabee House.

"You can make a beginning there, sir!"

Five minutes later a tablecloth fluttered from the staff where Sumter had hoisted daily for sixteen years the flag for which he had suffered so much. He looked at this white thing dourly. It reminded him of Yorktown.

Medical enlightenment made progress now. Within two days (but not without argument) a general meeting of magistrates and townsmen in the courthouse decided to make inoculation compulsory. The indefatigable Bartelo took into his service Mr. Montgomery, the schoolmaster, and the New Light preacher, and showed them the mysteries of the rite. On January 30th, 1801, Sumter wrote in his diary (as always on this date), "Anniversary of King Charles his Martyrdom," and added, "The schooner *Three Brothers*, Jewers master, arrived with kine-pock matter for the Innoculation. My Family begin the Course of Physic in preparation. Tincture of Rhubarb & Calomel."

After two days they took rhubarb and calomel again, and salts on the following morning. Bartelo was a little doubtful about the black woman Hagar, who had "a touch of the Saint Anthony's Fire," but decided to go on with it. The next day was set for the inoculation of the household; but a blizzard swept in from the sea, blocking the streets with drifts, and Doctor Bartelo did not come. He had gone on snowshoes to the town pest-house at Oak Point, where the worst cases lay.

It was on the third day of February that the whole family assembled finally in the long parlour; Sumter himself, nineteen-year-old Allan, the daughters Priscilla and Flora, and three negro servants—Hagar, Black Philip, and the house-boy Juba. They were all very tense, and the blacks awed and afraid, as Doctor

Bartelo laid his apparatus upon a small maplewood table: a sharp and gleaming stiletto, a bowl of water, a small pile of clean rags and—the object of all eyes—a handkerchief in which the mysterious "kine-pock matter" was wrapped.

As became the head of the house, Colonel Larrabee stepped up first. He records the affair tersely in his diary:

> He made a Slitt in my left hand between the Fore Finger & Thum, not in the loose Skin there but in the Hand, & then laid a small Infected Thread about three eighths of an Inch in Length into the Slitt. This he covered with a square of Ragg doubled & then a bandage to Keep it in Place. He then Dipt the knife in Water & proceeded to my son Allan, & etc. All stood the Opperation Very Well, tho Priscilla was Rather Faint & asked Bartelo several times if the Disseease taken in this Way might leave Pocks upon her Face. Black Hagar & the boy Juba wept but Philip was very Good. Towards the end my friend Thomas Handiside & Wife & Daughter came in asking if they might have the Innocculation with us, which Bartelo did. They will stay with us till All is Over."

As he prepared to leave Bartelo said, "You must air yourselves—move about out-o'-doors as much as you can. Wrap well, mind. And drink plenty of water mixed with cream-o'-tartar—a spoonful to the quart." On the portico he paused. The town lay very quiet in the frosty air. Viewed in this way from Larrabee House the straggling main street and its alleys and lanes toward the water all seemed half-buried in snow. Above the Larrabee wharf the river itself was frozen and snow-muffled as far as the eye could reach. And as if all this whiteness were not enough, the townsfolk were busy hanging out their white infection-flags. Bartelo waved a mittened hand. "It's blooming like a field of daisies," he said.

And now the Larrabee household awaited the oncoming of the kine-pox. Faithful to Bartelo's instructions, Sumter, Allan, and Black Philip shovelled paths from the rear of the house, across the garden and into the woods for some distance; and there the women, muffled in furs and shawls, tramped patiently up and down for an hour or two each day. Once or twice the girls drove in the sleigh along the lonely west road toward Topsail Point. At the end of a week all noticed pains in arm and stomach, and the women complained of nausea. In another day they were feverish, and Black Hagar rather ill. And fever brought thirst. It was no longer an effort to drink Bartelo's cream-of-tartar and water.

In the following week Sheriff Mahon appeared at the gate, shouting up at the house. Sumter walked down the snow-path with his old cavalry cloak about his shoulders and a 'coon-skin cap on his head.

"How's it goin'?" Mahon said. It was a sunny February day, very cold and still, and the barking of dogs came up to them very clearly from the town. Sumter halted twenty feet from the gate. "Very well, Mahon, except my daughter Kate. She seems to have taken the smallpock itself, and Bartelo's afraid it's the confluent kind. What's in your mind?"

"It's the inoculations, sir. A good many o' the inoculated people's breakin' out in boils and ulcers, and some gone into a decline. Doctor Bartelo thinks 'twas something in the kine-pock matter that he got, but he's determined to keep on with it. A stubborn man that, sir. Some o' the people's murmuring."

"Um! Well, I see nothing now but to keep on with it, Mahon. How many are dead?"

"Only fourteen that I know, sir. But some's been buried in the woods, and there's graves dug at night in the buryin'-ground that nobody seems to know about. Some o' the poor people, sir, have a great fear o' bein' shut up, so they say nothin' o' their sick, and bury the dead ones secret-like."

At the end of the second week the whole Larrabee household had "Come out in the Pusteels, Verry Satisfactory to Doctor Bartelo"; but Catherine, Sumter's beloved Kate, sank into a violent secondary fever, "her dear Face much Swolen, red & purple Horible to See." On the 19th of February she died, and Allan and Black Philip hammered together a coffin of pine boards in the big echoing barn. The following afternoon, with the coffin resting on boards laid across the seats of the sleigh, they started for the burying-ground.

Black Philip drove slowly, the family walking in the snow behind, Sumter tall and stern in his old thrice-cocked hat and blue cloak, then Allan with Flora on his arm, and Mr. Handiside with Priscilla. Mrs. Handiside stayed behind to attend Black Hagar, and Sally Handiside was too overcome to go. As they descended into the town, faces diseased or faces merely pale and fearful stared at them through bull's-eyes rubbed in the frost of the windows. A few friends came out and joined the little procession, though Sumter tried to wave them off.

The service in the meeting-house was very brief. Nobody thought to toll the bell—the fine bronze bell taken out of a

Spanish brig off Caracas by an Oldport privateer in '98, and which looked so strange in that humble little heretic chapel. The preacher took his text from Job xxxiii; *His flesh shall be fresher than a child's*—and in the frosty air of that barren place the weeping of the women sounded very loud. Sumter would not mop his eyes as they did, and sat silent and motionless, with his cheeks wet.

When the cortège reached what was then known simply as The Burying Hill, a rough knoll still partly wooded, almost in the heart of the town, they found a narrow pit gaping in yellow earth at the bottom of a crater of trampled and blackened snow. The gravediggers had built a great fire of brushwood to thaw the ground. All about were fresh mounds, some under snow, some still showing heaped earth in the queer sooty snow-craters; and beyond they could see fresh stumps and littered twigs where Mahon's men had been clearing new ground. There was something very dreadful about that.

The decent dignity of the affair was marred by a curious incident as the mourners turned from the grave at last and walked two-and-two down the shovelled path to the town street. Old Deborah Tupps stood there in her soiled black skirts and cast-off army coat, the scarlet of which was dingy and threadbare, and a shawl about her head. For a reason nobody knew she hated all the loyalists. Some said she was a witch. In any case she was an outlandish character, even in the Oldport of that day, so full of odd humanity. She belonged a little farther back in history, and across the sea, hooting tumbrils and knitting beside a guillotine.

"Ha!" cried Deborah. "So the high and mighty Larrabees die just like the common folks!"

Sumter and Allan ignored her and passed on. Priscilla drew her skirts aside, and eloquent gesture, but Flora spoke.

"As even you must, some day, Debby; and a good riddance."

Sumter half turned, raising his eyebrows at that, but he recognized the Larrabee spirit and tongue in it and was silent. They moved on.

"There," Deborah Tupps cried, "goes Flora Larrabee, proud Flora, wedded but not bedded. Tell us! Tell us all, Flora Larrabee —be you maid, wife or widow?" The cackle of her laughter rang in the silent street.

Colonel Larrabee dropped back and took Flora's arm, and thus they walked through the peering town and up the west road to Larrabee House. In the long parlour, still in his old army cloak, Sumter faced the black ewe of his family and put his long hands gently on her shoulders. A fire of dry beech logs burned with a clear flame in the great hearth, and its crackle marked the great hush all through the big wooden house.

"God forbid," Sumter said, "that there be any more bitterness between you and me, my dear."

Twenty minutes later Priscilla, soft-footed in her caribou house-moccasins, found them thus, Flora close against her father's tall figure with her dark head on his breast, and Sumter staring up at the portrait of pretty Kitty Nesbit, painted in Carolina long, long ago, as if to ask his dead wife's guidance in the sorrows come upon her children.

Early in March Sheriff Mahon and Justice Bunt came to the gate of Larrabee House, and again Sumter talked from the path in the snow. The pocks on his face had filled, but were still visible, and his skin was yellow and lined. It occurred to Mahon with some astonishment that Colonel Larrabee, that imperishable man, was looking his age at last. The day was cold, with a low canopy of grey cloud puckered like a frozen sea, and a keen wind down the river moaning in the chimneys of the great house and rustling and tumbling the dull green mass of the pine woods beyond.

Justice Bunt was muffled in two fly-coats and a cape, with a red wool comforter tied over his blue tricorne hat and under his plump chin.

"Colonel Larrabee," he bawled pompously from the road, "it's the considered opinion of the magistrates an' gen'lemen that this inoccerlation had better stop. People's all broke out in sores, as if the pox ain't bad enough. Missus Tobias Jameson had a swellin' in her thigh that bust an' bled three pints o' noxious matter. Morgan's boy died this mornin', makin' fifteen that was inoccerlated." Sumter was watching the form of Doctor Phineas Bartelo come up the hill on a horse of Major Blount's. He was wearing the tall beaver hat—he had worn it throughout the siege, like a battle standard.

"That your opinion, too, Mahon?" Sumter said.

"Yes, sir, 'tis so."

They turned at Bartelo's approach and regarded him glumly. Black Philip came running to lead the horse off to the stables. The doctor looked at Mahon and Bunt—and read their errand in their faces.

"A very good day to you, gentlemen."

Sumter announced bluntly, "The people say you must give over the inoculations, Doctor Bartelo." Bartelo swept them with his cool grey eyes. He surprised them by offering no objections. He looked very tired.

"The voice of the people is the voice of God. Besides, if they've lost faith in inoculation it may do little for 'em after all. A great pity, gentlemen. Suppose there *are* fifteen dead that were inoculated. Out of seven hundred! Isn't that proof of its virtue? How many are dead that took it in the natural way?"

"Kelston's boy," said Justice Bunt heavily, "has got a sore from the inoccerlation that's et to the bone. See his collar-bone, ye can. That's a fact."

"Better sore than dead," Bartelo said, and strode past them into the house. After inspecting the household he told Sumter, "I think maybe we've seen the worst in Oldport, Colonel. But it's not done yet, by a long shot." He added, musing, as if Sumter were not there, "I'd like to meet that man Jenner, compare notes with him—these secondary inflammations, for instance. Something wrong there. Something to be corrected. mind—I still maintain the thing is right in principle. Some day the world will know."

"Some day," Colonel Larrabee declared unexpectedly, "our people will know your own true worth, sir, at the least. I don't know what to make of your inoculations, but notions aside you've been a godsend, and there's my hand on it."

Perhaps the town truly had seen the worst then, but as Bartelo foresaw, many were to sicken and some to die before spring. As late as mid-April we find Sumter complaining in his diary that "the General Sessions & Inferior Court of Common Pleas opened this day, but Grand & Petit Jurors are deficient on Account of the Small Pock & those who have not Had the Dissease are Afraid to Come for Fear of Geting It. The Courts are Adjourned to the first Tuesday In May, hoping by that Time the Place may be Clear of It."

But we are not concerned with the rest of that siege, the marks of which a whole Oldport generation carried to their graves. Something shattered its cold and grim monotony on March 7th, 1801, when the snow still lay deep, although the sun now was warm in the clear noons, and the icicles on south-facing eaves and windows grew long and thick as old men's beards with the alternate freeze-and-thaw of night and day, and the ice on the river turned dark and rotten so that people could cross on foot no more.

On that March day, in the warm afternoon, one Joel Parks came stumbling up the hill to Larrabee House, splattering the slush in the sled tracks. His old eyes were popping. He burst in upon Sumter gasping, "A furrin ship, sir, off the battery! They fired a gun an' put off a boat toward Tops'l Point."

Sumter sprang up at once, shouting for Allan and buckling on his old cavalry belt and the heavy sabre he had swung so heartily for his King in Carolina long ago. Allan took a musket from the moose horns over the chimneypiece in the small south parlour, the gunroom of the house.

"French!" Sumter snapped as they ran for the horses. "Bony's up to something, depend on it!" Since Napoleon acquired Louisiana the previous year Sumter had envisioned all sorts of dark French schemes for the recovery of the West Indies and Canada.

"Might be no more than a raiding privateer," argued Allan.

"No more! Ha! No more than a pair o' Yankee privateers captured the battery here in the old war—before my time in Oldport. Caught 'em all asleep. The town had to buy 'em off, a damned disgraceful affair. All the militia arms were in the blockhouse at the battery. Begad, I've kept 'em stored in the town itself since I took command.

They found a knot of men and boys gathered in the lane beside the King's Store—that very store where Parson Oliphant had married Flora Larrabee to Aquila Denby four months before. The meeting-house bell was ringing the alarm and someone had gone a-horseback to warn the people at The Falls

Sumter unlocked the door in a great hurry, and he and Allan and Mahon passed out the militia equipment—muskets, bayonets, cartridge pouches, cross-belts—to a growing company in the lane. Major Blount came dashing up in his sleigh from The Falls. All told it was a sorry muster, thirty boys and old men, some in sea-boots, some in shoes, some in moccasins; and there were homespun jackets and breeches, and hats cocked and uncocked, and fur caps, and the red flannel nightcaps of the fishermen.

"Begad," muttered Blount, lest the men hear, "they've caught us nicely, Colonel—most of the militiamen abroad in the privateers or home sick o' the pox."

"We'll give 'em a fight for it, none the less," Sumter said fiercely, running an eye over the faces, young and old. The healed or healing scabs gave them a look of ferocity that pleased him. He tramped at their head along the road to the battery, hearing their straggle and shuffle in the snow behind, and smiling grimly. They couldn't march in step but egad they could shoot better than regulars, and they'd fight like wildcats for their town!

The battery was a crude affair on the point commanding the harbour bar; a low rampart of logs and earth, with embrasures for the three eighteen-pounders which now stood naked and forlorn in the snow; and the blockhouse, a small two-storey structure of squared hardwood logs, the upper storey projecting six feet beyond the lower on all sides and giving the whole a top-heavy look. The white infection flag was flying over it but Sumter went in at once.

The place was kept by an old loyalist soldier and his wife. The townsfolk called him Mad Ben, for he had received a ball in the head at Catawba Ford, and when in drink paraded the street shouting and singing the marching songs of Tarleton's Legion, and daring hosts of imaginary rebels to come and fight. He was now very ill of the smallpox, and his wife met Sumter at the door, a gaunt sour woman who had never ceased pining for the warmth and ease of Carolina. The sick man lay delirious upon a cot. Sumter went over and spoke to him, and Ben muttered something unintelligible. He was far gone.

The Colonel and Blount climbed through the trap-door into the upper storey, a bleak place with the northwest wind thrusting in the loopholes. From one of these they surveyed the mysterious invader lying at anchor off the point.

"Ice along her larboard side," Sumter muttered, "and an off-shore wind. She's come from the west'ard, then. Lateen rig—looks Spanish. Are we at war with Spain?"

"She's pierced for guns," Blount observed, "and I can see the sun on cannon as she rolls; but I see no men."

"Um. She's riding to her bowers—and we're to windward. They'll have to get springs on their cables if they want to bombard us properly."

They tramped out to examine the guns in the drifted snow.

"Damme!" cried Sumter, dismayed. "Some rascals of boys have been playing here. See, the tampions are out!"

Out they were, and a trickle of snow and ice lay in each barrel. Barnabas Tolley, the old privateer gunner, took a sponge rod and thrust it in and out again. The snow came with it but the ice clung to the frosty metal.

"As good as spiked, Colonel, sir. Daresn't fire 'em wi' that ice inside. Bust, they would. Got to thaw 'em out wi' a hot sponge fust."

"Then," roared Sumter, "heat your sponges at the woman's

fire in the blockhouse, and quick about it! Where's Joel? You, boy, there!—did you see 'em put off a boat?"

"Ay, sir, they manned a boat," declared the boy, sixteen and full of importance. The militia musket stood as high as his head. "Half a dozen of 'em, and armed they were. 'Peared to me like they was goin' fer to land right yonder"—he pointed to the southeast, where the pine woods came down to the shore.

"Ha! That means they intend to reconnoitre the town before they tackle the battery, Blount!"

"And that," said Allan Larrabee quickly, "means they'll strike in by the west road—it comes close to the shore there."

The men looked at Sumter then, in a profound silence, all thinking how Larrabee House stood lonely on the hill where the west road entered the woods.

"May be a trick," Sumter muttered. Duty urged him to hold his garrison together in the battery, where they could command the river entrance. But his bold military instinct, leaping in him like a flame as if the Southern campaign had been yesterday, told him to take a few marksmen and ambush these prowling foreigners somewhere in the woods beyond Larrabee House.

Blount's mind ran along the same line. "You take a party, Colonel. I'll hold the battery. We've time to thaw the guns— yon fellow seems in no hurry to attack."

Sumter set off at once with Allan and half a dozen men of his choice, trotting back along the way they had come. The alarm bell was ringing still but the town looked peaceful in the cold sunshine, the white flags snapping on sticks and staffs, the chimney-smokes whirling away to nothingness on the wind. At the town pump they met a quaint reinforcement—Major Blount's wife, her wide skirts dabbling in the snow, a man's hat on her head, marching toward the battery at the head of twenty Indians from The Falls. They came up and halted, the Indians grouping themselves about her, their black eyes glittering.

"James told me to rouse out the Indians," she said calmly. "These are all I could find. The rest are off hunting. I sent a squaw after 'em."

"Good!" exclaimed Sumter warmly. "Are they ready to fight?"

"They want powder, that's all."

"Um! They always do! Well, we'll get some at my house. Forward!"

The motley troop halted in the snow before Larrabee House while Flora and Priscilla filled the Indian's powder-horns from the keg in the gunroom cupboard. And at this moment appeared the omnipresent Bartelo, with his beaver hat, his leather case and his cynical eyes.

"Well met!" cried Sumter, eyes alight. He had doffed twenty years like an old hat. "There'll be some patching to do here, Bartelo, before this day's work is done!"

"There'll be some inoculating, too," Bartelo said coolly, "if these poor savages aren't to die like flies. D'ye realize the town's one mass of infection?"

"A matter of necessity," Sumter barked. "The defence of the town, sir!"

"Bah! That's the worst of a military mind! All ye think about is powder and shot. Look!"—he stabbed a finger at the white flags fluttering on the houses below. "There's your best defence, Colonel, and no blood spilled. Cry 'Smallpox!' and ye'd frighten Bonaparte himself. Begad, sir, I'll do it myself. Let me go up the road!"

Sumter checked a sulphurous retort. There was something in this pill-grinder's notion. Smallpox! Why not? He had seen men—a whole regiment of men—run at a cry, at a single white-faced man with a finger pointed to the rear, all stricken to sheep in a moment by the voice of fear.

But now they heard a challenge and a shot from the pine-woods up the road, and one of the Indians came trotting into sight. He pointed.

"*Ag-la-se-a-oo!*"

"English?" Mrs. Blount cried. "*Kul-oos-koo-ok-un!*" ("What nonsense!")

"*Ag-la-se-a-oo!*" the Indian repeated.

Now they heard voices just around the bend of the road.

"Into the bushes, lads!" rapped Sumter. "Don't fire, mind, till I give the word, or all's spoiled. I'll flog the man that disobeys."

Allan Larrabee appeared, walking easily, musket trailed, with half a dozen men clad in check shirts and duck trousers and a variety of jackets and headgear. Cutlasses dangled at their belts and they carried muskets and pistols in hands curiously covered against the cold—a pair of socks pulled on for want of mittens. Sumter walked up the road toward them and his little force emerged from hiding. The two groups halted and surveyed each other in mutual astonishment From the group of seamen stepped a tall man with a strong nose and a pair of keen blue eyes in a sunburned face.

"The bad penny," Aquila Denby said.

"What's the meaning of this?" snapped Sumter Larrabee.

"Well, sir, to begin with it means I'm prize-master of the *San Cristo del Graz*, a Spanish merchantman taken by your privateer *Nymph* in the Mona Passage two weeks back. I've anchored her in the bay."

"So we've seen, and a devilish scare she's given the town! What's all this damned foolishness about? Why didn't you signal? What are ye doing here, all armed like this, eh? Come sir, let's have it."

Aquila Denby gave him a gaunt brown grin. "Faith, sir, we fired a gun and got no answer from the battery. We had to wait the tide to get over the bar. Then we noticed a white flag on the blockhouse. More than that, from the masthead we could see white flags flying all over the town. That took us aback, I tell you, for we'd spoken a Yankee schooner off the Virginia capes and heard that Bony's fleet had crossed the sea. So—well—we reckoned the town was taken."

"And so," Colonel Larrabee snorted, "ye landed your paltry half-dozen to take it back. Denby, you're a fool."

"No more than you, sir, if ye thought *I* was Napoleon and *that's* your garrison. What's happened to their faces? They look like the beggars of Havana."

"We've had a siege," Doctor Bartelo said. "A seige of smallpox. Each of those white flags means a house infected. You'd best go back to your ship and stay there."

"Not till I've seen my wife," Aquila said stubbornly. "Besides, I've had the smallpox."

Flora appeared, running down the snow-path from the house, head bare, skirts flying, and crying as she came, "Aquila! Darling, darling Aquila! Oh, Aquila, I thought you'd never come." She checked herself just short of him, and her eyes went wide and frightened. "The smallpox! Aquila! We've all had something from a sick cow—and—and Cathy's dead—oh, Aquila!"

She burst into tears. Aquila Denby dropped his musket in the snow and threw his arms about her fiercely. Sumter's army and the seamen from the Spanish prize stood all about them, embarrassed and wondering. Mrs. Blount had tears in her eyes, knowing the tale of that romantic marriage and separation, and looking at Sumter's stern face. But there was a softness in Colonel Larrabee's black eyes. The winter's events had taken something out of him.

"Humph!" he said at last. "You'd best be getting your prize over the bar, Denby. The tide must be making now. She's a queer-looking thing."

"Ay, sir, and as queer as she looks. A xebec or polacca, I

don't know which to call her. Lateen rigged on the fore and mizzen and square-rigged on the main—a deuced unhandy rig, if you ask me. Missed stays twice tacking up the bay and pretty nigh put us ashore. But she's built o' some sort o' light hardwood from the Spanish Main, hard as iron and slick in the water—sails like a witch. Give her some decent rigging and she'd make a fine privateer for you, sir. And if ye want a captain—"

"Um. What's she got?"

"Cocoa, mostly. You'll have to take it out pretty smart or it'll spoil—got hot, somehow, on the way north. I went to have a look at it this morning, and the fore scuttle smoked like a chimney."

"Anything else?"

"Some dyewood—not much—and twenty seroons of indigo—and about a thousand dollars Spanish silver. She's fair prize, I guess. The master claimed she was Spanish and neutral, and in these times you never know whether you're fighting the Spanish or not; but she was bound for Martinico, which is French enough—and makes her contraband."

"Ah! But have ye got a davy-man? The Vice-Admiralty Courts are deuced strict, Denby. We must have a prisoner to go davy she was bound for Martinico."

Aquila Denby stroked his wife's hair. "I thought of all that. I've got a Spaniard for davy-man—speaks a little English and will serve the turn. I put the rest ashore on the coast of Hispaniola." He jerked his thumb at a small dark man amongst his seamen, shivering in the unaccustomed cold.

"That's him."

"With a musket?" Sumter roared.

"To be sure! I told him he'd got to fight for us like seven devils if he wanted see La Guayra again. I'd only five of a crew, sir. Had a brush with a French privateer off Cabo Engano on the way home, and lost a man—young Medad Burney from The Falls, a good lad."

"You're thin," Flora said, her voice muffled against his shoulder.

"Faith, we've had nothing to eat but tortillas and ship-beef all the way north, my dear."

"And you've worked, I venture," uttered Sumter grimly.

"Ay, sir. Two thousand miles in a thing that luffed like a cheese-box, in the winter season, and six of a crew. I hauled wi' the rest, and stood my turn at the tiller, good weather and bad—mostly bad—and did all the navigatin' besides. I've earned the command of her now that she's yours, if I may speak so bold."

"You're bold enough," Sumter said a little wryly. But he liked his son-in-law's truculent self-respect—had always liked that about him. "I promise nothing, Denby," he added. "There are the other shareholders to consult. We shall see. In the meantime, Flora my dear, get indoors out o' the cold—*and take your husband with you and look after him.*"

And then, as if in indignation at this whole affair, Colonel Larrabee strode fiercely to the flagstaff, threw the halliards off the cleat, hauled down the tattered tablecloth and cast it on the snow.

"Allan," he roared, "fetch you the flag of our country. I'll have no more of this white rag over my house!"

NOVA SCOTIA, in 1794. Winter. Snow on the ground. Two feet of it in the woods, less by the shore, except in drifts against Port Marriott's barns and fences; but enough to set sleigh bells ringing through the town, enough to require a multitude of paths and burrows from doors to streets, to carpet the wharves and the decks of the shipping, and to trim the ships' yards with tippets of ermine. Enough to require fires roaring in the town's chimneys, and blue wood smoke hanging low over the roof tops in the still December air. Enough to squeal under foot in the trodden places and to muffle the step everywhere else. Enough for the hunters, whose snowshoes now could overtake the floundering moose and caribou. Even enough for the always-complaining loggers, whose ox sleds now could haul their cut from every part of the woods. But not enough, not nearly enough snow for Miss Kezia Barnes, who was going to Bristol Creek to marry Mr. Hathaway.

Kezia did not want to marry Mr. Hathaway. Indeed she had told Mr. and Mrs. Barclay in a tearful voice that she didn't want to marry anybody. But Mr. Barclay had taken snuff and said "Ha! Humph!" in the severe tone he used when he was displeased; and Mrs. Barclay had sniffed and said it was a very good match for her, and revolved the cold bue eyes in her fat moon face, and said Kezia must not be a little fool.

There were two ways of going to Bristol Creek. One was by sea, in one of the fishing-sloops. But the preacher objected to that. He was a pallid young man lately sent out from England by Lady Huntingdon's Connexion, and seasick five weeks on the way. He held Mr. Barclay in some awe, for Mr. Barclay had the best pew in the meeting-house and was the chief pillar of godliness in Port Marriott. But young Mr. Mears was firm on this point. He would go by road, he said, or not at all. Mr. Barclay had retorted "Ha! Humph!" The road was twenty miles of horse path through the woods, now deep in snow. Also the path began at Harper's Farm on the far side of the harbour, and Harper had but one horse.

"I shall walk," declared the preacher calmly, "and the young woman can ride."

Kezia had prayed for snow, storms of snow, to bury the trail and keep anyone from crossing the cape to Bristol Creek. But now they were setting out from Harper's Farm, with Harper's big brown horse, and all Kezia's prayers had gone for naught. Like any anxious lover, busy Mr. Hathaway had sent Black Sam overland on foot to find out what delayed his wedding, and now Sam's day-old tracks marked for Kezia the road to marriage.

She was a meek little thing, as became an orphan brought up as house-help in the Barclay home; but now she looked at the preacher and saw how young and helpless he looked so far from his native Yorkshire, and how ill-clad for this bitter trans-Atlantic weather, and she spoke up.

"You'd better take my shawl, sir. I don't need it. I've got Miss Julia's old riding-cloak. And we'll go ride-and-tie."

"Ride and what?" murmured Mr. Mears.

"I'll ride a mile or so, then I'll get down and tie the horse to a tree and walk on. When you come up to the horse, you mount and ride a mile or so, passing me on the way, and you tie him and walk on. Like that. Ride-and-tie, ride-and-tie. The horse gets a rest between."

Young Mr. Mears nodded and took the proffered shawl absently. It was a black thing that matched his sober broadcloth coat and small-clothes, his black woollen stockings and his round black hat. At Mr. Barclay's suggestion he had borrowed a pair of moose-hide moccasins for the journey. As he walked a prayer-book in his coat-skirts bumped the back of his legs.

At the top of the ridge above Harper's pasture, where the narrow path led off through gloomy hemlock woods, Kezia paused for a last look back across the harbour. In the morning sunlight the white roofs of the little lonely town resembled a tidal wave flung up by the sea and frozen as it broke against the dark pine forest to the west. Kezia sighed, and young Mr. Mears was surprised to see tears in her eyes.

She rode off ahead. The saddle was a man's, of course, awkward to ride modestly, woman-fashion. As soon as she was out of the preacher's sight she rucked her skirts and slid a leg over to the other stirrup. That was better. There was a pleasant sensation of freedom about it, too. For a moment she forgot that she was going to Bristol Creek, in finery second-hand from the Barclay girls, in a new linen shift and drawers that she had sewn herself in the light of the kitchen candles, in white cotton stockings and a bonnet and shoes from Mr. Barclay's store, to marry Mr. Hathaway.

The Barclays had done well for her from the time when, a skinny weeping creature of fourteen, she was taken into the Barclay household and, as Mrs. Barclay so often said, "treated more like one of my own than a bond-girl from the poorhouse." She had first choice of the clothing cast off by Miss Julia and Miss Clara. She was permitted to sit in the same room, and learn what she could, when the schoolmaster came to give private lessons to the Barclay girls. She waited on table, of course, and helped in the kitchen, and made beds, and dusted and scrubbed. But then she had been taught to spin and to sew and to knit. And she was permitted, indeed encouraged, to sit with the Barclays in the meeting-house, at the convenient end of the pew, where she could worship the Barclays' God and assist with the Barclay wraps at the beginning and end of the service. And now, to complete her rewards, she had been granted the hand of a rejected Barclay suitor.

Mr. Hathaway was Barclay's agent at Bristol Creek, where he sold rum and gunpowder and corn meal and such things to the fishermen and hunters, and bought split cod—fresh, pickled or dry—and ran a small sawmill, and cut and shipped firewood by schooner to Port Marriott, and managed a farm, all for a salary of fifty pounds, Halifax currency, per year. Hathaway was a most capable fellow, Mr. Barclay often acknowledged. But when after fifteen capable years he came seeking a wife, and cast a sheep's eye first at Miss Julia, and then at Miss Clara, Mrs. Barclay observed with a sniff that Hathaway was looking a bit high.

So he was. The older daughter of Port Marriott's most prosperous merchant was even then receiving polite attentions from Mr. Gamage, the new collector of customs, and a connection of the Halifax Gamages, as Mrs. Barclay was fond of pointing out. And Miss Clara was going to Halifax in the spring to learn the gentle art of playing the pianoforte, and incidentally to display her charms to the naval and military gentlemen who thronged the Halifax drawing-rooms. The dear girls laughed behind their hands whenever long solemn Mr. Hathaway came to town aboard one of the Barclay vessels and called at the big house under the elms. Mrs. Barclay bridled at Hathaway's presumption, but shrewd Mr. Barclay narrowed his little black eyes and took snuff and said "Ha! Humph!"

It was plain to Mr. Barclay that an emergency had arisen.

Hathaway was a good man—in his place; and Hathaway must be kept content there, to go on making profit for Mr. Barclay at a cost of only £50 a year. 'Twas a pity Hathaway couldn't satisfy himself with one of the fishermen's girls at the Creek, but there 'twas. If Hathaway had set his mind on a town miss, then a town miss he must have; but she must be the right kind, the sort who would content herself and Hathaway at Bristol Creek and not go nagging the man to remove and try his capabilities elsewhere. At once Mr. Barclay thought of Kezia—dear little Kezzie. A colourless little creature but quiet and well-mannered and pious, and only twenty-two.

Mr. Hathaway was nearly forty and far from handsome, and he had a rather cold, seeking way about him—useful in business of course—that rubbed women the wrong way. Privately Mr. Barclay thought Hathaway lucky to get Kezia. But it was a nice match for the girl, better than anything she could have expected. He impressed that upon her and introduced the suitor from Bristol Creek. Mr. Hathaway spent two or three evenings courting Kezia in the kitchen—Kezia in a quite good gown of Miss Clara's gazing out at the November moon on the snow, murmuring now and again in the tones of someone in a rather dismal trance, while the kitchen help listened behind one door and the Barclay girls giggled behind another.

The decision, reached mainly by the Barclays, was that Mr. Hathaway should come to Port Marriott aboard the packet schooner on December twenty-third, to be married in the Barclay parlour and then take his bride home for Christmas. But an unforeseen circumstance had changed all this. The circumstance was a ship, "from Mogador in Barbary" as Mr. Barclay wrote afterwards in the salvage claim, driven off her course by gales and wrecked at the very entrance to Bristol Creek. She was a valuable wreck, laden with such queer things as goatskins in pickle, almonds, wormseed, pomegranate skins and gum arabic, and capable Mr. Hathaway had lost no time in salvage for the benefit of his employer.

As a result he could not come to Port Marriott for a wedding or anything else. A storm might blow up at any time and demolish this fat prize. He dispatched a note by Black Sam, urging Mr. Barclay to send Kezia and the preacher by return. It was not the orthodox note of an impatient sweetheart, but it said that he had moved into his new house by the Creek and found it "extream empty lacking a woman," and it suggested delicately that while his days were full, the nights were dull.

Kezia was no judge of distance. She rode for what she considered a reasonable time and then slid off and tied the brown horse to a maple tree beside the path. She had brought a couple of lamp wicks to tie about her shoes, to keep them from coming off in the snow, and she set out afoot in the big splayed tracks of Black Sam. The soft snow came almost to her knees in places and she lifted her skirts high. The path was no wider than the span of a man's arms, cut out with axes years before. She stumbled over a concealed stump from time to time, and the huckleberry bushes dragged at her cloak, but the effort warmed her. It had been cold, sitting on the horse with the wind blowing up her legs.

After a time the preacher overtook her, riding awkwardly and holding the reins in a nervous grip. The stirrups were too short for his long black-stockinged legs. He called out cheerfully as he passed, "Are you all right, Miss?" She nodded, standing aside with her back to a tree. When he disappeared ahead, with a last flutter of black shawl tassels in the wind, she picked up her skirts and went on. The path climbed and dropped monotonously over a succession of wooded ridges. Here and there in a hollow she heard water running, and the creak of frosty poles underfoot, and knew she was crossing a small stream, and once the trail ran across a wide swamp on half-rotten corduroy, wind-swept and bare of snow.

She found the horse tethered clumsily not far ahead, and the tracks of the preacher going on. She had to lead the horse to a stump so she could mount, and when she passed Mr. Mears again she called out, "Please, sir, next time leave the horse by a stump of a rock so I can get on." In his quaint old-country accent he murmured, "I'm very sorry," and gazed down at the snow. She forgot she was riding astride until she had passed him, and then she flushed, and gave the indignant horse a cut of the switch. Next time she remembered and swung her right leg back where it should be, and tucked the skirts modestly about her ankles; but young Mr. Mears looked down at the snow anyway, and after that she did not trouble to shift when she overtook him.

The ridges became steeper, and the streams roared under the ice and snow in the swales. They emerged upon the high tableland between Port Marriott and Bristol Creek, a gusty wilderness of young hardwood scrub struggling up amongst the grey snags of an old forest fire, and now that they were out of the gloomy softwoods they could see a stretch of sky. It was blue-grey and forbidding, and the wind whistling up from the invisible sea felt raw on the cheek. At their next meeting Kezia said, "It's going to snow."

She had no knowledge of the trail but she guessed that they were not much more than halfway across the cape. On this high barren the track was no longer straight and clear, it meandered amongst the meagre hardwood clumps where the path-makers had not bothered to cut, and only Black Sam's footprints really marked it for her unaccustomed eyes. The preacher nodded vaguely at her remark. The woods, like everything else about his chosen mission field, were new and very interesting, and he could not understand the alarm in her voice. He looked confidently at Black Sam's tracks.

Kezia tied the horse farther on and began her spell of walking. Her shoes were solid things, the kind of shoes Mr. Barclay invoiced as "a Common Strong sort, for women, Five Shillings"; but the snow worked into them and melted and saturated the leather. Her feet were numb every time she slid down from the horse and it took several minutes of stumbling through the snow to bring back an aching warmth. Beneath her arm she clutched the small bundle which contained all she had in the world—two flannel nightgowns, a shift of linen, three pairs of stout wool stockings—and of course Mr. Barclay's wedding gift for Mr. Hathaway.

Now as she plunged along she felt the first sting of snow on her face and, looking up, saw the stuff borne on the wind in small hard pellets that fell amonst the bare hardwoods and set up a whisper everywhere. When Mr. Mears rode up to her the snow was thick in their faces, like flung salt.

"It's a nor'easter!" she cried up to him. She knew the meaning of snow from the sea. She had been born in a fishing-village down the coast.

"Yes," mumbled the preacher, and drew a fold of the shawl about his face. He disappeared. She struggled on, gasping, and after what seemed a tremendous journey came upon him standing alone and bewildered, looking off somewhere to the right.

"The horse!" he shouted. "I got off him, and before I could fasten the reins some snow fell off a branch—startled him, you know—and he ran off, over that way." He gestured with a mittened hand. "I must fetch him back," he added confusedly.

"No!" Kezia cried. "Don't you try. You'd only get lost. So would I. Oh, dear! This is awful. We'll have to go on, the best we can."

He was doubtful. The horse tracks looked very plain. But Kezia was looking at Black Sam's tracks, and tugging his arm.

He gave in, and they struggled along for half an hour or so. Then the last trace of the old footprints vanished.

"What shall we do now?" the preacher asked, astonished.

"I don't know," whispered Kezia, and leaned against a dead pine stub in an attitude of weariness and indifference that dismayed him.

"We must keep moving, my dear, mustn't we? I mean, we can't stay here."

"Can't stay here," she echoed.

"Down there—a hollow, I think. I see some hemlock trees, or are they pines?—I'm never quite sure. Shelter, anyway."

"Shelter," muttered Kezia.

He took her by the hand and like a pair of lost children they dragged their steps into the deep snow of the hollow. The trees were tall spruces, a thick bunch in a ravine, where they had escaped the old fire. A stream thundered amongst them somewhere. There was no wind in this place, only the fine snow whirling thickly down between the trees like a sediment from the storm overhead.

"Look!" cried Mr. Mears. A hut loomed out of the whiteness before them, a small structure of moss-chinked logs with a roof of poles and birch-bark. It had an abandoned look. Long streamers of moss hung out between the logs. On the roof shreds of birch-bark wavered gently in the drifting snow. The door stood half open and a thin drift of snow lay along the split pole floor. Instinctively Kezia went to the stone hearth. There were old ashes sodden with rain down the chimney and now frozen to a cake.

"Have you got flint and steel?" she asked. She saw in his eyes something dazed and forlorn. He shook his head, and she was filled with a sudden anger, not so much at him as at Mr. Barclay and that—that Hathaway, and all the rest of menkind. They ruled the world and made such a sorry mess of it. In a small fury she began to rummage about the hut.

There was a crude bed of poles and brushwood by the fireplace—brushwood so old that only a few brown needles clung to the twigs. A rough bench whittled from a pine log, with round birch sticks for legs. A broken earthenware pot in a corner. In another some ash-wood frames such as trappers used for stretching skins. Nothing else. The single window was covered with a stretched moose-bladder, cracked and dry-rotten, but it still let in some daylight while keeping out the snow.

She scooped up the snow from the floor with her mittened hands, throwing it outside, and closed the door carefully, dropping the bar into place, as if she could shut out and bar the cold in such a fashion. The air inside was frigid. Their breath hung visible in the dim light from the window. Young Mr. Mears dropped on his wet knees and began to pray in a loud voice. His face was pinched with cold and his teeth rattled as he prayed. He was a pitiable object.

"Prayers won't keep you warm," said Kezia crossly.

He looked up, amazed at the change in her. She had seemed such a meek little thing. Kezia was surprised at herself, and surprisingly she went on, "You'd far better take off those wet moccasins and stockings and shake the snow out of your clothes." She set the example, vigorously shaking out her skirts and Miss Julia's cloak, and she turned her small back on him and took off her own shoes and stockings, and pulled on dry stockings from her bundle She threw him a pair.

"Put those on."

He looked at them and at his large feet, hopelessly.

"I'm afraid they wouldn't go on."

She tossed him one of her flannel nightgowns. "Then take off your stockings and wrap your feet and legs in that."

He obeyed, in an embarrassed silence. She rolled her eyes upward, for his modesty's sake, and saw a bundle on one of the low rafters—the late owner's bedding, stowed away from mice. She stood on the bench and pulled down three bearskins, marred with bullet holes. A rank and musty smell arose in the cold. She considered the find gravely.

"You take them," Mr. Mears said gallantly. "I shall be quite all right."

"You'll be dead by morning, and so shall I," she answered vigorously, "if you don't do what I say. We've got to roll up in these."

"Together?" he cried in horror.

"Of course! To keep each other warm. It's the only way." She spread the skins on the floor, hair uppermost, one overlapping another, and dragged the flustered young man beside her, clutched him in her arms, and rolled with him, over, and over again, so that they became a single shapeless heap in the corner farthest from the draft between door and chimney.

"Put your arms around me," commanded the new Kezia, and he obeyed.

"Now," she said, "you can pray. God helps those that help themselves."

He prayed aloud for a long time, and privately called upon heaven to witness the purity of his thoughts in this strange and shocking situation. He said "Amen" at last; and "Amen," echoed Kezia, piously.

They lay silent for a long time, breathing on each other's necks and hearing their own hearts—poor Mr. Mears's fluttering in an agitated way, Kezia's as steady as a clock. A delicious warmth crept over them. They relaxed in each other's arms. Outside, the storm hissed in the spruce tops and set up an occasional cold moan in the cracked clay chimney. The downswirling snow brushed softly against the bladder pane.

"I'm warm now," murmured Kezia. "Are you?"

"Yes. How long must we stay like this?"

"Till the storm's over, of course. Tomorrow, probably. Nor'easters usually blow themselves out in a day and a night, 'specially when they come up sharp, like this one. Are you hungry?"

"No."

"Abigail—that's the black cook at Barclay's—gave me bread and cheese in a handkerchief. I've got it in my bundle. Mr. Barclay thought we ought to reach Bristol Creek by suppertime, but Nabby said I must have a bite to eat on the road. She's a good kind thing, old Nabby. Sure you're not hungry?"

"Quite. I feel somewhat fatigued but not hungry."

"Then we'll eat the bread and cheese for breakfast. Have you got a watch?"

"No, I'm sorry. They cost such a lot of money. In Lady Huntingdon's Connexion we—"

"Oh well, it doesn't matter. It must be about four o'clock—the light's getting dim. Of course, the dark comes very quick in a snowstorm."

"Dark," echoed young Mr. Mears drowsily. Kezia's hair, washed last night for the wedding journey, smelled pleasant so close to his face. It reminded him of something. He went to sleep dreaming of his mother, with his face snug in the curve of Kezia's neck and shoulder, and smiling, and muttering words that Kezia could not catch. After a time she kissed his cheek. It seemed a very natural thing to do.

Soon she was dozing herself, and dreaming, too; but her dreams were full of forbidding faces—Mr. Barclay's, Mrs. Barclay's, Mr. Hathaway's; especially Mr. Hathaway's. Out of a confused darkness Mr. Hathaway's hard acquisitive gaze searched her shrinking flesh like a cold wind. Then she was shuddering by the kitchen fire at Barclay's, accepting Mr. Hathaway's courtship and wishing she was dead. In the midst of that sickening wooing she wakened sharply.

It was quite dark in the hut. Mr. Mears was breathing quietly against her throat. But there was a sound of heavy steps outside, muffled in the snow and somehow felt rather than heard. She shook the young man and he wakened with a start, clutching her convulsively.

"Sh-h-h!" she warned. "Something's moving outside." She felt him stiffen.

"Bears?" he whispered.

Silly! thought Kezia. People from the old country could think of nothing but bears in the woods. Besides, bears holed up in the winter. A caribou, perhaps. More likely a moose. Caribou moved inland before this, to the wide mossy bogs up the river, away from the coastal storms. Again the sound.

"There!" hissed the preacher. Their hearts beat rapidly together.

The door—you fastened it, didn't you?"

"Yes," she said. Suddenly she knew.

"Unroll, quick!" she cried. "No, not this way—your way."

They unrolled, ludicrously, and the girl scrambled up and ran across the floor in her stockinged feet, and fumbled with the rotten door-bar. Mr. Mears attempted to follow but he tripped over the nightgown still wound about his feet, and fell with a crash. He was up again in a moment, catching up the clumsy wooden bench for a weapon, his bare feet slapping on the icy floor. He tried to shoulder her aside, crying "Stand back! Leave it to me!" and waving the bench uncertainly in the darkness.

She laughed excitedly. "Silly!" she said. "It's the horse." She flung the door open. In the queer ghostly murk of a night filled with snow they beheld a large dark shape. The shape whinnied softly and thrust a long face into the doorway. Mr. Mears dropped the bench, astonished.

"He got over his fright and followed us here somehow," Kezia said, and laughed again. She put her arms about the snowy head and laid her face against it.

"Good horse! Oh, good, good horse!"

"What are you going to do?" the preacher murmured over her shoulder. After the warmth of their nest in the furs they were shivering in this icy atmosphere.

"Bring him in, of course. We can't leave him out in the storm." She caught the bridle and urged the horse inside with expert clucking sounds. The animal hesitated, but fear of the storm and a desire for shelter and company decided him. In he came, tramping ponderously on the split-pole floor. The preacher closed and barred the door.

"And now?" he asked.

"Back to the furs. Quick! It's awful cold."

Rolled in the furs once more, their arms went about each other instinctively, and the young man's face found the comfortable nook against Kezia's soft throat. But sleep was difficult after that. The horse whinnied gently from time to time, and stamped about the floor. The decayed poles crackled dangerously under his hoofs whenever he moved, and Kezia trembled, thinking he might break through and frighten himself, and flounder about till he tumbled the crazy hut about their heads. She called out to him "Steady, boy! Steady!"

It was a long night. The pole floor made its irregularities felt through the thickness of fur; and because there seemed nowhere to put their arms but about each other the flesh became cramped, and spread its protest along the bones. They were stiff and sore when the first light of morning stained the window. They unrolled and stood up thankfully, and tramped up and down the floor, threshing their arms in an effort to fight off the gripping cold. Kezia undid her bundle in a corner and brought forth Nabby's bread and cheese, and they ate it sitting together on the edge of the brushwood bed with the skins about their shoulders. Outside the snow had ceased.

"We must set off at once," the preacher said. "Mr. Hathaway will be anxious."

Kezia was silent. She did not move, and he looked at her curiously. She appeared very fresh, considering the hardships of the previous day and the night. He passed a hand over his cheeks and thought how unclean he must appear in her eyes, with this stubble on his pale face.

"Mr. Hathaway—" he began again.

"I'm not going to Mr. Hathaway," Kezia said quietly.

"But—the wedding!"

"There'll be no wedding. I don't want to marry Mr. Hathaway. 'Twas Mr. Hathaway's idea, and Mr. and Mrs. Barclay's. They wanted me to marry him."

"What will the Barclays say, my dear?"

She shrugged. "I've been their bond-girl every since I was fourteen, but I'm not a slave like poor black Nabby, to be handed over, body and soul, whenever it suits."

"Your soul belongs to God," said Mr. Mears devoutly.

"And my body belongs to me."

He was a little shocked at this outspokenness but he said

gently, "Of course. To give oneself in marriage without true affection would be an offense in the sight of heaven. But what will Mr. Hathaway say?"

"Well, to begin with, he'll ask where I spent the night, and I'll have to tell the truth. I'll have to say I bundled with you in a hut in the woods."

"Bundled?"

"A custom the people brought with them from Connecticut when they came to settle in Nova Scotia. Poor folk still do it. Sweethearts, I mean. It saves fire and candles when your courting on a winter evening. It's harmless—they keep their clothes on, you see, like you and me—but Mr. Barclay and the other Methody people are terrible set against it. Mr. Barclay got old Mr. Mings—he's the Methody preacher that died last year—to make a sermon against it. Mr. Mings said bundling was an invention of the devil."

"Then if you go back to Mr. Barclay—"

"He'll ask me the same question and I'll have to give him the same answer. I couldn't tell a lie, could I?" She turned a pair of round blue eyes and met his embarrassed gaze.

"No! No, you mustn't lie. Whatever shall we do?" he murmured in a dazed voice. Again she was silent, looking modestly down her small nose.

"It's so very strange," he floundered. "This country—there are so many things I don't know, so many things to learn. You—I—we shall have to tell the truth, of course. Doubtless I can find a place in the Lord's service somewhere else, but what about you, poor girl?"

"I heard say the people at Scrod Harbour want a preacher."

"But—the tale would follow me, wouldn't it, my dear? This—er—bundling with a young woman?"

" 'Twouldn't matter if the young woman was your wife."

"Eh?" His mouth fell open. He was like an astonished child, for all his preacher's clothes and the new beard on his jaws.

"I'm a good girl," Kezia said, inspecting her foot. "I can read and write, and know all the tunes in the psalter. And—and you need someone to look after you."

He considered the truth of that. Then he murmured uncertainly, "We'd be very poor, my dear. The Connexion gives some support, but of course—"

"I've always been poor," Kezia said. She sat very still but her cold fingers writhed in her lap.

He did something then that made her want to cry. He took hold of her hands and bowed his head and kissed them.

"It's strange—I don't even know your name, my dear."

"It's Kezia—Kezia Barnes."

He said quietly "You're a brave girl, Kezia Barnes, and I shall try to be a good husband to you. Shall we go?"

"Hadn't you better kiss me, first?" Kezia said faintly.

He put his lips awkwardly to hers; and then, as if the taste of her clean mouth itself provided strength and purpose, he kissed her again, and firmly. She threw her arms about his neck.

"Oh, Mr. Mears!"

How little he knew about everything! He hadn't even known enough to wear two or three pairs of stockings inside those roomy moccasins, nor to carry a pair of dry ones. Yesterday's wet stockings were lying like sticks on the frosty floor. She showed him how to knead the hard-frozen moccasins into softness, and while he worked at the stiff leather she tore up one of her wedding bed-shirts and wound the flannel strips about his legs and feet. It looked very queer when she had finished, and they both laughed.

They were chilled to the bone when they set off, Kezia on the horse and the preacher walking ahead, holding the reins. When they regained the slope where they had lost the path, Kezia said, "The sun rises somewhere between east and southeast, this time of year. Keep it on your left shoulder a while. That will tak us back toward Port Marriott."

When they came to the green timber she told him to shift the sun to his left eye.

"Have you changed your mind?" he asked cheerfully. The exercise had warmed him.

"No, but the sun moves across the sky."

"Ah! What a wise little head it is!"

They came over a ridge of mixed hemlock and hardwood and looked upon a long swale full of bare hackmatacks.

"Look!" the girl cried. The white slot of the axe path showed clearly in the trees at the foot of the swale, and again where it entered the dark mass of the pines beyond.

"Praise the Lord!" said Mr. Mears.

When at last they stood in the trail, Kezia slid down from the horse.

"No!" Mr. Mears protested.

"Ride-and-tie," she said firmly. "That's the way we came, and that's the way we'll go. Besides, I want to get warm."

He climbed up clumsily and smiled down at her.

"What shall we do when we get to Port Marriott, my dear?"

"Get the New Light preacher to marry us, and catch the packet for Scrod Harbour."

He nodded and gave a pull at his broad hat brim. She thought of everything. A splendid helpmeet for the world's wilderness. He saw it all very humbly now as a dispensation of Providence.

Kezia watched him out of sight. Then, swiftly, she undid her bundle and took out the thing that had lain there (and on her conscience) through the night—the tinderbox—Mr. Barclay's wedding gift to Mr. Hathaway. She flung it into the woods and walked on, skirts lifted, in the track of the horse, humming a psalm tune to the silent trees and the snow.

THE valley lay shimmering green under the June heat. The red-clay banks of the river shone like paint in the sun and its water flowed like a clear red wine. The narrow dirt highway was a hot red snake cut in twain by the river. One part of it, the part that lay toward Windsor and Halifax, came down the steep east bank and ended at the waterside; the west part ran off through the birch woods toward Fort Anne. From an oak stump on the west bank a stout rope stretched a taut three hundred feet across the river to a great yellow birch on the far side. On the west bank lay a small flatboat, and moored to the west bank was a small scow whose planking was scarred and splintered by the hoofs of restive horses. Above them, beside the dusty red road, stood a pine clapboard house with a gambrel roof, and a barn and stable formed with the house a little three-sided yard. There was a well in the middle of the yard, and a long balance-pole dangled a bucket over the well's mouth.

The house was quite large for those parts in those times, but it had a shabby and downcast look, as if the times had not measured up to the builder's hopes. The unpainted clapboards had drawn their nails in the bitter frosts of winter and warped in the hot summer suns, so that the loose ends rattled like castanets whenever a wind blew down the river. The roof shingles were curled like old leaves, with a new one here and there, crudely split from a cedar log with mallet and frow, and thrust under the old to stop the worst of the leaks. From their midst rose a brick chimney, very square and squat, breathing a wisp of blue wood smoke toward the sky. For the rest, a crazy pole fence staggered around three or four acres of clearing, and beyond, in the shade of the trees, sounded a thin clang of cow-bells. A few hens dusted themselves in the Great West Road; otherwise there was no sign of life but the smoke and the drowsy bells.

Into this languid scene from the west came a sudden horse-man, shooting out of the gap in the woods like a bullet in a discharge of choking red dust. He was a stout man in a blue coat whose dusty tails flapped in a breeze of his own making.

and the sweat down his florid round face made a comical mask of the red valley grime. He pulled up outside the shabby wooden house, scattering indignant hens, and bellowed, "Hullo, there!"

There was no answer. The dust settled. The hens stalked about the well ruffling their feathers and clucking their disgust.

"Job!" roared the man, rising in his stirrups and throwing his voice all round the clearing. "I say Job! Job Rogers! Oi! Rogers!"

No answer.

The horseman tried another key to the silence. "Oi! Thankful! Thankful Rogers! Oh, Thanky! Oh-h-h Thanke-e-e-e!"

A girl scrambled into sight from the alders by the river. She was what Mr. Dawkins in younger days—before he became a magistrate and *Custos Rotulorum* and deacon of the New Light congregation—would have called a fine well-set-up piece. She wore a plain gown of some light-coloured stuff, very neatly patched in places, and, Mr. Dawkins suspected, not very much underneath. What Mr. Dawkins could see of her was in various tints of brown. Her bare feet and ankles were brown, so were her smooth arms, and her face was the warm golden brown of good ale; her eyes were hazel, with lively glints as they took in his dust and discomfiture, and her hair, a shower of long tangled curls, was the dark brown that looks black by candle-light. She had a birch pole in one hand, and from the hooked fingers of the other, thrust under the gill, drooped a fresh-caught shad.

"D'ye want over?" she asked, nodding her head toward the ferry.

Mr. Dawkins took off his hat and with it beat some of the dust from his garments. "Nunno, my dear. I wanted to see Job, but you'll do. I guess ye do most o' the ferrying anyhow, eh?"

"I guess so," said Thankful diffidently.

"'Slike this," Mr. Dawkins said, putting on his hat and looking important. "The Jook's on the road."

"Jook?"

"The Prince—the Jook of Kent—a son o' King George hisself —surely ye've heard o' the Jook? Commander o' the forces at Hal'fax, and ridin' down the valley now—this minute—with some o' his staff."

The girl arched her eyebrows and looked past him up the west road.

"Not that way," snapped Mr. Dawkins. "He's comin' from Hal'fax way, headin' fer Annapolis. A sloop come in from Hal'fax 'smornin' with the word. She's to carry him over Fundy

Bay to Saint John, and he's goin' to inspect the garrison at Fredericton."

"Whyn't he sail all the way from Hal'fax in the sloop?"

Mr. Dawkins clucked impatiently. "Because he likes ridin', that's why. They say to Hal'fax that he's a reg'lar devil a-horse-back, forever galloping over the countryside and wearin' out good horse flesh. Rein and spur, flog and spur—that's the Jook; and he treats his men the same. Or so they say," he added carefully.

The girl cocked an eye at him saucily. "You come here to ride with him?"

"Nunno, gel. I'm here doin' my dooty. As *Custos* o' this county, I mean to say, I got responsibilities. Things must go without a hitch, I tell ye, for the Jook don't like delay; and the road bein' what it is, and rivers to cross and no bridges to speak of, why, I want the ferrymen to look sharp and act smart when the Jook comes along."

Thankful sniffed. "Well, His Royal Nob'll have to get along without Pa. Pa's gone over to Brandy Brook for a rest."

"A rest from what?" snorted Mr. Dawkins, running a cynical eye over the down-at-heel inn, the small garden patch and the idle ferry.

She gave her curls a toss. "Never mind Pa. I'll keep a sharp lookout for your Jook. How many in the party?" she asked shrewdly.

"Um," grunted the magistrate, squinting an eye down at her. "There'll be five or six. And don't ye go chargin' mor'n ye ought, Thankful Rogers. The Jook knows what's what, and ye'll get a lick wi' the rough side o' his tongue."

"He'll pay his sixpence, same as the rest," Thankful said defiantly. "What's he look like?"

"I dunno. I"—Mr. Dawkins drew himself up and loyally took off his hat—"I never had the great privilege o' seein' His Royal Highness. You keep a sharp eye, see? He always has a trumpeter ridin' well ahead, to give notice at the ferries and have 'em ready to take him over prompt. You keep an eye peeled for that trumpeter."

"Trumpeter" she repeated, with a pleased little twist of her mouth. "That's more like it. That's more my style."

"You be careful o' trumpeters and such," advised Mr. Dawkins primly. "Not that the trumpeter'll have much time for dallyin'. But so'gers is always too ready with a chuck under the chin and a squeeze o' the knee. Give 'em an inch and they'll take an ell. Mind what I say . . . . Giddup, Wildfire!"

And off he went in another cloud of dust.

"Well!" said Thankful Rogers, hands on hips. She threw the shad into the kitchen and walked down to sit in the grass above the scow.

She was sitting there, knees up, chin propped, when a horseman came thundering down the opposite bank and pulled up with a jerk at the very edge of the river. He wore a green riding-coat and a gold-laced hat, cocked high in the military fashion with a long fold at the back and two short ones coming to a peak at the front, with a black cockade at the left side. She saw that he wore a short yellow waistcoat, a white shirt and stock, tight white breeches, and a pair of black riding-boots with the turned-down tops showing brown, all soiled with the red dust of the Great West Road. A riding-crop hung from his wrist, but what took her eye at once was a gleaming brass trumpet slung by a cord about his neck.

He gave a tug at the thing, and she cried across the river to him, "All right, trumpeter, all right! Save your breath. I'm a-comin'!"

She jumped into the scow and pulled it across, hand over hand along the rope. There was not much current in the river now that the spring freshet was well past and the summer's drouth begun. As she drew in to the east bank she looked them over critically. The horse was a fine beast. The man was a little disappointing. She had fancied all soldiers young. This one looked five-and-thirty at the very least. He was tall and the uniform fitted him as a lynx fits its pelt, and there was something fierce and lynx-like in the play of his large light eyes. He was all impatience, she could see. He kept looking at the deep red river as if he had half a mind to swim the horse over and chance it.

"Don't ye dast!" she called out to him. "Ain't a-worrit about you, mind—I guess His Royal Nob's got lot's o' trumpeters—but ye've got that horse in a lather and a souse in cold water'll fix his flint quick, I tell ye. I'll be there in a minute."

"Ha!" said the trumpeter loudly.

He jumped in as soon as the scow touched the bank, with the reins in his hand, and coaxed the big brown hunter aboard.

"He goin' to stand quiet?" Thankful asked wisely, "or shall I fasten him?"

"He'll be quiet," the trumpeter said.

On the way over, Thankful asked, "When shall I expect His Nob and the others?"

"His Nob? Oh!" The trumpeter seized a large dangling seal

and jerked a watch out of his fob. "I doubt if you see 'em inside the hour. Is this Rogers' Ferry? D'you keep an inn yonder? How far to Fort Anne?"

"It is. We do. And it's a rough twenty mile. Better stop and bait."

"What's in the larder, my dear?"

"Nothin'. But I can kill a hen if ye want to wait a bit. Or I can give ye fresh fried shad. And I'm not your dear, not by no means. I could fancy a nice handsome young so'ger now, but not you."

He turned his light eyes and seemed to notice Thankful for the first time.

"What's wrong with me, Miss?"

"My name's Thankful—Thankful Rogers. Job Rogers is my Pa—he's off somewhere. Ma's dead this twelve-month so I keep the house. What's wrong with ye? I dunno. Ye're too like a musket, I guess—all flint, snap, and bang. I fancied a nice young so'ger that I could talk to, cozy-like—but no liberties, mind."

He laughed, and when he laughed the fierceness went out of his face. He looked almost human, but not quite.

"Aren't there any young men to suit you hereabouts?"

"No. And nobody comes this way but bag-men—they're too cheeky. Most folk hate to pay sixpence for the ferry and go round by Pratt's Ford—that's two-three miles up-river. So, it's lonesome."

"You seem pretty self-sufficient, Thankful Rogers. What d'ye want a soldier for?"

"For a husband, I guess." The teeth flashed white in her brown face but her eyes were serious.

"Pooh! Soldiers don't make good husbands, they're black-guards all."

"Ye don't look 'zactly a blackguard yourself, trumpeter. I'll tell ye. I want to find a husband so that we—me and him—can make this place what it ought to be. There ain't any richer land in the valley. All it wants is a man that's strong in the arms and knows how to use 'em. Give me that kind o' man and a few shillings' worth o' tools and I could make this the best farm 'tween Wilmot and Fort Anne—clear another ten or fifteen acres, keep more cattle, raise some grain along wi' the root crops, plant an orchard, fix up the house and barn. That's what I want a husband for."

"Nothing else?"

She caught the look in his eyes and tossed her head. "Oh, I'd want him to make love to me, when work was done. Tired o' bein' lonesome. If I'd a man I could live, why"—she wrinkled her snub nose and laughed—"I reckon he'd find the sugar was worth the pill. I'm a lot better made for teasin' and pleasin' than the fine officers' ladies I've seen to Fort Anne."

"Umph! But soldiers' wives have to live in barracks, or follow the drum in a tilt-cart, my dear. Have you thought of that?"

"Ah, but I wouldn't barrack nor follow anybody's precious drum. I'd stay here and keep the place a-goin' till the war's over. Wars don't last forever, and Pa told me Nova Scotia was made by so'gers settlin' after wars. Come the war's end and the French beat, why, there's no one like a so'ger to 'preciate a lovin' wife and a good bit o' land. You know any nice so'gers? My age, I mean."

"None worth your little finger, Thankful Rogers." His mouth clamped hard when he said this and she felt a little chilled. His lips looked cruel.

She pulled in to the west bank and the trumpeter led his horse up the road to the well trough, and dipped water with the bucket on the pole. Thankful fastened the scow, fetched a cloth from the house and rubbed down the hunter's sweating flanks. His lower belly was scored by the trumpeter's spurs.

"Does the Prince know ye use a horse like this?" she asked.

"His Nob? My dear girl, he won't have a man on his staff who spares a horse. Always swears if ye want the best out of man or beast ye must show no mercy to one or the other. He's never shown mercy to me, I can tell ye—I'd as lief have the devil for master."

"Tut! Hold your tongue!" cried Thankful sharply. "People's pretty scattered in this country, but gossip gets about. One o' these days that tongue o' yours'll take the skin off your back."

The trumpeter nodded bitterly. "Ay, a great one for flogging, is His Nob. What do the gossips say?"

She shrugged. "Oh, ye can't believe half the tales that drift up the Great West Road. But they say he used to be wild, like the rest o' the King's sons, till he came to Canada and took up with Madame."

"Who's she?"

"Madame Saint Laurent? Nobody knows much about her, I guess. The name's a made-up one—she's from Quebec way, d'ye see?—and some say they're marrit by a Romish priest, and some say she's just his doxy. Anyhow, he's got her set up in a fine country house by the shore o' Bedford Basin, a few mile out o' Hal'fax, with servants galore, a park to walk about in, and a comp'ny of so'gers in a barrack by the road to see there's privacy. But you must know all this—you're his trumpeter."

"A trumpeter, my dear, don't look past the end of his trumpet if he's wise. The more he blows, the less he knows. But tell me—what do you think of His Nob and Madame?"

She pushed out her red lips and considered, gravely. "Well, my notion is they truly love each other—there! She's a little dark dumpy woman, so I've heard, and that makes me sure. If she was beautiful, I'd be 'spicious. And they say she's modest and gentle and keeps away from that shameless Hal'fax high life—and what's more, keeps him out of it. As for him, he's a good soldier they say, though a strict 'un. Fought agin the French in the West Indies afore he come to Canada, and minded bullets no more'n skeeters. If ye ask me he's a whole lot better'n those other scapegrace sons o' His Majesty. But they say the King won't let him come home—not with Madame—and the Jook won't leave her, so he's sent from one garrison to the other in the colonies—the hotter or colder the better—till he comes round to His Majesty's way o' thinkin' .... You want somethin' to eat?"

"No, I think not, my dear." His impatient eye was on the road again. "I'll sup in the mess at Fort Anne."

"That's twenty miles on. Mind ye don't founder that horse. I'll look out for your Jook. Is there anything else?"

The trumpeter hesitated and looked at her carefully. "Can you read?"

"Yes. Not right well, but well enough. Why?"

"I wish to leave a small packet addressed to one of His Nob's party. Show me to ink and a pen, if you please."

She led him into the bare little parlour, where his spurred heels gritted on clean sand from the river bed, and sat him before ink and paper at a small maple desk in a corner. She dived into the barnyard, and there was a clamour of geese at the rear. She came back with a pair of quills, and he took one and whittled the tip to his liking with a pen-knife out of his waistcoat.

"You may leave me for a bit, if you've work to do," he said over his shoulder. As she went out the pen was scratching furiously. He wrote the way he rode, at a round spattering gallop. She was still rubbing down the horse when he came out and put a small packet in her hands.

"That's for a fellow named Bauer, one of His Nob's staff. Get Bauer aside when they come, and put the packet in his hands—no one else's, mind that—and see what he has to say. It's a matter of importance."

He swung into the saddle and jammed his hat down firmly on his forehead.

"Goodbye, my dear."

"What about my sixpence for the ferry?"

"Oh, that!" he laughed. "You'll have to get that from Bauer," and he spurred the hunter into the road. Wrathfully she watched him out of sight, the riding-crop rising and falling in a rush of red dust that filled the cleft in the birch woods.

"That's for trustin' a so'ger!" she said aloud in the silence.

She had a good mind to throw his precious packet in the river. But it was done up in a handkerchief, a fine bit of silk, worth a shilling at the least—the price of two fares. Inside, there was a crackle of paper, and something heavy and hard. Um! Well, she would get her shilling from Bauer before she let go the packet. So'gers!

But now she thought of the Prince, and hurried to the well and sluiced bucket after bucket of water over her dusty feet; and in her chamber she washed face, neck, bosom, and arms with great care, and combed her dark curls to a gleaming fall, and put on her one whole gown. Then the bodice left behind by a careless lady traveller last year, a green velvet thing laced with a black ribbon that, drawn taut, made the least of Thankful's slim waist and the most of her plump young breasts. She pulled on her best white stockings, and her shoes with the gilt buckles bought in Halifax, and as a final concession to His Nob she rubbed the shoe-leather with a greased rag till it shone. She examined all this, with the usual female contortions, in her small looking-glass, and announced several times to the image there, "Please, Your Highness, the fare is sixpence each."

Satisfied at last, she went down to the scow and pulled it across to the east bank. She did not have long to wait. The road made a notch in the woods at the crest of the slope, filled with blue sky, and suddenly the wedge of sky was blotted out by a whirl of horses and men that seemed to leap out of the ridge itself. They made a picture coming down the red road to the river, five big sweating horses and five laughing men in fine uniforms laden with dust. One wore a blue coat and one a green; the rest were in red coats with buttoned-back tails. There was a good deal of polished brass about them, and gold lace and epaulets, and the green coat had silver buttons, and their hats were all cocked like the trumpeter's, and their breeches and riding-boots were plastered red by the splash of the fords and the dust of the road.

They came down the slope at a gallop and reined up hard at the brink, like the trumpeter before them, and flung themselves off, crying out to her, "Where's Aitcharaitch, eh? How far ahead?"

"If ye mean that trumpeter," she answered, "he's over and gone this half-hour." They laughed a good deal at that, and declared to each other that, by Gad, 'twould make a pretty jest in the mess at Fort Anne—Aitcharaitch blowing his own trumpet all down the Great West Road.

She had to make two trips of it, taking three horses and two men the first time; and as she busied herself at the ferrying she studied the officers, wondering which was Bauer and which the Prince. Three were quite young, and their names seemed to be Rickbarton, Captain Weatherford and "Jemmy." No prince there. Blue Coat was older, and the others quipped him merrily about the riding style of the artillery. The fifth must be Prince Edward, Jook of Kent. They called him simply Colonel, but there was a note of respect in their voices and she knew the Jook to be colonel-in-chief of the fusiliers at Halifax. He was a big man with a long face, and a long hooked nose like a sabre hung between two cold blue fires; and he had little to say. Indeed he seemed a bit impatient with the hilarious chatter of the younger men.

"Aitcharaitch—did he stop for a sup at your inn?" he asked the girl coldly.

"Please sir, no," she said, awed, not lifting her gaze from the gold rope on his left breast.

They all looked at the inn and nodded their dusty hats together. It was not much of an inn, even for the Great West Road, that pitiful track in the wilderness.

"He'll not stop short of Fort Anne," declared the young captain named Jemmy.

"Nor shall we," said Sabre Nose fiercely. He slipped a hand to his belt and detached a leather-covered bottle, and drank thirstily. The others followed suit, a great fumbling for leather bottles, and heads thrown back, and eyes squinting into the afternoon sun.

"Which o' you gentlemen is Mister Bauer?" asked Thankful cautiously.

They were putting their bottles away and preparing to mount again.

"Bauer?" said one of the red-coats. "He's behind."

"Poor devil!" clucked Captain Weatherford. "He'll catch it for laming his nag. Shouldn't wonder if there's two dozen o' the cat's best awaiting him at the triangle when he gets to Fort Anne."

"The man rides like a sack of potatoes," snorted Sabre Nose. "Demned shame. For the horse, I mean."

The youngest officer tossed Thankful a crown piece, which she caught deftly at the end of its glittering arc in the sunshine, and they all rode off in a great hurry toward the west.

The sun was sitting round and red on the birch tops when the last lone traveller appeared, leading a lame horse and carrying a plain cocked hat in his hand. He was dust from his pigtailed head to his limping boots. He wore a green coat with brass buttons and looked very hot and weary as Thankful pulled the scow across to him in the scarlet flare of the sunset. He led the horse aboard gently and crossed over without a word.

On the west bank he asked, "How far am I behind them— the Prince and the others?" He said this in an accent that reminded Thankful of the settlers behind Bear River, old soldiers of the Waldecker Line.

"Far enough that you'll never catch 'em," she answered promptly. "As for that trumpeter—"

"Trumpeter?"

"The one they call Aitcharaitch—a furrin name if ever I heard one—he's to Fort Anne by now, I reckon, riggin' two dozen triangles or somethin' like that for a feller named Bauer. You him?"

"*Ja*," the young man said heavily. "That is me."

"Two dozen o' the best, the Prince said—what a nose he's got! Well, I reckon ye'd better stay the night and rest that horse."

"You got no horses, you?"

She shook her head. He looked up the road in a desperate sort of way, as if he would go on afoot.

"You see, *Fräulein*, I am trumpeter to the Prince and—"

"Land o' Goshen, another! His Royal Nob travels in style, I must say—trumpet before, trumpet behind, and four high cockalorums in gold lace for company! Well, it's twenty mile to anywhere, and nigh on dark, and ye look as lame as your horse. Where's your trumpet?"

"Mine trumpet? He took it—Aitcharaitch—when I had to fall back. The Prince, he does not like to wait at ferries, he does not like to wait anywhere."

"I could see that—him and his nose. Go into the house and

make yourself to home while I tend your horse. D'ye like shad? It's a fish," she added, seeing the lift of his brows.

"Fish!" he exploded. "You talk about fish, *um's Himmels willen*, when I am wishing I am dead!"

His hands were large and strong and his shoulders filled the dusty green coat, but he had a dreamy unhappy face and his blue eyes were full of trouble. He sat by the roadside and stared gloomily around the clearing.

"Good land," he observed tonelessly, as if trying to take his mind off something else. "This earth is rich like blood. In Halifax the earth is grey, the sky is grey. In Halifax always it rains. I talk with *deutsche* farmers there and they tell me that grey earth is too wet for a bed, too sour for a crop, and too full of rock for a grave. But here! Your earth is red and fat—see the bank of the river—and how the sun shines, *lieber Gott!* That is the way the sun shines on the banks of our Eder at the end of the day."

Thankful regarded him, brown fists on hips. "Don't tell me you're a farmer! You? What are ye doing in that uniform?"

The young man made a wry mouth and threw out his hands, palms up.

"I come from a farm, *ja*. In the old country my father has cattles and swines and he sends me to school to learn moosic. That is good, *ja*? But in the town I am taken by the landgrave for the regiment he is hiring to the English king. So I go to England, I go to Ireland, I go *Gott* knows where, and at last I go to Halifax to be trumpeter for the Prince. There is a war somewhere. I do not want to kill nobody but I do not mind to fight, that is something. To play moosic, that is something. But bump, bump, bump—so!—up and down on the horse, the poor horse, blowing my trumpet for ferries, trying to keep pace with this prince who rides like the Wild Huntsman in the tales. *Ja*. That is what I do in this uniform. That is why I wish to be dead."

"What you need," said Thankful kindly, "is a drink o' good Demerary under that belt, and a platter o' fried shad. Go into the house!"

The sharp note of command in this last fetched him to his feet in a hurry. Obediently he limped indoors, while the girl watered his horse and led it to the stables. When she came in, Bauer was sprawled in her father's old oak chair, staring at the cold ashes on the hearth. She had her gown pulled up and filled with chips for kindling, which she dropped in the fire-place hastily, feeling his puzzled stare on her garters. She was piqued, for if his face meant anything he had seen nothing pleasant or even interesting. She said sharply, "If ye were any good ye'd go out to the wood-pile and bring in some split maple for frying."

He got up in the same obedient way, and with the same woebegone countenance, and came back after a time with an armful of oak billets—just as she might have expected. Oak, that would take all tarnation to burn down to frying coals! He put them down carefully on the hearth and sank into the chair once more with a groan of relief. The groan turned away Thankful's wrath and gave her a twinge of pity. She dropped on her knees, pulled off his stiff riding-boots and coarse woollen stockings, and ran her fingers lightly over the chafed and blistered feet. He had hobbled several miles along the Great West Road in those clumsy things.

She went out for maple wood split small, and got her fire going, with a kettle on the crane and the frying-pan warming; and she cleaned the shad with a slit and a jerk and a splash from the kitchen water-pail. Then she took an earthenware basin and filled it with water, fetched a saucer of soft soap from the barrel and a clean rag from the press upstairs, and began to bathe his sore feet.

She expected some expression of gratitude, or at least relief; but he sat dumb. She grew more and more indignant until at last she looked up and saw his blue eyes glittering with tears.

"That iss goot," he said thickly. "You are kind, *Fräulein*. Nobody iss kind with me since I leave my poor modder by the Eder."

The maple wood blazed and snapped and sank into coals, and she put the pan on, threw in a chunk of butter and then the shad. It began to sputter and give off savoury smells. She fetched a noggin of rum from the keg in the cellar and bade him drink it down. Then she remembered the trumpeter's packet, tucked between her breasts. "Here," she said, putting it warm into his hand, "is a message o' some kind from that other trumpeter. He didn't pay his fare."

"Other?" he said stupidly, turning the packet in his big fingers.

"Yes, you know—Aitcharaitch."

The kerchief was fastened with tight knots which Bauer untied clumsily. He drew forth and unfolded a sheet covered with the trumpeter's furious scrawl. Another sheet was folded inside that. He read the first slowly, and she watched amazement spread over his tanned blond face. He glanced at the noggin suspiciously. At last he mumbled, "This other paper is addressed to Mistress Thankful Rogers. Is that you?" He passed it to her and she began to read, moving her lips silently over the more difficult words:

My dear little Charon,

The young man who presents this note is well known to me and I heartily recommend him to your consideration. His name is Diedrich Bauer, he reads and writes English quite as well as he speaks it, and can play a very fair tune upon the French horn; but much more important, he is healthy and not ill-looking and comes of solid farmer folk in Germany, where I received much of my military education.

I have heard poor Bauer sigh more than once for a soldier's grant in this province when the wars end. But peace with these tempestuous French seems as remote as the moon, and as the young man will never make a soldier, and on the other hand might make a loving and faithful husband, I have given him a paper which places him in your capable brown hands. Your choice is your own. But if and when I pass this way again, I shall hope to find you Mrs. Bauer or even Mamma Bauer, and simply Thankful to,

THE TRUMPETER

"Well!" she cried. "Yours—what's yours say, Diedrich Bauer?"

Dazed, he hitched the paper into the last of the daylight, and read slowly and aloud:

Roger's Ferry, N.S.

To WHOM IT MAY CONCERN:

This is to certify that Diedrich Bauer has served His Majesty faithfully for eight years, in the German Legion, as a private in the 7th Fusiliers, and lately as my trumpeter. I hereby grant him full and honourable discharge. There is one condition—that immediately upon receipt of this document he go down upon his knees and ask the hand of Miss Thankful Rogers in marriage.

Given under my hand and seal this 16th day of June, 1798.

EDWARD.

Over the trembling paper their eyes met, and Diedrich Bauer slid out of the chair with an air of solemn purpose. In his blue eyes was the hopeful look of a small boy begging sweets. Thankful looked down modestly—and saw a postcript on the note in her lap. It said:

> P.S. As a memento of the happy meeting which gave me such a heart-warming vote of confidence, I enclose in the kerchief some useful implements, each of which has on its back a portrait of my esteemed father. I regret I have none of myself.
>
> E.

At that moment the handkerchief slipped from her grasp and five spade guineas rolled and gleamed on the floor about Diedrich Bauer's knees.

THE farm lay lonely by a dusty track known as the Great West Road, in the forest wilderness between Halifax and Windsor, where nothing passed but an occasional drove of sheep or oxen on their way from the Valley to market, a few bag-men, pedlars and other wanderers, now and then a red-coated despatch rider flogging a sweaty horse to the next post station, and sometimes in summer a coach or a little fleet of coaches carrying officers' wives or other high folk from the provincial capital to the fashionable air of Fundy Bay. Now the fall had come again and in Challoner's orchard the apples hung ripe and the swamp maples down by the brook were turning the bright massed scarlet of a Halifax garrison parade. In a few days Challoner's farm hands would begin the last of the autumn chores, stacking the wild hay in the forest meadows ready for winter.

It was one of the warm still days which made the autumn of '99 a time to be remembered in the countryside, with a Saint Luke's summer of surpassing heat and haze and drowsiness, as if the eighteenth century were throwing a smile over its old sinful shoulder as it crept away. Challoner had slung a saddle on the chestnut mare and ambled down the road for a pipe and a talk with Major Crompton, a half-pay officer like himself. They would discuss the crops but mostly they would talk about the war and that fellow Buonaparte, and Major Crompton would have up a decanter of wine and Mr. Challoner would come home in the early dusk full of Madeira and gloomy convictions.

Mrs. Challoner had retired to her chamber, after her habit, to nap through the afternoon heat. Miss Celia was in the posy garden with a book, reading in the sunshine by the rose arbour where the roses had perished long since and gone to brown rags like the bloom of her own romance. Juno the cook was in the kitchen putting away the last of the dinnerware, her hands very bony and black against the pale sheen of the crockery. She noticed the hired girl Jenefer sidling toward the back door, and chuckled. Her whole flesh shook. With a grin and a roll of eyes toward the chamber where Mrs. Challoner now delicately snored she passed Jenefer a fresh-baked apple pie. Not a word was uttered. Jenefer thrust the pie under her apron and slipped out the back door, closing it carefully.

Behind the barn and outhouses the land dipped a little and then rose steeply through pastures and clumps of maple and fir to the crest where the signal station stood. The station had been there more than a year, and the signallers had worn a brown path down through the pastures to the Challoner well, but its appearance was still very new to Jenefer. It seemed like yesterday. What a mystery it had been! First a party of Royal Engineers passing slowly up the Great West Road with surveying instruments, visiting every hill-top and climbing trees and peering through telescopes, this way and that. Then a solitary rider on a fine horse, a brisk young officer from Halifax, splendid in white breeches and London riding-boots and a scarlet coat garnished with gold lace, calling on Major Crompton and then on Mr. Challoner, quoting mysterious orders "from H.R.H. himself" in the hushed tone of one who has talked with God. The two gentlemen farmers had looked astonished but they kept mum about his mission.

Then a sudden swarm of soldiers from the Halifax garrison, armed not with muskets but with axes, their red coats darkly blotched with sweat, slashing a straight and narrow way through the forest along the crest of the ridge, a slot in the pinewoods aimed like a musket at Major Crompton's windmill six miles to the southeast and at the top of Sickles' Hill ten miles to the northwest. Then the carpenters and masons and their wagons of boards, bricks, and tools. Apparently Major Crompton's windmill suited their mysterious purpose, for they built a platform on the roof and erected a mast on the platform as if it were a ship, and rigged a sort of topsail yard on the mast.

But on Challoner's ridge they found no such convenience, and had to build a whole structure, a kind of blockhouse, using the logs felled by those sweating soldiers in their passage along the crest. There was a square platform on the blockhouse roof, and upon the platform sat a watch-cabin like a roundhouse on a ship's deck; and braced against the building itself rose the short mast with its yard and sheaves for the signal halliards. A brick chimney, four feet square, went up from the wide hearth in the midst of the lower barrack-room, through the ceiling, through the platform, and straight up through the middle of the little cabin and its conical roof. When all was done, and as they packed their tools and rattled off along the road toward Windsor, one of the carpenters let fall the strange word "tellygraft."

Finally came Corporal Sleed and four privates of the Royal

Nova Scotia Regiment with muskets slung, green jackets unbuttoned for comfort on the route, trudging in the dust behind a wagon which contained a barrel of salt beef, another of army biscuit, a half-barrel of dried peas and a firkin of rancid butter —their rations for a month—and a large box of bunting and several large objects of basketwork shaped like balls, cones, and drums, and painted black.

The corporal had paid his respects to Mr. Challoner and his squad had taken possession of the tower on the hill, where at once they began hoisting and lowering the flags, balls, cones, and drums in various combinations, and staring intently through a spyglass toward Crompton's mill or in the opposite direction toward Sickles' Hill. That day Mr. Challoner revealed the secret to his family at dinner.

"A notion of the Duke of Kent's, my dears. It seems the French have developed some means of sending intelligence very swiftly to Paris from the farthest outposts by signals from one hilltop to another. Frenchmen always talk with their hands, and it's said that their system consists of two wooden arms on a high pole; they wag these arms by means of cranks somehow, and some fellow with a telescope miles away reads what they have to say, very ingenious, very ingenious indeed, and probably half the reason of that fellow Buonaparte's success. Of course, that arm-wagging business would never do for *us*, it's against our temperament, d'ye see—but soon after Prince Edward came to Halifax in '94 he set his engineers experimenting with a signal system. By the spring of '98 they had it perfected, a station at the harbour mouth, another on the Citadel, and one at the Prince's lodge by Bedford Basin, so that . . . ."

"So that," Mrs. Challoner said in her flat voice, "Prince Edward, Duke of Kent, could spend a week at a time in the arms of his *chère amie* without . . . ."

"Madame," returned Mr. Challoner violently, "I will not hear you speak in that fashion of His Highness at our board—and before the servants, too!"

"It's the talk of Halifax," broke in Miss Celia, acidly.

"That is no concern of ours," responded Mr. Challoner heavily. "Let me remind you, Madame, and you too, Miss, that the Duke is an energetic and ambitious soldier, and we must consider it a boon that he was made commander of the forces here at this time when God knows what the enemy will be doing next. They design to recover Canada one of these days, that's sure."

"Pooh!" Miss Celia kept her thin lips pursed and closed her black eyes. Her father was riding his hobby-horse.

"I tell you, Miss, they're over-running the whole of Europe and they'll over-run the world if we don't look out. That fellow Buonaparte's made a good start in Egypt—planted his rascally army on the road to India, damme!"

"All the wide ocean . . ." Mrs. Challoner murmured in a bored voice.

"Wide fiddlestick! The French have got troops and guns and stores to the West Indies without trouble since this war began, and we're closer by a thousand miles or so!"

Mrs. Challoner shrugged and devoted herself to the roast beef and cabbage. She had a voracious appetite. Miss Celia picked disdainfully. There was a cool smile on her lips. Crossed in love in her twenties, she had come to regard all men as fools or rogues, and her father a man like any other.

Jenefer stood slim and straight in her clean cotton gown and apron and mob-cap at the sideboard, waiting to serve the dessert when Juno pushed it through the slide. The talk meant little or nothing to her. She knew vaguely that the French had turned the world upside down with their godless ways—killing their king and queen and such-like, and beating armies of their betters, the British with the rest.

"Well, as I was saying," Mr. Challoner went on, after a long pull at his port, "the Duke's determined to extend his telegraph stations all along the road to Fort Anne. We shall see messages passed from Halifax to Annapolis in no more than an hour—two hours at most."

"Stuff!" said Mrs. Challoner casually. "It's a hundred and thirty miles."

"We live in an age of marvels, Madame, and stand upon the threshold of a new century. Who are you to say what is or is not to come?"

All that was more than a year ago, and to Jenefer, stealing up the hill with the pie beneath her apron, the most marvellous thing about the age had already occurred. The telegraph had brought her a sweetheart. Beside that, nothing mattered; the telegraph itself was already a commonplace, the country folk had stopped talking about it, the chain of wooden towers and their flutter of bunting and their black drums and balls going up and down had become a part of the landscape; you might say the soldiers were old inhabitants.

Jenefer had been an early and eager visitor to the tower on the hill. From its top, she explained to the Challoners pathetically, she could see the roof of her home on Sickles' Hill. Mrs. Challoner grumbled over her gadding about the telegraph, and Miss Celia had said tartly that Jenefer doubtless enjoyed showing her legs to those good-for-nothing soldiers—climbing that steep ladder inside the tower every fine afternoon—and Mr. Challoner had said, with a twinkle, that Jenefer must be careful for she was seventeen and a big girl now.

Jenefer accepted these comments meekly, though her cheeks burned. To be sure there had been some difficulty with the corporal at first, a lean man sly of eye and glib of tongue, with a certain boldness about the hands; but all that ended when Jenefer met the gaze of Private Harry Beckitt and something kindled in their eyes and passed between them like a message on the telegraph. Beckitt was a middle-sized young man, country-born, with lank brown hair and a pair of dark blue eyes that looked at you very straight. He had been raised on a small farm in the woods like Jenefer's own home on Sickles' Hill, and had a ploughboy's hands and a woodsman's rangy gait that four years of yelling drill sergeants had not mended very much. But he was a good soldier, even Corporal Sleed admitted that. Harry had the countryman's knack of remembering hard-learnt things. He could read off whole messages without once consulting the signal book, and his steady eyes could pick out distant flags and pennants when the wind was wrong or what was worse when there was barely enough breeze to stir them away from the halliards.

And now Jenefer had chosen a fortunate afternoon for her call. The corporal and two of his men had taken their muskets and gone through the woods to Pockwock for a day's moose-hunting with the Indians. She opened the door carefully and entered the lower room of the tower. It was a bare place with the chimney and hearth in the middle, where the soldiers took turns at cooking, and a narrow pine table stained by hot pots and the round marks of wet bottles and mugs, and burned by spilled pipes, and carved with the names of girls in Halifax and sentiments that did those young women no credit. It was a gloomy place too, for the narrow windows were set in splayed niches cut through the logs for use as loopholes in case of emergency. Against the north and south walls were the wooden berths of the soldiers, and in one of them, on a straw paillasse, lay Private Sawyer snoring mightily with his grey hair untied and his shoes off. He was too old a soldier to look upon a day's hunting as anything but a route march in disguise, and he was preparing himself for the long night watch in the tower.

Jenefer tiptoed across the plank floor and went on up the ladder. It was a little awkward with the pie but she had done it a good many times now. She emerged in the signal room, a sunny place lit by large windows facing exactly northwest and southeast. In winter weather the men kept their watches inside, trying to warm their backs against the chimney and rubbing the frost from the panes. It was hot now and full of buzzing flies. She opened the door and stepped out upon the platform. Harry was sitting in the shadow cast by the watch-cabin, looking toward the south. He scrambled to his feet and smiled. His teeth were white and strong—he had not been very long in His Majesty's service. Most of the soldiers had bad teeth from eating salt junk all the time.

"Guess what I've got," said Jenefer archly.

He scratched his brown head dutifully. She played this game every time she came up. He was twenty-four, an immense age, and she seemed a child, but a very charming one with her eyes shining like that, and the flush in her cheeks.

"Somethin' to eat?"

"Pooh! You saw!" She whisked the pie into view.

"Jenny," he said in his slow voice, "you look good enough to eat, yourself, that's a fact"—taking the pie nevertheless and slipping an arm about her waist. He had been awkward about that at first. She had placed her inviting person very close to him whenever the corporal wasn't looking but it had been a long time before he touched her at all. She was blessed with the art of coquetry which comes to all healthy young women with the air they breathe, but she had found what all women find, that only the wrong men know instinctively the right things to do. The right ones have to be taught. Well, she had taught him. Not with words. Not with anything noticeable. He had learned to slip his arm about her waist because somehow it was there within reach, whenever she came rattling artless questions about the telegraph—for that was what he liked to talk about—and he had learned to kiss her because when she stood thus her head came against his shoulder, and when she turned her face upward with some smiling remark there was her small red mouth like—like something to eat.

He kissed her now with a lingering ardour that pleased her and puzzled her a little. There was something thoughtful about him today, a kind of determination on his mouth that was strange. They leaned against the locker where the signal flags were kept. The signal slate and pencil lay on top of it beside the brass spyglass and the worn and much-thumbed signal book.

Harry kept looking toward Crompton's mill, very small and sharp against the skyline to the southeast, and she saw that his face was grim. There was a queer set to his jaw.

"Are you expecting a message from Hal'fax?"

"Yes."

"Important?"

"To me—yes."

"What's the matter? You sound queer."

Without shifting his gaze he said quietly, "They're movin' some of us right soon. A man from each station. I'm to be the one from here—the corporal 'commended me."

"What for?"

"The Duke's decided to go on with the tellygraft—all around Fundy Bay and up to Fredericton. All the way to Quebec, prob'ly, when he's got enough men. He wants a 'sperienced man from each station here to send up Fundy Bay and teach the others."

The pink had fled from her cheeks and her lower lip came out. Her eyes were full of tears. She looked stunned, and so she was.

Pitifully she said, "When?" in a voice no more than a whisper.

"That's what'm waitin' to find out."

A long silence. At last he said, without taking his gaze from Crompton's mill, and biting off the words, "I ain't a-goin'. I 'listed to fight ag'in the French, not to sit and stare in some little ol' log tower in the backwoods like a fool owl that's got nothin' better to do."

"What are you going to do? You're a soldier—you've got to go where you're sent, or the Duke'll have you taken to Hal'fax for a whipping. He's an awful one for that. Mrs. Challoner says the Duke got sent away from Gibberaltar 'cause he flogged the men there so, and she says that when he was to Quebec there was whole companies that could show the drummer's receipt on their backs. She says . . . ."

"When the message comes orderin' me up the Bay I'll pack my knapsack an' shoulder my gun an' set off all proper-like for Windsor—but they'll never see me in Windsor, nor Cape Chignecto nor the Wolf Rocks nor none o' those places they got picked around Fundy Bay. Not me, they won't."

"No!" cried Jenefer, turning and throwing her arms about his neck. "Oh no, Harry, you can't, you mustn't! They'll catch you—yes, they will!—and send you down to Hal'fax, and the Duke'll have you hanged on the common in front of all the soldiers and people, like he's threatened to do with deserters."

"They have to catch deserters first. Besides, the Duke don't hang good signalmen—they're too scarce. Give me two or three hundred at the triangles, more likely, an' put me on some station where I couldn't run away, like Haut Island. But they ain't a-goin' to catch Harry Beckitt! Soon as I'm out o' sight o' Challoner's, off comes my regimentals an' on goes a suit o' homespuns an' the ol' leather cap I've got in my knapsack. An' I won't stick to the road—not me! I'll head through the woods for Saint Margaret's Bay, an' get a passage down the south shore in a coaster."

"Are you—are you going to run away to the States?" Jenefer faltered.

"Not that far, no. Down the south shore there's a place called Liverpool, and a horse path lately cut into the backwoods at the head o' the river there—the middle o' nowhere. They'll never think o' lookin' for me there."

"How do you know?"

" 'Cause I know two or three men o' my reg'ment that's gone there already—cut out farms for 'emselves an' married girls from down the river. They're all right. The squads that hunt deserters always foller the coast."

"Won't you be awful lonesome?" Jenefer said.

He looked at her swiftly and turned his eyes to the south again.

"That's what I want to talk to you about, Jenny. I ain't much hand to beat about the bush. D'ye like me, Jenny? A lot, I mean —an awful lot."

Her breast leaped in the too-tight bodice—she was still growing out of her clothes. "Oh, Harry . . . Harry! I like you more than anybody in the world. I never knew anybody, 'specially a man, could be so nice as you. When I'm working in the kitchen I think about you all the time, and when I go to bed I dream about you sometimes—lots of times. Juno says that's love."

Watching his gaunt profile she saw a softening of the lips. He did not look at her as he said in a low voice, "D'ye love me enough to run away and go to a rough country like—like the backwoods o' Queens County, say?"

"Anywhere! I'd go anywhere!" She stood on the toes of her worn cobbler's brogues and kissed his cheek, his chin, his neck, the corner of his mouth, in such a rapture that he was amazed. He turned to her then and kissed her mouth, her eager happy mouth, and said, "Listen then, Jenny. Here's what you must do. You must wait till I'm gone a month. That'll give me time to get there and fix up a place to live, an' by that time the Challoners won't suspicion anything if you say you want to go home a few days afore winter sets in. Then you must start off, an' make your way to Hal'fax, an' get passage in a coaster down to Liverpool. I've got a sister marrit to a Copley there—John Copley, remember the name—you go an' stay with her till I can come down the river to get you."

"But how?" she cried, distressed. "I've never been anywhere, not even to Hal'fax, and I've no money for lodgings nor packet fare nor anything."

He drew a worn buckskin purse from his breeches pocket. "Here's thirty-five shillings I saved out o' my pay. That'll see you through."

"But you—how will you get to Liverpool without money?" He gave his brown head a fierce shake as if her doubts were flies.

"I'll make my way, depend on't. I'm country born and raised in the woods, an' in my common clo'es they'll never know me for a so'ger—folk won't be afeared to give me a bed and a bite or a lift on the road. Will you do it, Jenny? Say you'll do it! Say it!"

The departure of Private Beckitt for Windsor and his failure to arrive there, avowed by an indignant flutter of signals from the northwest, created a small sensation at Challoner's Farm. This was increased by the discovery, two days later, of the missing man's regimentals, tucked behind a rock along the Great West Road. Miss Celia watched Jenefer for some sign of dismay— and saw nothing but a rapt look, which puzzled her. Mrs. Challoner observed with her customary vinegar that one thing was sure; the girl wouldn't go trapesing up to that tower any more, and a good thing, too. Soldiers were a bad lot and they were not improved by this telegraph nonsense—this was for Mr. Challoner's ears—scattered in idle squads about the country-side where there was nothing to do but hunt and fish and make love to silly servant-girls on the farms. If the Duke persisted in this fad of his there'd be an end to his precious discipline. And in another year, the way things were going, he'd have the entire garrisons of Nova Scotia, New Brunswick, yes, and all Canada, loafing in little wooden towers through the woods, and who'd defend the coast when Bony came, as Mr. Challoner so confidently expected? At once Mr. Challoner mounted his hobby-horse with a snort, and Miss Celia rolled her fine black eyes to the ceiling resignedly.

Jenefer was always a little afraid of Miss Celia's sharp tongue, though she admired her good looks and even felt sorry for her at times—five-and-thirty, an old maid with no prospects ever since young Dick Crompton jilted her twelve years back to marry a girl in Halifax. Mrs. Challoner always said in her bored voice that it was all Challoner's fault—burying his family along with his money in this lonely hole in the Nova Scotia wilderness. Farm! What did he know about farming? Nothing! Even the land was worthless! And where were the neighbours, and what kind? That poverty-stricken brood of Sickles—poor Jenny's family—miles away in one direction, and the Cromptons—parents of that scoundrel who jilted Celia—miles away in the other. There was a noticeable frost in Miss Celia whenever this was mentioned, but of course Miss Celia was a frosty person in any case, for all her good looks and handsome figure.

Her voice was as cold as the weather outside when, one morning in late October, with the wind in the north and specks of snow flying, she found the girl Jenefer weeping quietly in a corner of the kitchen.

"She's undone," thought Celia; just what she had suspected when that good-for-nothing soldier ran away.

Aloud she said, "Well! It's that wretched Beckitt, I suppose."

Jenefer looked up, a little startled. She was a woebegone object, her eyes all red and swollen and her cheeks daubed with tears and the dust of her sweeping.

"Yes, ma'am. They've caught him. He's up for punishment at Halifax barracks."

"Oh! How do you know?"

"Corporal Sleed. He was waiting at the well to tell me. The word came up the tellygraft. The Duke is in Annapolis, staying to Fort Anne, and they have to notify him about court martials and such-like and he sends back what the punishment's to be."

"The Duke will have him hanged, as like as not," Miss Celia said cruelly. "You're rid of a scamp, my girl."

Jenefer wept afresh. Her world had gone to pieces and she sobbed out her poor little story. Miss Celia was aghast.

"D'you mean to say, poor foolish girl, that you were going to run away from a comfortable home and a kind mistress to join that scapegrace soldier in some wild place in the woods? Have you any notion what sort of life you'd lead?"

"Yes, ma'am," Jenefer said.

Miss Celia thought of Jenefer's shiftless father and hopeless mother and the ragged and barefoot Sickles brood, the crowded log hut and the tottering barn and the miserable stony fields.

"But why?" she cried in a high and rather wild voice. "Why?"

"Because I love him, ma'am."

"Love!" Miss Celia walked to the window and looked up the hill at the signal station. "When does Corporal Sleed expect the reply from Fort Anne?"

"In two or three hours, ma'am, maybe less. The Duke always sends his orders very prompt, they say."

"What else did Sleed say?"

"He said . . ." Jenefer choked. "He said I'd better take up with him now and forget Harry Beckitt. He said he'd get me some new ribbons from the next pedlar up the road. He said I was too likely a piece for a fellow like Beckitt that didn't know how to make love."

"Humph! Anything else?"

"He wants me to slip over to the tower, and bring something to drink. He's let all the men go hunting for the day."

"Pooh! That old soldier—what's his name, Sawyer?—he never goes hunting or fishing, he's too lazy."

"He's sent Sawyer up the road to Sickles' Hill to borrow a couple of flags. Sawyer won't be back till night, he said."

Miss Celia stared up the hill and drummed her slender fingers on the window frame. Her foot tapped, and kept tapping very quickly and softly. For a long time she stood thus, with her back to Jenefer and her chin high and a queer tight smile on her lips. Then, "Jenny!"

"Yes, ma'am?"

"Take the brown jug to the cellar and run it about three parts full from Mr. Challoner's rum keg."

"But," gasped Jenefer, eyes very wide, "Mr. Challoner doesn't like anyone . . . ."

"Faddle! Do what I say! And listen carefully. I'm going up the hill to entertain poor lonely Mr. Sleed. After all, I'm lonely and quite a likely piece myself."

"Oh, ma'am!"

"Yes, indeed. Why should you have all the pleasure, Jenefer? I haven't been kissed in twelve years and it's time. Besides, I'm curious. Do corporals drink first and then kiss, or does the kissing come first? 'Twill be interesting to find out, and very exciting too, I'm sure."

"Ma'am!"

"Don't sit there saying Ma'am! Time's precious. Go fetch the rum—and mark this well—you're to watch the tower while I'm gone. When I come to the door and wave my handkerchief —run up the hill at once. At once, you hear?"

No one ever knew what transpired in the signal tower when

Miss Celia went up the hill with the jug. If Corporal Sleed ever told, it was far away and to unbelieving ears. And Miss Celia never breathed a word. When Jenefer ran breathless into the tower in response to a fluttered handkerchief she found Miss Celia standing in the middle of the floor scrubbing her lips with that same handkerchief, and the corporal sprawled half-in and half-out of his berth, with his mouth wide open and snoring loudly through his nose. The jug stood nearly empty on the table. There was a powerful reek of rum. Miss Celia looked very calm and triumphant and she turned to Jenefer briskly.

"Quick! Up to the signal platform!"

She followed the girl's worn heels up the rungs. It was cold outside the watch cabin with a strong north wind whipping their skirts.

"Now," said Miss Celia crisply, "we're going to send a message to Halifax. How do they start?"

"Well . . . most of the messages come from the Duke. When he's at Fort Anne they start, 'Commander in Chief to Headquarters.'"

"Yes, yes, but how do we get the attention of those men at Crompton's mill?"

Jenefer ran to one of the great black wicker balls. "You have to hoist this on the west yard-arm." She fastened it to the halliards and Miss Celia helped her hoist it. Jenefer rested the spyglass in the niche in the rail and stared toward Crompton's mill.

"You seem to know a good deal about this," observed Miss Celia grimly.

"I've watched my Harry lots of times," said guileless Jenefer. "They're hoisting a ball now. That means Begin."

"Good! . . . 'Commander-in-Chief to Headquarters,' eh? . . . C! . . . What's C?" Jenefer flipped pages in the signal book. "It's a square flag on top and two balls below."

"Quickly, then!"

They were awkward and the things went up slowly.

"What now?"

"You leave them up while you count twelve and then run up another letter."

"That's O. . . . What's O?"

Jenefer put her finger on it in the book. "A ball above, then a pennant, then the square flag."

Miss Celia hauled C down while Jenefer rummaged the flag locker for the pennant. And up went O.

"M's next."

"A ball first, then another, and the pennant below."

At the sides of the clearing on the hill the tops of the pines were bending and hissing in the cold breeze, and the squalls went ruffling over the forest like cloud shadows over a meadow. Down in the farm hollow the apple trees were bare and the birch woods on the other side were stark and white, and the maples a bristle of dark limbs and twigs. The leaves had gone with the fall gales and the first frosts and all the countryside was bleak and comfortless. Dark clouds piled up the sky from the northwest and now and again a few specks of hard snow stung their faces. They were chilled to the bone.

N called for the drum, a black wicker thing shaped like a barrel and quite as big. The flags and pennants went up easily, snapping out in the wind, but the balls and drums were unwieldy in the wind and seemed to grow heavier with every letter they made. At the end of each word they waited, shivering, Jenefer at the spyglass, until the answering ball went up on Crompton's mill. A slow business. Once Miss Celia gasped, "Telegraph, ha! I could mount a good horse and carry a message to Crompton's just as quick!"

"The men do it a lot faster," said Jenefer mildly.

Painfully, with frozen fingers and aching arms and the raw wind blowing up their skirts, they spelled out Miss Celia's message—

PRIVATE HARRY BECKITT TO FORFEIT ANY BACK PAY AND BE DIS-CHARGED FROM HIS MAJESTY'S SERVICE AT ONCE REPEAT AT ONCE SIGNED KENT.

At last it was done, each word acknowledged, and the signalmen on Crompton's mill already were running balls and pennants and flags and drums up and down in a very smart fashion, passing that outrageous forgery to the next station down the line. Jenefer turned, awed, to Miss Celia. It was beginning to dawn on her what an awful thing they had done to His Majesty's Service. But Miss Celia was looking toward the north. She snatched up the spyglass.

"Ah! They've got a ball up on Sickles' Hill!"

"Oh Lor," moaned Jenefer. "That must be the real message from the Duke. Whatever shall we do?"

Miss Celia put down the spyglass carefully. "Nothing. Just nothing."

"But what will they think—the men on Sickles' Hill?"

"They'll think Sleed's drunk. Well—he is! His men will testify to that when they find him here tonight."

"Testify?"

"At the court martial, goose! There's sure to be a fine touse over this. The Duke's probably ordered three or four hundred lashes for your precious Harry Beckitt and he'll jump a foot off the floor when he learns what happened. The hunters will testify that they found Sleed beastly drunk, after he'd let 'em go for the day, and the old soldier Sawyer will testify that Sleed sent him off on a fool's errand to Sickles' Hill."

"But suppose they send a man from Sickles' Hill—now—to find out why Challoner's doesn't answer?"

"Pooh! He'd have to travel the road on foot—that's nearly sixteen miles, the way the road winds. But they won't send a man. I know soldiers. I wasn't brought up a captain's daughter in army cantonments for nothing! They'll stay right where they are, and make an entry in their logbook or whatever it's called, to clear 'emselves—and wait for this station to sober up and take the consequences. I'll wager they don't like Sleed. No one could like that man. Ugh! but you waste time, girl! Go on down to the house and pack your bits of things and tell Black Ambrose I want him to drive you down to Crompton's. Mama will snore till five and there's nobody else to question you. The Major's starting for Halifax right after noon in his gig with the pig-yoke springs. Tell him you've got a sick brother in Halifax—tell him anything you like. He'll take you. Have you any money?"

"Oh yes, ma'am, thank you ma'am. Oh, Miss Celia—I don't know what to say, I don't know how to thank you. It's wonderful. I didn't know you could be so kind."

"Kind! My poor goose, I'm doing this to please myself, not you, nor your precious Harry. Get on with you!"

Jenefer vanished. Miss Celia put the flags away carefully with her chilled blue fingers, took a last sardonic look through the spyglass at the small black ball going up and down indignantly on Sickles' Hill, and climbed down the ladder. Corporal Sleed sprawled where she had left him, making sawmill noises. She caught up the jug and scattered what was left of the rum in judicious spurts over his green jacket and the berth, and closed the door quietly and triumphantly upon that queer little tableau. She walked down the hill jauntily, swinging the empty jug by the handle. There was a light in her eyes. She had done a good deed in a naughty world, but she was not thinking of Jenefer and that good-for-nothing Beckitt.

She was calling up a scene from her childhood: a barrack

square, and the triangle rigged for a punishment but with a sheepskin stretched where the defaulter usually stood, and the tall drummers practising with their long whips, first with the right hand, then with the left, to make a perfect diamond pattern on the skin; and the drum major standing by with his cane, ready to dust their own shoulders if they failed to whip the fleece off the hide in the process. And she thought of Sleed and his sly eyes and his wet mouth and the soiled paw at her waist; and she thought of the hot-tempered Duke and his passion for discipline and the smart working of his telegraph.

She came with long strides down the hill, whistling the air of *Would You Know My Celia's Charms* and looking like Boadicea.

IN SHARDSTOWN they sing ballads no more. Nor will you hear a chantey, for the chanteymen have vanished and the tall grass shines where once the shipyards lay under a snow of chips and shavings.

It is a village enchanted. There is the yellow dust of the street, the procession of dwellings down to the broad sheltered bay, where a fleet could anchor and only the lone fishing-boat flashes a riding sail; and there is the little church and the store and the dry-rotten fish wharf asleep in the sun, all still as death. Half the houses are empty, with blinds drawn and faded and forgotten, and grass in the kitchen path.

The people are pleasant but silent. They smile and vanish. Down by the waterside, in the lee of a tottering shed, you may find an old man on a cushion of discarded net, with worn boots thrust out before him, with a frown to shield his old eyes from the shine of the sea, and a dream on his face.

"A ballad? People don't sing ballads now. A chantey? Ha! Where's the need—and no sails to haul?" If you persist he will swear great oaths that have a strong taste of the sea, and he will say, "Och, man, yes; but that's too long ago. That's back in the time of Blind MacNair."

And who was Blind MacNair?

Before Shardstown became enchanted, the village stood pretty much as it stands now, but alive, with a smell of new-sawed wood in the air, and the sounds of hammer and adze, and the clack-clack of calking mallets. They built good ships in Shardstown then. The hulls grew by the waterside with their bowsprits reaching over the road. A blockmaker and three families of coopers carried on business in sheds behind their homes, and a busy sailmaker squatted with palm and needle amongst billows of canvas up there in the long sail loft. The village blacksmith made ironwork for vessels three parts of the year; in winter he shod oxen and horses and fitted sled runners and peavey hooks for the loggers.

The tall iron stack of the sawmill poured blue wood smoke at the sky, and from dawn to dark within its grey wooden walls rang the death-scream of logs. There was a wisp in every chimney then, and children played by the dusty road, and women came out of the kitchen doors and set the well windlasses rattling. Too many women; for in those days men went out upon the broad world in the wind ships and the world did not always give them back. The sea took many, and there was the gold rush to California, and then the gold rush to Australia; and thirty men went to the American war. All that within twenty years.

So there were lonely women in Shardstown. For a time, in one part of the long street lived six widows side by side. Three married again as the years went by; but the others were Bullens and counted unlucky, their husbands gone—blown off a topsail yard, washed overboard, stabbed by a drunken foremast hand—each within fifteen months of the wedding. In a village like Shardstown men could pick safer wives.

There was a fourth Bullen sister, the youngest, but she lived with old Chris on the Bullen farm, a lonely hillside clearing by the Revesport road, fourteen miles out of Shardstown. There was a scandal about Nellie Bullen. She had gone to work in Revesport in '60 or '61, a slim blonde girl of two-and-twenty with the self-willed Bullen mouth, and came home late in '62 and had a baby. A fine wagging of tongues there was, to be sure, in that village of too many women. But one Sunday old Chris Bullen came down in his buggy and nailed to the church door a paper for all to see—Nellie Bullen's marriage lines, with a date that defied the gossips' arithmetic.

After that the matter dropped, and nobody even remembered the husband's name, and Nellie Bullen stayed close to the lonely farm with her boy and called herself Nellie Bullen. Things like that happened very easily in the old times, when men came and went from the sea like visitors from the moon.

People sang ballads then, except on Sunday when the minister came over in a buggy from Revesport and there were hymns to be sung. And the best of the singers were chanteymen from the brigs and barks and barkentines, the lovely wind ships that lay at the waterside. Nowadays men say the wind ships were hell ships and well lost; and they say the chanteys had no music and the ballads no poetry. Blind they are, more blind than Blind MacNair, who knew the beauty of those things.

Och, yes, Blind MacNair, who came to Shardstown in the fall of 1872 aboard a potato schooner from Prince Edward Island. Square-built he was, with brown hands and a brown face and a curly black beard, and hair long and black as night. He wore a band of green silk across his eyes and carried a stick and bundle. His black frieze trousers were called shag trousers in those days, and he had a pair of stout brown sea boots under their wide bottoms, and a sailor's red shirt tucked in the top, and he wore an old long coat with skirts that hung wrinkled and loose at his knees; but he had no hat and the sea wind stirred the black hairs of his head.

The tide was out and the ship lay low, and Blind MacNair climbed the forerigging to the level of the wharf and a sailor gave him a hand and pointed him for the wharf's end. That was the way Blind MacNair came to Shardstown, with his staff striking a hollow sound from the planks of the wharf, and the sea wind blowing the skirts of his coat, and the long hair streaming about his head, like a blind prophet out of the Bible.

Shardstown folk were shy of strangers, and Blind MacNair was an awesome man to see; so they stood off and watched him up the village street and down, without a word. But the children saw the gentleness in him and sang out "Hello," as he passed, and Blind MacNair paused in the dust and asked their names in the deep slow voice he had. And after a time Taggart's wife—Taggart of the forge—called her youngsters to supper and saw them squatted about MacNair in the grass at the wayside.

MacNair was singing softly, and the song was *Fair Margaret and Sweet William*. That is a sad song and a sweet song; the children stayed to the end, and Taggart's wife came to the gate and listened, too. At the end she said, "Won't you come in, man, and have a bite with us?"

MacNair rose gravely and bowed. "Thank ye, ma'am, and I will."

After the supper things were cleared Taggart sat with MacNair by the stove in the parlour, and while Mrs. Taggart shushed the children off to their beds the blacksmith said, "Where's your home? If that's a fair question."

"I've none," said Blind MacNair; "no more than the birds."

"It's fall," Taggart said, "and the birds gone to the South for winter."

"South!" said the blind man. "It's a great country, the South, but a sad one, and I've had my fill of sadness. Ten years I've been wandering, and there came on me suddenly a great longing to be in my own country. This was my landfall. There's birds must winter in the North, for that is the way of them."

"Ah!" Taggart said. He was a tall man and spare, with a red beard square as a shovel, and his eyes were kind. "Would ye take a bed in the garret the winter?"

"Man, man," said MacNair, "the winter bird's no beggar. The bush by the pasture wall, the red berry left by God on the bare wild rose, a crumb at the kitchen door if it's offered, and chance the rest. That's the winter bird, and that's Blind MacNair."

"You're proud, man, and I respect ye for it," Taggart said. "There's a spare bedroom over the parlour that's fixed up fine for ministers and such."

"Is there no loft to your stable?" demanded MacNair.

"What place is that for a man?" cried Taggart's wife, for she had come into the room and stood by Taggart's chair with her hands on his shoulder.

"I'm only half a man," said MacNair, "and a stable was good enough for the child of God."

So MacNair slept the winter in Taggart's loft, with the quilts from Taggart's spare bed, and caught his meals as the birds do, a dinner here and a supper there; with Fraser the blockmaker, with Lowrie the fishing-captain, with Shard the ship chandler, and now and again at Taggart's—but not often, for "I'm beholden enough for the loft," said Blind MacNair.

He was a welcome guest wherever he went. There was never a speck on his clothes nor a whiff of the stable about him; for he was clean, that man, clean as the brook that fell from the hill, and he ate as neat as a man with eyes. Like everybody in Shardstown he had the Gaelic, and when he said the grace before meat you felt that God was in that house.

After the meal Blind MacNair would sing, with the menfolk at their pipes and the women waiting the dishes, and the children sitting about his feet. A grand strong voice he had, and could roar a chantey with the best of the sailors. But he liked ballads best; for ballads he would drop his voice to the size of the room, till it was like a man speaking music, and his voice was deep and sad on the low notes like the southerly pipes of the Presbyterian organ at Revesport.

Daytime he spent at Taggart's forge. That was Shardstown's clubroom in winter, the bellows roaring under the red coals, the old men on the benches that Taggart had made for them, and the teamsters leaning or squatting while their beasts were shod. He loved to get the men singing chanteys, himself giving the by-line in a great round voice and the men roaring in on the chorus. And when they struck up a real rouser like *The Drunken Sailor*, Taggart himself would join in, singing free like a man that enjoyed himself, hammering *rang-tang-tang* on the live iron, and the golden fire spurting. Those were singing times, and

Shardstown men were great men to sing; but there was never such singing as they had that winter in Taggart's forge.

With the turn of the year the cold grew and there was good snow for the log hauling. Ox bells rang up and down the beaten sled road from the woods, and the birch wood yokes creaked and the runners squealed on the snow, and the teamsters grinned and cracked their little whips.

When March came the loggers came out of the woods. They had hauled their cut, and a turn of the wind now would bring the thaw and the break-up. And there was work now at the wharves, with schooners to fit out for the spring voyage to the Banks, and a bark from Revesport to load with shooks from McLaughlan's cooperage. There was great singing in the forge then, for the chanteyman of the bark was a big, handsome negro man with a voice like the sound of great bells, and Singing Johnny Hanigan had come over from Revesport to go in the fishery.

The negro man had a great store of songs, and Singing Johnny was famous in forty miles of coast, and when the Shardstown men began to brag of Blind MacNair one thing was certain.

It came of a Saturday morning, with the old men sitting each in his place, and sailors and loggers and fishermen and ship carpenters standing or squatting wherever was room for their heels. Taggart's was a big forge and dark, though the sun flamed on the snow outside; for the inside walls and the high gloomy rafters were black with the smoke of a century, and the little windows thick with dust, and the big double doors closed for the sake of the old thin blood on the benches.

There was a smell of hot iron in that place always, and a smell of horses and oxen and scorched hooves; and now such a smell of men and tobacco as the forge had rarely known, for Singing Johnny and the negro man had set out to sing down Blind MacNair.

Taggart had Donald MacAllan's big ox in the shoeing stall when the singing began, and he went on with it, for he was no man to let pleasure meddle with business. So he thrust the ox down on its knees in the open frame of the stall, and made each foreleg fast with rope to the shoeing ledge, hoof upward, and moored the beast bow and stern like a ship, with a rope to the yoke and a high rope to the off hind foot. And he passed the broad canvas band under the hard brown belly and put the wooden pin in the windlass socket, and hoisted the beast off its hind feet for the shoeing of them.

Each part of that wooden stall was dark and smooth from

the grasp of Taggart's hands, and the hands of his father and grandfather before him. The chimney stood at the back of the forge with the brick block of the fireplace waist-high before it, and the black beam of the bellows and the anvil and work bench by the window to left of it. To the right was a litter of long iron stretched along the floor, and a bench for wheelwright work.

That space was full of men standing, the iron a-clank with the shift of their feet, and the bench laden with sitters. And the space between the fire and the big double doors was full of men too, except the ox stall in the corner where Taggart knelt at his work. And in the midst of it all sat Blind MacNair on a three-legged stool, with his coat skirts in the dust on the floor, and his big hands on his knees. And the smiling negro sat on the earthen floor, and Johnny Hanigan stood.

They began with chanteys as a matter of course, to get them out of the way, singing the solo lines in turn and chanting the chorus together. The first was *Reuben Ranzo*, and they sang twenty verses about that famous dirty sailor who shipped aboard a whaler.

Then it came Johnny Hanigan's turn for the verse. He hesitated, and no wonder, for nobody had ever heard so many verses to *Reuben Ranzo;* but he saved himself in time with a poor patched-up sort of verse out of his own head that fitted the tune badly and rhymed worse.

There was no rule against such, for a good chanteyman could make a new verse to an old tune, and sometimes the verse pleased other ears. That was how chanteys grew. But there was ill taste in offering a trumped-up verse, and a poor one, to sing down another man. Everyone expected MacNair to say something, for he knew no more, but he shrugged and opened his hands; and the negro man said "No more here," and the chalk went on the board on the wall with a mark for Singing Johnny.

Then MacNair began *Shenandoah*, and the negro man sang the next verse, and Johnny followed after. That is a great chantey, to be sung slowly, and so they sang it; you could shut your eyes and see sailormen stamping round a capstan with hard brown hands on the bars, and the chanteyman perched on the cat-head, and the cable coming in wet from the tide. MacNair had the last of it, for the negro man grinned and said, "No more here," and Singing Johnny could not say better.

So they went on through *Leave Her Johnny*, and *Blow, Boys, Blow*, and *Banks of Sacramento*, and *Blow the Man Down*, and

Paddy Doyle's Boots, and *Stormalong* and the other workaday chanteys, and turned at last to the less familiar ones. And when it came to *Sally Brown*, and *Johnny Come to Hilo*, and *Bound to Alabama*, and those other cotton-rolling songs that drifted out to sea in the bosom of Mississippi, the big negro man went far ahead in the score, singing verse after verse when the others had dropped out and his mark was up on the wall, singing just for the pleasure of it, and his voice ringing through the crowded forge like a music of hammered brass.

From behind came the sounds of Taggart's work as he tapped home the little half-moon shoes on the ox, snipped the nail points with a twist of the sharp hammer claw, and cast loose the foot lashings, and took the pin from the windlass barrel and lowered the great drooling beast to its new-shod feet. But there the big ox stayed. His owner was part of that listening throng, lost to the world and the waiting sled on the hillside. And Taggart stood on the shoeing ledge of the stall for better hearing, and hung there silent with a hand on the yoke of the ox.

It was strange; the big ox patient in the corner, and the tall red-bearded man above him, and the silence of gathered men, and the singers chanting in the midst, like something barbaric and old as the world.

Outside, the sun stood at noon, but no one in Taggart's forge gave a thought to food. Food was a thing you got three times a day. Singing like this might not come again in a month of Sundays.

They turned to ballads now, as men turn from the morning chores to the real work of the day. Any fool could sing chanteys, and the man with the most verses won the score. But with the ballad it was as with hymns, a proper set of verses handed down from the past, and woe to the man who altered so much as a word. There were keen old ears on the benches, and tongues to chide, and a score to lose on the board of the wall.

Singing Johnny began with *Bold Jack Donohue*; and at the song's end Blind MacNair said quietly, "That is a good ballad and an old one, for it came out of the country of Australia long before the gold-finding; but ye have the names of the bush-rangers wrong in the third verse." And the old men nodded and said it was so.

The negro man had a try at the third verse, but the old men wagged their heads. Then sang MacNair; and the names Walmsley, Weber, Underwood rang true in the old heads; the blind man's score went up on the board.

And they went on to *The Golden Vanitee*, and *Farewell to Ye Spanish Ladies*, and *High Barbaree*, and other old, old ballads of the sea, and Blind MacNair held his own with Singing Johnny, and the black man held his lead. But when they came to *The Tiger and the Lion*, which tells of a sea fight in the olden time, the negro man dropped a point to Singing Johnny. And they came to *Hame, Dearie, Hame*, and the black man dropped a point to Blind MacNair, for he did not know those songs; and from then on the negro man was lost, for all his fine voice and the good nature of him.

"I never saw the nigger yet could sing ballads!" cried Singing Johnny Hanigan.

"Nor the braggart," answered Blind MacNair, and Singing Johnny laughed; but there was no pleasure on his tongue— then or after.

So the negro man dropped out of the game, and Johnny and MacNair went on through *The Chesapeake and Shannon*, and then *The Fighting Chance*, and the score between them even. Blind MacNair sang *The Captain and the Maiden*, and Singing Johnny followed with *Young Johnson*: and MacNair sang *Lord Bateman*, and Johnny sang *The Banks of Newfoundland*.

And Blind MacNair said, "That was a good ballad and well sung, and there's all the sorrow of the sea in the part that goes:

Oh, when they took us from the wreck we were more like
        ghosts than men,
They clothed us and they fed us and they took us home again.
But there was few of our company that e'er reached English
        land,
And the captain lost his limbs by frost on the Banks o' New-
        foundland.

And the man with the chalk scored one on the board for Blind MacNair, for Hanigan had it "The captain died o' frostbite on the Banks o' Newfoundland"—and all knew that was wrong. And again Singing Johnny laughed, and no pleasure in it.

Then Blind MacNair sang *The Ship Lady Sherbrooke*, which is a sad ballad of Irish folk wrecked on the voyage to Quebec. And Johnny Hanigan sang *On the Banks of the Brandywine*, a fine tune with romance and scenery and a sailor in it, and popular with the Shardstown men. But MacNair sang *Young Charlotte*, the ballad of the frozen bride, for the sad mood was on him; and the fishermen stirred uneasily, for they believed *Young Charlotte* an unlucky song, a Jonah song, and would never hear it sung aboard the vessels.

So Singing Johnny cheered them with *The Rambling Irish-man*, a jolly thing that set them tapping their feet on the hard earthen floor, and Blind MacNair saw that he must keep his sadness to himself. So he sang *The Braes o' Balquhidder*.

That song has a lilt to its music like the lilting of bagpipes heard afar on the hills in the morning, and the men were glad to see MacNair put his sadness down. And Johnny Hanigan, not to be outdone in a song of old Scotland, sang *The Pride of Glen-coe*, a grand song about a soldier MacDonald and the lassie that waited home for him. But there was no pleasure in Johnny's singing any more, because he was behind in the score and he knew he could not sing down Blind MacNair.

The afternoon was far gone, the dinners parching on the stoves of Shardstown and the wives all peering out of doors to know what man-foolishness was afoot in Taggart's forge. The sun drooped low in a patch of mist over the western woods, with queer rays shining out to the four points of the sky's compass. That was a sign of snow; and the wind had come east and fetched now a cold breath from the sea, and set up a shudder in the rigging of ships, and moaned down every chim-ney in the village. There would be snow before morning.

Singing Johnny was beaten and he was hungry. He stared in the calm face of Blind MacNair and found something terrible about it, the face of an image that could sing, sing forever, and not be moved by earthquakes. He could not sing that image down; but Johnny Hanigan had made a boast, and a boast is a hard thing to swallow when you are famous in forty miles.

"Can ye sing *The Blind Sailor*?" asked Singing Johnny.

"I can," said Blind MacNair, and sang it. A verse of that song runs:

Before we reached the mainmast cap a heavier flash came on,
My God, I well remember it, my last glimpse of the sun.
Our main topmast in pieces split, all in a pelting light,
And me and four more seamen bold by lightning lost our sight.

"And," asked Johnny Hanigan, "is that how ye lost yours?"

" 'Twas not," said Blind MacNair.

"How then?"

"In war," said Blind MacNair.

"The American war—the Civil War?"

"Call it that if ye like."

"Will ye sing for us *The Fifer of the Cumberland*?" demanded Johnny Hanigan.

"I will not," said Blind MacNair.

"I wonder ye don't know it. 'Tis the song of a brave boy."

"Ay, a brave boy, and a Yankee boy, and a good brave song."

"I was on the Yankee side in that war," Johnny Hanigan murmured, and ran his glance about the men, for half the gathering had fought in the Northern army in that war.

"No doubt," said Blind MacNair. "The war was across the border and nothing of ours, in a manner of speaking. But our talk was all of the North and the South, and from argument men go to deeds if their heart's in what they say. The war's past and done with now, and they were brave men all; but I fought by the side of the Southern men and I will sing no Yankee song."

And now men noticed that Singing Johnny had come to a stoop, and now he was leaning forward, and his long fingers licking out to the face of Blind MacNair.

"I doubt ye fought in any war and I doubt you're blind!" he cried, and whipped the silk from MacNair's eyes while the whole forge gasped and stared.

MacNair might have been an image of stone. Not a muscle moved. His lips were firm. The lids of his eyes were closed, and white as a woman's, for they had known no sun since the fall of '64. Just beneath the thick black brows ran a scar from side to side, straight as a ruler—straight as a slash of a sword.

Singing Johnny stood dumb, with the green wisp in his fingers.

"I got that," MacNair said quietly, "from Sheridan's cavalry in the Valley of Virginia. A good fight, and my last."

"Sorry," mumbled Johnny Hanigan.

"Sorrow's not enough," said Blind MacNair. He stood up then, a fine strong figure of a man, awesome with the bleached stripe in his dark skin, and the shining scar, and the white closed eyes.

"Many Nova Scotia men went to that war—ten thousand, they say—and some fought for the one side, some for the other, according to their opinions. There's no knowing now which had the right of it, for a brave man makes a brave cause, and blood's the one colour, North or South. But whichever jacket he wore, the Bluenose was an honest man and a fighting man and a credit to Nova Scotia. Now there must always be an exception to prove a rule, and there were certain ones that crossed Fundy Bay to pluck what cash they could from the agony of other men. In Boston ye could get two or three hundred dollars from the sons of the rich, to substitute on the draft, and another hundred bounty from the state. And 'twas easy to desert

then to another state and 'list again with another name for
another shower of Yankee dollars. Some were caught, and some
got away home with their blood-money—though it couldn't
buy enough soap to take the judas smell from their hands. I'm
truly blind, Johnny Hanigan, but the eye of the mind sees
through the stones of the wall. I will sing you a Yankee song.
'Tis a good song, and a jolly song, and a fine song for the feet
on the road." And he began :

"Come all you fine young fellows, I am going to sing a song:
I pray you give attention and I won't detain you long.
'Tis of a fine young fellow, and Johnny was his name:
He was tried in Alexandria for the doing of this same."

Now that was a song called *The Bounty Jumper*, known to
every man in the forge, and they joined MacNair in the chorus.

So come join my humble ditty as from town to town I steer.
Like every real good fellow I am always on the beer:
Like every real good fellow I prefer my whiskey clear,
I'm a rambling rake of poverty and the son of a gamboleer.

And Blind MacNair sang on :

"Oh, he jumped in Philadelphy and he jumped into New York;
He jumped in the City of Boston, it was all the people's talk.
Oh, he jumped and he jumped all along the Yankee shore,
But the last place he jumped was in the Town of Baltimore."

It was made for the laughter of marching men, that song; but
Blind MacNair sang it with a strange violence, like the chanting
of a curse.

Singing Johnny Hanigan stood, white and red by turns, a thin
sweat on his long clever face, with the chorus pouring upon
him like scalding water. And whenever the tune struck the high
note some iron rods vibrated thinly on the beam overhead, as
if the old forge itself had come to life for the scorn of Johnny
Hanigan.

Oh, now we'll dig poor Johnny's grave, we'll dig it wide and
*   deep.*
We'll bury him in the valley where the bounty jumpers sleep.
We'll put him in his coffin and we'll carry him along,
And we'll all join the chorus of the bounty jumper's song.

But Singing Johnny did not wait for the end. He slunk out of
the forge like the shadow of a man, and nobody ever saw him
in Shardstown again.

He left one of the big doors open, with a broad wedge of daylight pouring into the forge and blinding them all. There was a great silence. Then a woman's shadow fell across the floor and Nellie Bullen's voice was crying, "Mr. Taggart! Mr. Taggart!"

Taggart stepped down from the shoeing stall and thrust through the blinking men to her.

"The mare's got a loose shoe, Mr. Taggart; will you look at it, please? The road's a glare of ice—and I must get home before the snow."

Taggart went outside and Nellie Bullen turned to follow him, and just then James McCuish said, "Sing us one more song, MacNair, afore we go."

Nellie Bullen paused.

She was a tall woman with grey eyes, and she had the slim proud back of the Bullen women, and thick coils of hair with a dull gold shine like a hempen hawser new from the ropewalk.

"Can ye sing *The Desolate Widow*?" asked James McCuish, for he was a thoughtless man.

"Not I," said Blind MacNair. He faced the open door with his feet together and his hands at his trouser seams, like a soldier—or a prisoner before judgement. The cold light was full on his face.

"Any song, then! A Gaelic song—we've had no Gaelic songs today."

"I know a song," said Blind MacNair, "but there's no more music in me, and no rhyme to the words. A poor thing it is."

"Give us the hang of it," insisted James McCuish.

"An old tale, James, old as the sorrows of the world. A young man with a hot head, and a young wife with spirit. There's the quarrel, and the young man saying things no lassie of spirit would take, and there's the separation, with the young wife home to her own folk and the young man off to the wars. You see how old a song it is. Now in those old songs always the young man comes home a hero from the wars, and finds the wife forgiving and waiting true, and there's an end of it. But this song of mine goes wrong somehow, for the man comes blind and a beggar, no fit company for man, woman, or dog. A judgement on him, d'ye see?—for in the parting he'd said 'May I never see you again!'—and never he will, except with the eye of the mind."

"Cruel judgement, that, for a few foolish words," objected Lowrie, the fishing-captain.

"The judgement of God?" murmured old John MacLaughlan reprovingly.

"But what's the end of the song?" asked Nellie Bullen from the doorway, and the men pressed back, none knew why, until she was standing alone in the shaft of light that fell upon MacNair, and all the men hushed in the shadows.

"It has no end, it goes on forever," cried Blind MacNair.

"Forever?" she said. "There's only one song goes on forever." There was a flutter of skirts, and suddenly Nellie Bullen had her arms about Blind MacNair and her shining head on his shoulder, and her hat in the dust of the floor.

"Ah, Colin, Colin!" cried Nellie Bullen.

Tears ran down his face, strange and terrible, as if you saw waters spring from a barren rock.

"I've nothing to give ye, Nellie."

She kissed him then, and the men began stealing out of Taggart's forge with a strange look on their faces, as if they had seen ghosts.

"Will you give your son the sound of his father's voice, Colin?"

"My son!"

"Will you sing for your wife the song that goes without end?"

Och, yes, it was a great singing that day in Taggart's forge, but long ago, and who remembers the old time now? The old Bullen farmhouse, where Nellie MacNair took her husband that night of the big March snow, is gone from the Revesport road, with nothing to mark it but a dent in the green turf.

Some in Shardstown hold the place haunted, and say how on nights of the full May moon you can hear Blind MacNair plowing the windy hillside behind the old white Bullen horse, and singing the old Gaelic song *Mo Run Geal Dileas—My Faithful Fair One*. But that is an old wives' tale; and how could they know that song? For in Shardstown only the old men in the sunshine remember, and they sing ballads no more.

THE air in the classroom was warm and rather stuffy, because it had snowed a little the night before, and Stevens the janitor had stoked up his great furnace fiercely. Grade Nine, coming in rosy-cheeked from the snow outside, found it oppressive, but nobody dared to open a window. Old Mr. Burtle, who conducted the educational fortunes of Grade Nine, was Principal of the school and a martyr to asthma.

The rest of the big brick school was empty and silent. The lower grades were not required to answer roll-call until half-past nine. It was just one minute past nine by the clock on the classroom wall when James hung his school-bag on the back of his seat and flung an arithmetic manual on the desk. He also produced two pencils and sharpened them with his jack-knife, dropping the shavings on the floor and keeping a wary eye on Old Gander Burtle, who disapproved of that procedure. All about him was a bustle of preparation. Fifty boys and girls were busy with books, pencils, and erasers.

"Attention!" demanded Old Gander, with his asthmatic cough. Everybody sat up very straight. "We shall sing the morning hymn." The class arose with a clatter, shuffled a little, and then burst raucously into "Awake my soul and with the sun" as Old Gander raised his bony forefinger. James had a point of vantage when they stood up to sing; for his desk was near the windows and he could look down into the street, two storeys below. It was certainly too nice a morning to spend indoors. The sky was blue, without a speck of cloud anywhere, sun very bright on the snow, and wisps of smoke rising straight into the air from a forest of chimneys that stretched away southward. The snow was not deep enough for sleighing. There were a few wheel-tracks in the street, and the sidewalks were a mess of brown slush already, and when the several hundred kids of the lower grades had scampered in, there would be nothing but thin black puddles. Grade Nine intoned a long "Ahhh-men!" and sat down. It was five minutes past nine by the clock on the wall.

The act of sitting down in unison always produced a clatter, but this morning the effect was astounding. The hardwood floor began to move up and down very rapidly, like a gigantic piston of some sort; the walls swayed drunkenly to and fro, so that the blackboards came down and were followed by plaster, crumbling away from the walls in lumps and whole sheets. The great clock dropped from its fastening high on the wall, missed Old Gander's head by an inch, and spewed a tangle of springs and cogs over the heaving floor. The opaque glass in the door of the boys' coat-room sprang across the classroom, sailing over James's head, and went to pieces in a mighty splatter on the wall in front of him. The windows vanished, sashes and all. Not only the inner everyday windows, but the big storm-windows that were screwed on outside every fall and taken off in the spring. The room, the big echoing school, the whole world, were filled with tremendous sound that came in waves, each visible in breakers of plaster dust.

Then the sound was gone, as suddenly as it had come, and in its place there was a strange and awful hush that was emphasized, somehow, by distant noises of falling plaster and tinkling glass. Grade Nine was on its feet, staring at Old Gander through a fog of plaster dust, and Old Gander stared back at them, with his scanty grey hair all on end, and his long seamed face the colour of snow when rain is turning it to slush. A waft of cold air came in from the street, where the windows should have been, and the fog cleared before it. A girl broke the silence, screaming shrilly. James perceived that her cheek was laid open from ear to mouth, with a great red river pouring down her chin, and that others were putting fingers to cut faces and heads, and staring strangely at the stains. Grade Nine was covered with plaster dust, and looked like a company of startled ghosts, and when James saw the thin red trickles running out of those white masks he knew he was dreaming, because things like that did not really happen. The girl with the red mask screamed again, and there was a chorus of screams, and then with one impulse the class turned and fled, as if it were Friday afternoon fire practice. James heard them clattering down the stairs into the street, with glass grinding and tinkling under their shoes. For a moment James was poised for similar flight, but in that moment he remembered the time he was frightened by a signboard groaning in the wind at night, and Dad's deep steady voice saying, "Never run from anything, son, till you've had a good look at it. Most times it's not worth running from."

Old Gander was standing beside his desk like a statue, staring at the lone survivor of his class. His watery blue eyes seemed awfully large. They looked like Mum's breakfast saucers. James moved jerkily toward him, licking plaster-dust from his lips. "What is it, Mister Burtle?" His own voice seemed queer and very far away, the way it sounded when you talked in your sleep and woke yourself up. Old Gander gazed at James in enormous surprise, as though he had never seen James before, as if James were speaking some foreign language not authorized by the School Board. Then he said in his old asthmatic voice, "James! Is that you, James?" and without waiting for a reply he added, as though it were the most ordinary thing in the world, "Some of the little boys have been playing with dynamite in the basement." James nodded slowly. Old Gander knew everything. The kids in the lower grades said he had eyes in the back of his head. He was a very wise old man.

They stood silent, in the wrecked classroom for a space of minutes. Another gust of chill air stirred the thin hairs that stood out like a halo from the schoolmaster's head.

"You are a good boy, James," murmured Old Gander in a dazed voice. James squared his shoulders instinctively. After all, he was a sergeant in the school cadet corps. It was all right for the others to go if they wanted to. Old Gander passed a shaking hand back over his head, smoothing down the straggled hairs. Bits of plaster fell upon his dusty shoulders in a small shower, like a brittle sort of dandruff. "I think," he said vaguely, "we'd better see if there is any fire."

"Yes, sir," James said. It occurred to him that Mr. Burtle ought to look in the basement where the little boys had played with the dynamite. "I'll go through the upstairs classrooms, sir."

"Very good," murmured Old Gander, as if James were a superior officer. "I will search the lower floor and then the basement." And he added, "Don't stay up here very long, James." They separated.

James passed from room to room on the second floor. Each was like the one he had left, with blackboards tumbled off walls, heaps of plaster, doors hanging splintered in the jambs. Along the south side of the school the windows had disappeared into the street, but on the north side the shattered sashes were festooned over desks, and shards of glass in the tumbled plaster gave it a glitter of snow. The big assembly hall occupied most of the north side. Miraculously, the doors were still in place, but they refused to open. One was split badly in the panel, and James peeped through at a tangle of wood, piled against the doors on the inside. He thrust an arm through the hole and pushed some of the rubbish aside. The hall was a strange sight.

The tall windows which occupied almost the entire north wall had come inward, had swept across the hall, carrying chairs with them, and the shattered sashes had wedged against the south wall and the side doors in a complete barricade. There was no trace of fire.

James walked down the stairs, along the lower hall, and out through the main entrance into the snow. The stained glass that formerly cast a prism of colours from the transom over the great main door had gone outward, and was littered over the snow in a jig-saw puzzle of many hues. Old Gander stood there in the snow amid the coloured fragments, staring up at the mute ruins of his school. James gave him a glance, no more. Something else had caught his eye. To the northeast, over the roofs of silent houses, a mighty mushroom was growing the sky. The stalk of the mushroom was pure white, and it extended an enormous distance upward from invisible roots in the harbour; and at the top it was unfolding, spreading out rapidly in greasy curls, brown and black, that caught the December sun and gleamed with a strange effect of varnish. An evil mushroom that writhed slightly on its stalk, and spread its eddying top until it overshadowed the whole North End, strange and terrible and beautiful. James could not take his eyes from it.

Behind him a voice was speaking, a woman's voice that penetrated the mighty singing in his ears from a great distance. Miss M'Clintock, the Grade Seven teacher, arriving early for the day's work. She was a tall woman, masterful to the point of severity. There was a wild look on her face that astonished James; for he had spent a term under her much-libelled rule and had never seen her anything but calm and dignified. ". . . all along the street. I can't tell you what I've seen this morning. Are you listening to me, Mr. Burtle?" Old Gander removed his wide gaze from the ravaged building. "My first really modern school," he murmured in that quaint asthmatic falsetto. "Dear, dear. What will the School Board say?"

James was watching that poisonous fungus in the sky again, but something Miss M'Clintock was saying made him look toward the houses about the school. They were like the school, void of window-glass, and in some cases of doors as well. There was a great silence everywhere, a dead quiet in which nothing moved except Old Gander and Miss M'Clintock and James and the mysterious mushroom that grew in the sky. But now over the whole city there came a great sigh, an odd breathless sound that was like a gasp and like a moan, and yet was neither, James saluted Old Gander awkwardly. "I—I guess I'd better go home now, sir." If Mr. Burtle heard him, he gave no sign. Miss M'Clintock said, "What a blessing the lower grades don't go in till half-past nine. All those big windows. Your hand is bleeding, James." James nodded and left them, walking out through the school and into the street.

Now there was a flurry of movement and a chorus of wild human sounds above the shattered houses. An oil wagon stood at the kerb, with a pair of great Percheron horses lying inert under the broken shaft. The teamster squatted beside them in the slush with his hands on their heads, addressing blood-stained people who scurried past without attention. "Dead!" he said to James in a queer surprised voice. "An' not a mark on 'em. Would you think a man could stand a Thing that killed a horse?" James began to run.

Home was not far up the street. The old brown house stood two hundred yards from the school. (Dad had said, "It'll be handy for the kids going to school. When I get back we'll look for something better.") Just now it was silent, without doors or windows. Ragged wisps of curtain dangled in the gaping window frames fluttering with every stir of the December breeze like signals of distress. James went up the front steps shouting, "Mum! Mum!" The house was cold and still. Like a tomb. James ran, frantic, through that ominous quiet. Margery's room was empty, the bed littered with broken glass. Mum's room. His own room. Broken glass, crumbled plaster, shattered doors. Slivers of glass thrust like arrows through the panels of Margery's door. Bare laths where the plaster should have been, like the naked ribs of a skeleton. In the lower hall the long stove-pipe from the big anthracite heater lay in crumpled lengths, with soot mingled in the littered plaster, and the painting of Fujiyama that Dad brought home from a trip to the East was half-buried in the rubble, broken and forlorn. Confusion reigned, too, in the living-room; a window-sash, void of glass, was wedged against the piano, and the dusty mahogany was scored deep by invisible claws. In the wrecked kitchen he heard voices at last. Mum's voice, outside, in the garden. The rear door and the storm porch were lying, splintered, in the tiny scullery, amid a welter of broken chinaware and tumbled pots.

Mum's voice again, "James! Is that you?, James?" James scrambled through the wreckage of the back door and ran into her arms, and they stood in the snow for several minutes, Mum and Margery and James, holding each other in silence. There was a bloody handkerchief about Mum's forehead, and little rivulets of blackish-red drying on her cheeks. Margery wore a coat over her nightdress.

Mum said, "I was looking out of the kitchen window, and suddenly across the way all the windows glowed red, as if they'd caught a gleam of sunset. Then our windows seemed to jump inward." James said quickly, "Are you hurt, Mum?" but she shook her head. "Just cut a little about the forehead, I think, James. The window in Margery's room came right in on her bed, and she walked downstairs in her bare feet without a scratch. Over all that broken glass! It's a miracle, really."

"Why are you standing out here?" James demanded. It was cold, there in the snow without a coat. Mum waved her hand vaguely toward the street. "Somebody shouted, 'They're shelling the city—get behind your house!' So we came out here."

"I don't see how that could be," James considered gravely. "All the houses along the street are just like ours—doors and windows blown to pieces, and all the plaster down. The school, too. They couldn't do that. Not all at once, I mean."

There were sounds from next door. Old Mrs. Cameron appeared, embracing her husband in a strange hysterical way. He was breathing very heavily, for he was a fleshy man. Sweat made little clean streaks in the grime of his face. Mr. Cameron was something in the railway.

"Station roof came down!" he shouted across to them. "All that steel and glass! Crawled out somehow! Ran all the way!" They came slowly to the garden fence, arms about each other, and Mum walked to meet them flanked by Margery and James.

"You hurt, Mrs. Gordon?" Mum shook her bandaged head again. "Nothing serious. Mr. Cameron, what does it all mean?" Mr. Cameron took an arm from his wife's waist and wiped his streaming face with a sleeve. "There was a terrible explosion in the harbour, down by the Richmond wharves. A munitions boat, they say. A French boat with two thousand tons of T.N.T. on board. She came up the harbour flying the red flag—the powder flag—and ran into another ship in the Narrows. She caught fire and blew up. It was like an earthquake. The whole North End of the city is smashed flat. Houses like bundles of toothpicks. And the boat went to pieces about the size of a plum—that big ship! When I ran up North Street the sky was raining bits of iron. I don't think many got out of the station alive."

Mum shivered. "No use standing here," James said. They went into the house and tramped silently through the shattered rooms. A motor-truck went past, soldiers leaning from the cab, shouting something urgent and incoherent. The street emerged from its dreamlike silence for a second time that morning. Feet were suddenly splattering in the slush along the sidewalks, voices calling, shouting, screaming. Another truck went by, one of the olive-green army ambulances, going slowly. Soldiers hung from the doors, from the rear step, shouting up at the yawning windows. "What are they saying?" Mum said.

James said, "Sounds like, 'Get out of your houses.'" Mr. Cameron appeared on the sidewalk outside, shouting in to them through cupped hands. "... out! Magazine's on fire! Big magazine at the Dockyard! On fire!"

"Put on your coats and overshoes first," Mum said, her mouth in a thin white line. "Where's your coat, James?"

"In school," he mumbled, embarrassed. It was hanging in the coat room, covered with plaster dust, like all the others, and he had run away forgetting everything, like the other kids after all. "Put on your old one," Mum said. Margery went upstairs, and after a few minutes came down again, dressed in a woollen suit. They went down the street steps together, and beheld a strange and tragic procession approaching from the direction of the city. Men, women, and children in all sorts of attire, pouring along the sidewalks, choking the street itself. Some carried suitcases and bundles. Others trundled handcarts and perambulators laden with household treasures. Two out of three were bandaged and bloody, and all were daubed with soot and plaster. Their eyes glistened with an odd quality of fear and excitement, and they cried out to Mum as they stumbled past, "Get out! Out in the fields! There's another one coming! Dockyard's afire!"

Margery said, awed, "It's like pictures of the Belgian refugees." James looked at Mum's firm mouth and held his own chin high. They joined the exodus without words or cries. The human stream flowed westward. Every sidestreet was a tributary pouring its quota into the sad river. Open spaces began to appear between the houses, with little signboards offering "Lots for Sale." Then the open fields. The nearest fields were black with people already, standing in the snow with rapt white faces turned to the northeast, as in some exotic worship. The vanguard of the rabble halted uncertainly, like sheep confronted by a fence, and under the increasing pressure of those behind a great confusion arose. Their backs were to the stricken city. Before them lay the little valley of the Dutch Village Road, and beyond it the timbered ridges that cupped the city's water supply. Cries arose. "Here! Stop here!" And counter cries,

"Too near! Move on!" At last someone shouted, "The woods! Take to the woods!" It was taken up, passed back from lip to lip. The stream moved on with a new pace, but Mum turned off the road into a field. They halted in a group of those strange expectant faces.

At the roadside was a pile of lumber. James went to the pile and pulled down some boards, made a small platform for Mum and Margery. Some of the people turned from their fearful gazing and said, "That's good. Better than standing in the snow." The lumber pile disappeared in a space of minutes. The great retreat poured past the field toward the Dutch Village Road for half an hour. Then it thinned, disintegrated into scattered groups, and was gone. The street was empty. The field was a human mass. Many of the women were in flimsy housedresses, hatless and coatless. Two were clutching brooms in blue fingers. A blonde girl, with rouge-spots flaming like red lamps in her white cheeks, said, "Standing room only," with a catch in her voice. Nobody laughed. Most of the men were old. Northeastward rose fountains of smoke, black, white, and brown, merging in a great pall over the North End The weird mushroom of those first tremendous minutes had shrivelled and disappeared in the new cloud. People watched the biggest of the black fountains. "That's the Dockyard," they said.

Two hours went by; long hours, cold hours. Still the people faced that black pillar of doom, braced for a mighty upheaval that did not come. There were more smoke fountains now gaining in volume, creeping to right and left. A tall old man joined the crowd breathlessly, cried in a cracked voice, "The fire engines are smashed. The city is doomed." A murmur arose over the field, a long bitter sigh, like the stir of wind among trees. Someone said, "Nineteen days to Christmas," and laughed harshly. Three hours, and no blast from the burning Dockyard. Only the smoke poured up into the December sky. Old Mrs. Cameron came to them. She had become separated from her husband in the crowd and was weeping. "Joey! Joey!" she moaned, very softly. James thought this very strange. Joe Cameron had been killed at the Somme last year, and her other son's name was George. He was in France, too, in another regiment. But Mrs. Cameron kept moaning "Joey! Joey!" and wiping her eyes. She had no coat.

James said, "Looks as if we might be here a long time. I'll go back to the house and get some blankets, and something to eat." Mum caught him to her swiftly. "No," she said, through her teeth. Surprisingly, old Mrs. Cameron said, "That's right, James.

I'll go with you. Mrs. Gordon, you stay here with Margery."
Margery was not well. James looked at Mum. "Anywhere out-
doors we'll be just as safe as here. I won't be in the house very
long." Mum stared at him queerly. "You sound like your father,
James." They set off at a brisk pace, old Mrs. Cameron clutching
his arm. The snow in the field had been packed to a hard crust
under a thousand feet. Farther on, where the houses stood
silent rows, it was like a city of the dead. Blinds and curtains
flapped lazily in gaping window frames. Clothing, silverware,
all sorts of odds and ends were littered over hallways and door-
steps, dropped in the sudden flight. There were bloody hand-
prints on splintered doors, red splashes on floors and entries.
The slush on the sidewalks was tinged a dirty pink in many
places where the hegira had passed.

Home at last. Smoke curled, a thin wisp, from the kitchen
chimney. It was absurd, that faithful flicker in the stove, when all
the doors and windows were gone and the winter breeze wandered at will through the empty rooms. They paused outside for
a moment. Old Mrs. Cameron said, "We must rush in and snatch
up what we want. Don't stay longer than it takes to count a
hundred. Remember, James." She moved toward her doorstep,
drawing a deep breath. James nodded dumbly. He clattered up
the steps, making a noise that seemed tremendous in the stark
silence, then along the lower hall and upstairs, where his steps
were muffled in fallen plaster. All the way he counted aloud.
Numbers had a sudden and enormous significance. Margery's
bed was full of broken glass, cumbered with wreckage of the
window-sash. He stripped a blanket from his own bed and passed
into Mum's room. Mum's big eiderdown was there on the bed.
Her room faced south, and the window-glass had all blown out
into the street. A gust of chill air came through the empty frame,
and the bedroom door slammed shockingly. The interior doors
had been open at the time of the great blast, and had suffered
little injury. The slam gave James a sudden feeling of suffocation
and made his heart beat terribly. He went to the door quickly
and twisted the handle. It came away in his hand, and the
handle on the other side fell with a sharp thud, taking the shaft
with it. "Hundred-'n-ten, hundred-'n-'leven." James dropped his
burden and tried to force back the catch with bits of wood.
They splintered and broke, without accomplishment. Outside,
old Mrs. Cameron was calling, "James! James!" her voice very
loud in the awful silence. Fear came to James in a rush. He
fancied that sidelong earthquake again, and the big brown house
tumbling into the street, a bundle of toothpicks, as Mr. Cam-

eron had said about the houses up Richmond way. He went to
the window, and debated throwing the blankets into the street
and jumping after them. It looked a terrible distance down there.
Mrs. Cameron caught sight of him staring down at her, and
waved her arms awkwardly and shouted. She had a blanket
under each arm, a loaf of bread in one hand and a pot of jam
in the other. Inspiration came to James at last. Dad's rifle kit.
In the bottom drawer in Mum's big chiffonier. He snatched out
the drawer, brought forth a tiny screwdriver, prised back the
catch with it. Freedom! He came down the stairs in four leaps,
dragging blanket and eiderdown, and was out in the street,
sucking in an enormous breath. Old Mrs. Cameron scolded. "I
thought you were never coming, James. You should have
counted."

"I couldn't get out," James said. The breeze felt very cold on
his brow. He put up a hand and wiped big drops of perspiration.
As they approached the field again James stopped suddenly. "I
forgot to get something to eat." He was very close to tears. Old
Mrs. Cameron pulled at his arm. "I have bread and jam," she
said. Mum and Margery were standing on the little wooden raft
in the snow. Mum clutched James against her, and held him
there a long time. It was two o'clock in the afternoon.

At half-past three an olive-green truck appeared from the
city, stopped in the road by the field. Soldiers came. "Any badly
injured here?" There were none. All the people in the field had
walked there unaided. Most of them were bandaged roughly, but
nobody wanted to go to the hospital. The hospital was in the
city, too near that ominous pillar of smoke. Somebody said so. A
soldier said, "It's all right now. You'd better go back to your
homes. You'll freeze here. The magazine's all right. Some sailors
went in and turned the cocks and flooded it." The truck roared
away toward the city again. People stood looking at each other,
with many side-glances at the smoke over burning Richmond.
The old white-haired man wandered among them, shaking his
bony fists at the smoke, a fierce exultation in his long face.
"Woe unto ye, Sodom and Gomorrah! Alas, alas for Babylon,
that mighty city! she shall be a heap." Old Mrs. Cameron muttered, "God have mercy." The girl with the rouge spots said,
"You're getting your cities mixed, old man." A man cried,
"Better to burn than freeze," and shouldering his bundle, walked
off in the direction of the city, whistling "Tipperary." A few
bold ones followed him. Then people began to move out of the
field into the road in groups, walking slowly, cautiously, toward

the city. The old man went with them, crying out in his wild voice. Nobody paid any attention.

Mum, James, and Margery got home at half-past four in the afternoon. Mr. Cameron was standing outside his house, staring up at the sky. The sunshine had vanished. The sky had turned grey, like steel. "It's going to snow," he said.

Mum said, "We'll have to spend the night in the kitchen." James looked at the kitchen stovepipe. It was all right. He put coal on the faithful fire, and got the coal shovel out of the cellar and began to scoop plaster and broken glass from the kitchen floor, throwing it out into the snow. He counted the shovelfuls. There were seventy-five. "There's an awful lot of plaster in a room," Margery observed. Mum took a broom and swept up the fine stuff that escaped James' big shovel. They looked at the yawning window frames. "That old storm-window," James said suddenly. "It's still in the cellar." They carried it up to the kitchen, and Mum and Margery steadied it while James mounted a table and drove nails to hold it in place of the vanished west window. It was meant to go on outside, of course, but there was no ladder, and it was terribly heavy. "We must have something to cover the other window," Mum said. They stared at each other. The people in the field had said you could not get glass or tarpaper in the city for love or money. James said, "The lumber—back in the field." Mum thought for a moment. "That lumber's gone by now, James. Besides, you couldn't carry a board all that way." They gathered up the living-room carpet, tugging it from under the tumbled furniture and shaking it clean of plaster. They folded it double and nailed it over the north window frame on the inside, and James stuffed the gaps between nails with dish-cloths and towels. There were two doors to the kitchen. The one opening into the lower hall had been open at the time of the explosion, and was unhurt. The other, opening into the shattered scullery, had been blown bodily off its lock and hinges. Mum and James pushed it back into place and wedged it there tightly with pieces of wood. "The snow will drift into the house everywhere," Mum said. "But we can't help that." James nodded soberly. "The water-pipes are going to freeze and burst." They debated nailing a carpet over the bathroom window. Finally Mum said, "The hall stove is out and the stovepipe is down. The pipes will freeze whether we cover the windows or not. We must let the taps run and hope for the best. We can get help in the morning, I hope. Tonight it's everyone for himself."

Through the makeshift storm-window they could see snow

falling rapidly in the winter dusk. Mum made tea, and they ate bread and butter hungrily by the light of a candle. The stove created a halo of warmth about itself, but the rising wind began to whistle through the impromptu window coverings. Margery said, "Couldn't we go somewhere for the night?" Mum shook her head. "Everybody's in the same mess," James said. "Lots of the houses looked worse than ours." Mum looked at the fingers of fine snow that were growing along the kitchen floor under the windows. "We must keep the stove going, James." James carried chairs from the living-room, grouped them close about the stove, and stuffed a towel into the crack under the hall door. The candle on the kitchen table guttered blue in the cross draft from the windows. "Thirteen hours before we see daylight again," Mum whispered, as if to herself.

There was a knocking. James opened the hall door carefully, and saw the dim figure of a soldier framed in the front doorway, rapping knuckles against the splintered jamb. "Does James Gordon live here?" Mum stepped into the hall, shielding the candle with her hand. "Colonel James Gordon lives here. But he's—away, just now." The dim figure lifted a hand in a perfunctory salute. "I mean young James Gordon that goes to the big brick school down the street." James stepped forward, but Mum caught his shoulder firmly. "What do you want with James?" The soldier made as if to salute again, but took off his fur hat and ducked his head instead. He was a young man with a uniform far too big for him, and a long solemn face, rather sheeplike in the candlelight. "We—the sergeant, I mean—has been sent up to this here school for a—well, a special kinda job, ma'am. The awf'cer telephoned to the head schoolmaster's house. He lives 'way down in the city somewhere, but he said there was a boy named James Gordon lived handy the school an' would show us how to get in the basement, an' all like that."

James moved quickly, and Mum's hand slipped from his shoulder and fell to her side. "I won't be long, Mum," The soldier mumbled, "It's only a coupla hundred yards." Mum said, "Put on your coat and overshoes, James."

It was pitch dark, and the night was thick with snow. James led the way. The soldier plodded silently behind him. It was strange to be going to school at night, and the great silent building seemed very grim and awful with its long rows of black window-holes. A dark blur in the main doorway disintegrated, came toward them. Four men in fur hats and long flapping overcoats. Soldiers. "You find the kid, Mac?" James's soldier said, "Yeah. This is him. Where's the sergeant?" One man waved a vague arm at the dim bulk of the school. "Scoutin' around in there somewheres, lightin' matches. Tryin' to find the basement door." James said, "Which door do you want? You can get in the basement from the street if you like."

"Ah," grunted the second soldier; "that's the ticket, son."

A tiny point of light appeared within the school flickered down the stairs. James wondered why the sergeant looked upstairs for a basement door. A stout figure, muffled in a khaki greatcoat, was revealed behind the feeble flame of the match. The sergeant came out into the snow, swearing into a turned-up collar. With the shapeless fur hat on his head he looked strangely like a bear roused out of a winter den. "Here's the kid, Sarge." The sergeant regarded him. "Hello, son." James pointed. "The basement door is around there." He showed them. The door had been blown off its hinges and wedged, a bundle of twisted wood, in the frame. They pulled at the splintered wood stoutly, and the doorway was clear. On the basement steps the sergeant lit another match. Their voices echoed strangely in that murky cavern.

James knew them now for soldiers of the Composite Battalion, made up of detachments from various home-guard units. They wore the clumsy brown fur hats and hideous red rubber galoshes that were issued to the home guard for winter wear. Some people called them "The Safety Firsts"; and it was common for cheeky boys to hurl snowballs after their patrols from the shadow of alleyways, chanting—

> "Com-Po-Zite!
> They won't fight!"

Mum had cautioned James against such pleasantry. Somebody had to stay at home, and these men were mostly physical unfits, rejected by the overseas regiments.

"Big as all Hell," declared the sergeant, after a tour of the echoing basement. "Hold a thousand, easy." The soldiers said, "Yeah." The sergeant fumbled in the big pocket of his greatcoat and brought forth a dark bottle. He took a long swig, wiped his moustache with a sweep of mittened hand, and passed the bottle around. "Gonna be a cold job," he rumbled. "All the windows gone, an' snow blowin' in everywheres. Concrete floor, too." The sheep-faced soldier said, "What-say we tear up some floor boards upstairs an' cover some of these cellar winders?" The sergeant spat, with noise. "They gotta send up a workin' party from the Engineers if they want that done. We got dirty work enough." The soldiers nodded their hats again, and said "Yeah" and "Betcha life."

Wind swirled through the gloomy basement in icy gusts. The men leaned against the wall, huddled in their greatcoats, cigarettes glowing in the darkness. James walked up the concrete steps to street level and stood inside the doorway, staring into the snowy dark. He wondered how long he was supposed to stay. A glow-worm appeared down the street, a feeble thing that swam slowly through the whirl of snow toward the school. James experienced a sudden twinge of fright. There was a great white shape behind it. Then a voice from the darkness above that ghostly shape: "Hulloa!" James cleared his throat. "Hulloa!" A man rode up to the doorway on a white horse. A lantern dangled from the horse's neck, like a luminous bell. The rider leaned over, and a face became visible in the pale glow. He was a detective of the city police, and James recognized his mount as one of the pair that used to pull the Black Maria in the days before the war. He was riding bare-back, feet hanging down, and the big policeman looked very odd, perched up there. "Anyone else around, son?" James jerked his head toward the black hole of the basement entrance. "Some soldiers. Down there, sir. Do you want them?" The policeman turned his horse awkwardly. "Just tell 'em the first wagon will be right along." He kicked the glistening side of his mount and disappeared as silently as he had come, lantern a-swing. James shouted the message down into the darkness. "Okay!" There was a lull in the wind, and the bottle gurgled in the sudden stillness.

Another glow-worm came, as silent as the first. But as it turned in toward the school James caught a faint rattle of wheels, and a hoarse voice bellowed, "Whoa-hoa!" The soldiers came tumbling up the steps in the darkness, and James went with them toward the light. It was a wagon, one of the low drays that clattered along Water Street from morn to night. A man climbed stiffly from the seat. He was crusted with snow, even to his moustache and eyebrows. "Let's have the lantern, fella," demanded the sergeant. They walked to the back of the wagon, and the sheep-faced soldier held the lantern high while the sergeant whipped a long tarpaulin from the mysterious freight.

"Niggers!" rumbled the sergeant loudly. James, peering between the soldiers in astonishment, beheld six figures lying side by side on the dray: three men, two women, and a young girl. They were stiff and impassive, like the dummies you saw in shop windows. The women had dirty rags of cotton dress. One of the men wore a pair of trousers. The rest were naked. Ebony flesh gleamed in the lantern light. The snowflakes drifted lightly on the calm up-turned faces. Their eyes were closed, hands lay easily at their sides, as if they were content to sleep there, naked to the storm. "Looka!" called the sheep-faced soldier. "They bin hit, Sarge. But there's no blood!" The sergeant stooped over for a better look. Two of the dark faces were scored deeply, as if some vandal had gouged wax from the dummies with a chisel. "Concussion," announced the sergeant with immense assurance. "That's what. Drives the blood inward. They was dead before they got hit. That boat went to pieces like shrapnel." He called it "sharpnel."

The teamster was complaining. " . . . get a move on, you guys. This snow gets much deeper I gotta go back to the barn an' shift to sleds. There's work to do." Two of the soldiers picked up a dummy by head and feet, carried it awkwardly down the basement steps, and dropped it. There was a dull flap when it struck the concrete. They came up the steps quickly. "Froze?" asked Sarge. "Stiff as a board," they said. The wagon was cleared of its silent passengers and went away into the night. The sergeant struck matches while the men arranged the bodies in a neat row. "Once," a soldier said, "I worked in a meat packin' plant. In T'ronta, that was."

"Well," Sarge rumbled, "you're keeping your hand in."

Another lantern swam up the street. Another dray. More silent figures under the tarpaulin. White people this time. A man and four young women, nude, flesh gleaming like marble in the lantern light. There was blood, a lot of it, dried black like old paint. "Musta bin farther away," observed the sergeant. "Them niggers was from Africville, right by the place she went off." T'ronta said curiously, "Funny, them bein' stripped this way. Was their clo'es blowed off, would you say?" The teamster shook his head. "Nuh. These was all pulled outa the wreckage by the troops this afternoon. Clo'es caught an' tore off, I guess. Besides, lotsa people sleeps late winter mornin's. Prob'ly didn't have much on anyway." More wagons. The intervals diminished. The sheep-faced soldier said, "The awf'cer's forgot us. We oughta bin relieved by now." "Quit beefin'," said Sarge. "All the troops is up Richmond way, pullin' stiffs outa the wreckage, huntin' for livin' ones. If it's okay for them its okay for us." A teamster gave them a spare lantern which they stood on the basement floor, and in the fitful glow of that lonely thing the dummies lay in orderly rows, toes up, faces toward the dim ceiling. The shadows of the soldiers performed a grotesque dance on the walls as they went about their work. Sarge pulled something from his greatcoat pocket, and James gave it a side-wise glance, expecting to see the bottle. Sarge thrust it back into the pocket again, but James had seen the silver figure of a baseball pitcher, and knew it had been wrenched from the big cup his school had won last summer. He said nothing. Sarge said, "You still here, son? We don't need you no more. Better go home."

Mum greeted James anxiously in the candlelit kitchen. "How pale you are, James! What did they want? You've been gone three hours." James looked at the stove. "Nothing. Nothing much, Mum. I guess they—just wanted to fix up the school a bit." They sat in the cushioned chairs, huddling over the stove. Margery had her feet in the oven. James went upstairs and brought down blankets, and they muffled themselves up in the chairs. Mum said, "Don't you want something to eat, James? There's tea on the stove, and there's bread and butter." "Not hungry," James said in a low voice.

It was a long night. James had never known a night could be so long. Sometimes you would doze a little, and you would see the faces of the dead people on the drays as plain as anything. Then you would wake up with a start and find yourself sliding off the chair, and feeling terribly cold. Several times he took the hod and the candle down into the cellar and brought up more coal. When the candles burned down to the table he lit new ones and stuck them in the hot grease. After a while there was a pool of grease on the table, hard and wrinkled and dirty-white, like frozen slush on the street. Drafts came through the window-covers and under both doors, like invisible fingers of ice, and you had to keep your feet hooked in the rung of your chair, off the floor. The candles gave a thin blue light and made a continual fluttering sound, like the wings of a caged bird. Sometimes the house shook in the gusts, and twice James had to climb on the table and hammer more nails to keep the carpet in place. Snow drifted in between the carpet and the window frame, and formed thin white dunes along the floor next the wall. The heat thrown off by the kitchen stove was lost between the bare laths of the walls and ceiling.

"There must be a lot of dead, poor souls," Mum said.

"Yes," James said.

"In the morning, James, you must go to the telegraph office and send a cable to your father. He'll be frantic."

"Yes," James said.

Mum had washed the blood from her face and tied a clean

rag of bedsheet over the cuts on her forehead. James thought she looked very white and hollow, somehow. But when he looked in her eyes there was something warm and strong in them that made him feel better. When you looked in Mum's eyes you felt that everything was all right. Margery had drawn a blanket over her head, like a hood, and her head was bent, hidden in the shadow. Mum said, "Are you awake, Margery?"

"Yes," Margery said quickly.

"Are you all right?"

"Yes."

"It will be morning soon," Mum said.

But it was a long time. They sat, stiff and cramped, over the stove, and listened to the snow sweeping into the rooms upstairs, and the flap-flap of broken laths, and blinds blowing to rags in the empty window frames; and the night seemed to go on for ever, as though the world had come to a dark end and the sun would never come back again. James thought of Sarge, and the sheep-faced man, and T'ronta, carrying frozen dummies into the school basement, and wondered if the awf'cer had remembered them. Daylight crept through the storm-window at last, a poor grey thing that gave a bleak look to everything in the kitchen. Stove, blankets—nothing could ward off the cold then. The grey light seemed to freeze everything it touched. Outside, the snow still swept fiercely against the carpet and the glass. James found potatoes in the cellar, and rescued bacon and eggs from the wreck of the pantry. Mum brushed the snow and bits of plaster from the bacon and put it in a frying-pan. It smelt good.

The telegraph office was full of people waving bits of scribbled paper. The ruins of plate-glass windows had been shovelled out into the streets, and the frames boarded up. Outside, a newsboy was selling papers turned out by some miracle on battered presses in the night. They consisted of a single sheet, with HALIFAX IN RUINS in four inch letters at the top. Within the telegraph office, lamps cast a yellow glow. There was a great buzz of voices and the busy clack-clack of instruments. James had to wait a long time in the line that shuffled past the counter. A broad cheerful face greeted him at last.

"What's yours, son?"

"I want to send a cable to Colonel James Gordon, in France."

The man leaned over the counter and took a better look at him. "Hello! Are you Jim Gordon's son? So you are. I'd know that chin anywhere. How old are you, son?"

"Four—going on fifteen," James said.

"Soon be old enough to fight, eh? What's your Dad's regiment?"

James paused. "That'll cost extra, won't it?" he suggested shrewdly. "Everybody in the army knows my father."

The man smiled. "Sure," he agreed reasonably. "But France is a big place, son. It's their misfortune, of course, but there's probably a lot of people in France don't know your Dad."

James said, "It's the Ninetieth."

"Ah, of course. Jim Gordon of the Ninetieth. There's an outfit will keep old Hindenburg awake nights, son, and don't you forget it. What d'you want to say?"

James placed both hands on the counter. "Just this: 'All's well. James Gordon.' That's all."

The man wrote it down, and looked up quickly. "'All's well'? That counts three words, son, at twenty-five cents a word. Why not just, 'All well'?"

James put his chin up. "No. 'All's well.' Send it like that."

THOMAS H. RADDALL was born in 1903 at Hythe, near Folke-stone, England, and the family moved to Halifax when he was ten years of age. Five years later his father who was an instructor in the British Army was killed in action at Amiens, and young Raddall enlisted as a wireless operator at the age of fifteen. For four years he served as radio officer on board transports and at radio stations along the Nova Scotia coast and Sable Island where he acquired the background for his writing. In 1923 he became an accountant for a pulp mill on the Mersey River in Nova Scotia and it was at this time he began writing his stories.

Raddall's published works, which embrace short stories, novels, and histories, include *The Pied Piper of Dipper Creek*, 1939; *His Majesty's Yankees*, 1942; *Roger Sudden*, 1945; *Tambour and Other Stories*, 1945; *Pride's Fancy*, 1946; *The Wedding Gift and Other Stories*, 1947; *Halifax: Warden of the North*, 1948; *The Nymph and the Lamp*, 1950; *Tidefall*, 1953; *The Wings of Night*, 1956; *The Path of Destiny*, 1957.

Three times winner of the Governor-General's Award, he has also received the Lorne Pierce Medal from the Royal Society of Canada.

THE NEW CANADIAN LIBRARY